Elijah

S. A. Haycock

To my wonderful friends, family and girlfriend who have managed to put up with my incessant whinging and moaning.

"Unfortunately, the story I'm about to tell you is true."

"Is this why I'm here?" Corporal Jayne spits, "To listen to you tell a story?"

The cutthroat smiles a cruel grin, "Yes."

Corporal Jayne slams her hand on the table, "You're a terrorist and a mass murderer. Why should I listen to a single word that leaves your wretched mouth?"

"Because I am not the monster you've been led to believe." The snake hisses, "I am not your enemy; you're just fighting for the wrong side."

Chapter I

I bolt upright, drenched in sweat, checking my chest frantically expecting to feel three distinct stab wounds. Thankfully, no blood is oozing out of my torso, just another wretched dream. I prop myself up in bed and peer through the cracks in the shutters, taking in the first light of a fine summer's day.

Unbeknownst to me, today is the last day I would be able to enjoy the simple beauty of our quiet life in Rochton.

I climb out of bed and quickly change into a clean shirt and trousers. I then reach under my pillow and retrieve my prized possession, my knife. The length of my forearm from hilt to tip, my curious knife is unlike any other with the blade made of a strange, jet-black metal, as cold as ice and sharper than any razor. In the hilt of the dark wooden handle sits a blood-red ruby.

As soon as the worn leather grip of the handle touches my skin, I instantly feel better. It just feels right in my hand, other weapons made of steel feel heavy, unbalanced and plainly useless; but this knife is a part of me. I carefully place my knife in its scabbard on my belt and a feeling of calmness and serenity fills me as if the horrors of last night's dreams had been washed away.

Silently, I sneak out of my bedroom and tiptoe across to the front door. It creaks softly as I open it. I slip out as the cool, fresh summer's breeze greets me. I close my eyes and fill my lungs, ready to set off.

"Morning."

The voice catches me off guard. I instinctively draw my knife and whip around, finding my blade at the neck of a tall, slim, eighteen-year-old girl. Her long blonde hair falls down the side of her face covering her ears. She also possesses a knife, placed in her belt sitting gently on her hip. Although the shape of her blade is identical to mine, the blade is a radiant white and hilt is decorated with the bluest of sapphires. Pushing the point of my knife back carefully with the palm of her hand, her bright green eyes scan me quickly.

"Really Jacob," Maria mocks, "You don't recognise your own sister?"

"Very funny," I grumble. I pull my knife away, "What are you doing up so early?"

While plaiting back her long blonde hair Maria replies, "Going for a run. I assume you're following Dad's plan and doing the same?"

I nod in agreement, brushing my own messy blond hair out of my eyes.

Maria smiles, "Good, let's get this over and done with."

She turns on her heels and sets off running. I sheath my blade and follow her out the door.

We set off at a steady pace, leaving our small Kladoenian border village of Rochton behind and head North towards the Great Woods. After a half-mile of heading North, we turn West out of Klad's lands, wary to keep our distance from the Great Woods.

The uneven ground of the Rocky Pass on the Western horizon, along with the Northern deterrent of the Great Woods, helps isolate Klad from the rest of Valouria. This isolation is both a blessing and a curse in Klad's history. It has helped protect Klad and the Valouria's other four nations in stories such as the fabled War of Old, but now in these times of peace when Vlaydom, the largest nation, expects trade and taxes, our isolation can be a hindrance.

Maria keeps pushing us on towards the Rocky Pass. The morning sun warms our backs as it climbs over the mountains that encircle Valouria. We rest when we reach the small stream which marks the start of the Pass. I drop down and splash the cool water on my face. Maria smirks at me struggling.

Maria lets me catch my breath before saying, "Come on Jacob, we best get back and see Dad."

She turns back to face Klad and sprints towards the sunrise. I run after her, trying to keep her in sight.

By the time I manage to catch up with her, we are back Rochton. We walk through the quiet street, the market stalls on either side filled with fresh fruit and vegetables are abandoned. The cobblestone streets are bare. The small sandstone houses are lifeless. One of the mutts is eying up the empty butcher's stall. Where is everyone? The lack of vendors is disturbing, and I feel my back begin to prickle as I look around wondering where all the people are. "Damn, I forgot!" Maria exclaims causing my head to whip-round.

"Forgotten what?" I ask.

"We're meant to be at the tournament." She runs towards the arena. I relax, she's right. I had forgotten it started today, that's where everyone is. I leisurely jog to the arena.

We enter the arena through the back entrance and head straight to the changing room. On a bench, there are two light leather armour suits laid out; one for me, one for Maria. Turning away from each other we quickly begin change into the appropriate attire. I throw leather breastplate over my head and tie the straps tightly at my sides. I then slowly and carefully fasten braces to my forearms and greaves to my shins. I stretch in my armour. Good, I can still move easily. I look at Maria and nod. We hide our knives amongst our clothes and pick up our wooden weapons. I grab a bow, a spear, and a knife while Maria chooses a sword and shield. We run into the main hall of the arena where other competitors are lined up ready to be shown to the crowd. We join the back of the queue and listen. It's not long before I hear my Dad's booming voice addressing the crowd.

"The rules are simple. Teams must be of two or three. If you are in a team of three you must not possess a shield. All competitors must be eighteen or younger. The team that knock out their opponents win and go through to the next round until there is only one team left. Now; let me introduce you to the competitors." The small crowd roar in excitement.

Team One steps forward. Three seventeen-year-old Chevonic warriors, all carrying wooden swords. Why are these Chevonic riders so far from Chevon, I think to myself.

Plus, why would renowned riders opt to fight Kladoenians on foot? The people from the open plains of Chevon in the Southwest of Valouria are renowned for their mastery of horses, not their skill in combat.

The first two Chevonic teens are enormous and easily over six-foot-tall, with closely cropped brown hair and brutish faces. How their horses could carry them is beyond me. The third is considerably shorter, much more in line with your stereotypical Chevon. He has a mousy face which is drawn and skinny, but his physique still belies a lithe strength. The top and sides of his head are shaven and when he turns you can see on the back of his head; he possesses long hair which is braided with beads decorated in Kladoenian blue.

Next, a team of two typical Kladoenian eighteen-year-olds, towering at over six feet tall. Biceps bulging and stretching their armour, they raise their weapons to the crowd's applause; the Kladoenian staple of spear, shield, and sword. Years of constant fighting and training has turned these dark-haired teens into formidable warriors, bounded by honour and loyalty.

Our father continues to call out the names of our competitors; local Kladoenian youngsters from Rochton and its surrounding farms. Eventually, after what seems an age, I hear my Dad call. "Team eight, is last year's champions, Maria Da Nesta, age eighteen and Jacob Da Nesta, age sixteen. I can hear the crowd go wild when our names are called. It's not hard to work out we're still the tournament favourites. Maria gives the crowd a wave, but I remain stoic, eyes fixed in front ignoring them all.

Once the applause and anticipation dies down, Maria and I head into the market to quickly get some food before our first fight. The stalls are filled with expensive goods from Klad's closest ally, Arabia, who trade in silks, jewellery, and other luxury goods. Maria leads us past them to the bakers where she buys us fresh bread to go with a morsel of salty goat's cheese we had left in the house. I inhale my lunch as fast as I can and walk over to a poster nailed to the side of a grocer's stall.

I quickly scan the poster. "We're the last to fight and we're fighting the three Chevonic teenagers," I tell Maria.

"You sound scared," she jokes.

I smile, "We've never been beaten. What are three riders going to do when they have to fight us on foot?"

"There's always a first time for everything." Maria laughs, "Anyway, did that little Chevon guy seem familiar or was it just me?"

"I wasn't really paying attention to him." I admit, "I was more concerned about the two giants either side of him." Maria shrugs her shoulders and carries on eating her lunch.

After we finish, we casually stroll back to the arena, sun on our backs. We enter the arena and head down the corridors into the fighter's common room. I can faintly hear another fight going on in the distance. The boos and cheers of the crowd echo down the tunnel, causing the air to shift and warp.

Sitting in the arena's common room, my stomach is churning. Opposite us are the three Chevonic teenagers, the two giants talking in hushed voices as the smaller of the trio, the one with the blue beads in his hair, regards his companions in unbridled disgust. Without warning his head snaps up and finds me staring. Our eyes locked, I am shocked to find not repulsion in his gaze but pure sorrow. He's nervous but masking it with a smile. I take a closer look at his mousy face, Maria is right, I feel like I should know him. The diminutive Chevonic teenager drops his gaze awkwardly.

I usually savour silences, but this time it's different. This silence is unnerving. "Do you all have your steeds yet?" I ask the Chevonic teens.

The three of them look at each other before the small one pipes up. "Course we do, we're from Chevon. It is the horse kingdom." He has a regal yet kind voice and spares us an impish smile.

"What brings you to Rochton?" I ask.

The biggest Chevon rider answers, "Nothing in particular," he then turns to the other giant and smirks as if sharing an inside joke, "Only to face the mighty Da Nesta siblings, even if it means doing so without our horses." Before I can ask how he knows us, we are called to the ring. The Chevonic teenagers head to the far side of the arena, as Maria and I walk over to the near entrance.

Waiting inside the tunnel I feel my heartbeat begin to spike, feeding into the nerves I felt earlier. I can't help but think that there is more to the three of them than meets the eye. Why would they come all the way to Klad just to fight us? We've won many tournaments before but only ever in minor competitions. How did they know of us before the tournament? Maria and I had never left Rochton.

I need to think, but it's hard to concentrate with Maria rattling off hundreds of different battle plans. She always does this, but we never use any of them. Fighting together is instinctive and we always win, no matter what. As standalone warriors we are competent, but it is immediately obvious that we fight better as a pair. I let her talk through the plans, and I nod when she pauses, seeking my reassurance. I just want to get out there. I want the fight to begin.

Standing in the musky corridor, I can hear the cheering. They're waiting for us to appear. Anticipation is building rapidly, the crowd getting louder and louder with excited me.

"Jacob," Maria looks up, faint traces of worry in her eyes, "what if we lose this time?" I was going to reply but our names are called before I get a chance. She needs to calm down.

As we are walking to the gate, I can hear my Dad shouting, fighting to be heard above the roaring crowd.

"To my right, all the way from Chevon, is team one." I can hear a couple of cheers but nothing major. "And to my left, the current champions, team eight." The crowd explodes. Then comes the countdown to open the gates. My stomach starts to somersault. I nock an arrow into my bow, I'm ready.

"Ten... Nine... Eight... Seven... Six... Five... Four... Three... Two... One..."

The gates open. I let loose an arrow and hit the small, beaded Chevonic warrior square in the chest. He crashes into the dirt, eliminated from the competition. Suddenly wary of my arrows, the two, giant Chevon soldiers split up. Maria stays close. They're moving too fast for me to get another clean shot away. I let loose a second arrow and miss the biggest one by a fraction. The two of them advance. I drop my bow and ready my spear. The bigger one heads towards me, while the other charges at Maria.

The large Chevonic teen almost gets me with his first strike, but I somehow manage to roll under his sword at the last second. He spins and brings his sword downwards. I deflect the blow with my spear and counter with a jab to the face. He parries it, swinging his sword to my mid-section. I jump over it and hit him in the chest with the butt of my spear. He falls to the ground but before I can stab him, he's back on his feet, swinging his sword mercilessly. I block every strike but I'm unable to return an attack of my own.

I can feel myself tiring. Each strike is like a hammer blow. I rack my brains, he must have a weakness, so where is it? His strategy is only to attack, I can't get close enough to get a strike in. It suddenly dawns upon me. He must be used to fighting on horseback, he is used to fighting at more of a distance. The spear I'm holding is a lengthy weapon. I have an idea, a rash idea.

He swings his sword. I block it, spin into him, drop my spear, and pull out my knife. There is sheer disbelief when he feels the edge of my knife at his throat. The large rider curses as he chucks his sword to the side. I grin as I look over to Maria to see her disarming the last fighter.

"Team eight win!" the match referee booms, and I'm almost deafened by the crowd.

I walk over to Maria, jokingly I mock, "What took you so long?"

"I was busy," Maria moans. "Anyway, what are you complaining about, we won." Maria laughs as roses and confetti shower down from the adoring crowd. Maria blows kisses and applauds the audience. I shake my head and trudge out of the arena.

Walking down the corridor back to the changing room, the other fighters congratulate us. Maria catches up with me, a sombre look on her face. As soon as the others are out of earshot, Maria turns to me and fixes me with a stern glare, "You didn't applaud the crowd. Again."

"What? I mean, why should I?" I say, somewhat taken aback.

"Because people have paid good money to watch us fight and you show them no respect. It looks bad on us and Dad." Maria explains.

"How does it look bad on Dad?"

Maria rolls her eyes. "People will think that we think that we are above them just because Dad is the leader of the village."

"Everyone knows us here; they know what we're like."

She sighs, "Well people will think that we're like... like Mum."

That stung. "We are nothing like Mum!" I retort, "And besides, no one knew her. We never knew her. How are people supposed to know what she is like?"

"How do you know that Jacob? According to Dad, we look like her."

"We may look like her, but we are not her." The disgust in my voice is clear. Maria turns away and I'm almost certain I can see tears rolling down her face. I grab her arm; she looks up and fakes a smile. I lead her back into the now empty arena. Someone has cleared up the damned flowers and confetti that had been thrown in honour of our victory. It is quiet now, quiet enough for us to talk.

"Are you alright?" I ask.

"I'm fine Jacob." she sighs. She looks down at the wooden sword in her hand then looks at me and gives me a challenging smile. I know what she's thinking, she wants a duel. She tosses her shield to the side.

I look at her and shrug my shoulders, dropping the bow and quiver of arrows. Why not? I lower my spear. Maria paces around me. I keep the spearhead pointed towards her chest. She starts swinging her sword. I wait. The circles she is walking grow smaller and her pace quickens.

Then she strikes. I manage to parry the blow. She spins, swinging for my head. I drop into a crouch, watching the sword pass over me. I try to sweep her legs, but she anticipates it. She kicks my hands, sending the spear to the other end of the arena.

I slowly back up. Maria has the sword pointed at my face. Before she delivers the final blow, I draw my knife and swipe at the sword. She steps back off balance. I jump up. Maria laughs, "Really Jacob. Give up." I shake my head, grimacing through a smile.

Maria doesn't hesitate and brings her sword down towards my head. I sidestep and try to strike. But she is too quick. Maria spins and smacks me in the back sending me face-first into the dirt. She walks over and picks up my wooden knife.

"Looks like I win, again." She laughs. I curse her. Maria smiles as she picks me up. We head back into the changing rooms and, in an annoyed silence, I take off our armour. Maria turns to face me, "We need to get back." I nod in agreement. She picks up her knife and walks out of the arena. I grab mine and follow.

Unlike earlier in the day the marketplace is now bursting with life. The whole village of four hundred people must be here. We walk towards the market stalls in an attempt to buy produce, bumping and pushing into people on the way. There are so many people I crouch down and through the gaps in the crowd, I can see it's too little too late. The stalls are virtually empty, so we decide to head back home.

On the way back, we see the Chevonic teenagers brushing their steeds. Maria walks over to them. "That was a good fight we had. We must do it again one time."

"You got lucky," the biggest one growls. "By tomorrow you won't be laughing." He stomps off laughing to himself, the others quickly follow behind.

"Why won't we be laughing?" I ask, chasing after them. The three of them ignore me and keep on walking. "Hey, answer me, you Chevonic idiot."

The biggest of the three whirls around to face me and in one swift movement throws a punch. Without thinking I deflect the punch and my elbow connects with his nose. Blood gushes from his face as the one who Maria beat swings a fist. I duck under his arm sweeping his legs from under him. He falls, slamming his back on the ground.

I jump up preparing myself for the smaller Chevonic teen with the braids to attack but he stands still watching the others splayed out on the floor in front of him.

He turns to Maria. "I'm so sorry about them two." Then he mouths something I couldn't interpret and proceeds to jump on to the most magnificent horse I have ever seen. The braided Chevonic teen nods as he trots away, leaving his comrades lying on the ground.

I hadn't noticed the small crowd that has now gathered a few feet away. Maria aggressively grabs my arm and drags me to our house, chuntering to herself along the way. When we get to the front door, Maria throws me into the wall, her face inches away from mine. "Jacob, control your anger. You can't win every fight. One day you'll meet someone who will beat you, and I doubt they'll be fighting with wooden weapons."

I push my sister away from me. "That's why we train, Maria, so when someone attacks me with a sword, or a knife, or an axe, or any other weapon, we can defend ourselves."

16

Maria is furious. "You don't have to go looking for a fight. One day you will fight someone better, faster, and stronger and they will beat you. So, calm down and get into fewer fights." And with that, she storms into the house. I sigh, wiping the sweat from my brow and follow her inside.

The evening meal Maria prepares is delicious, a small portion of roast mutton, boiled potatoes, and plenty of vegetables. I notice that Maria has let her guard down. Between mouthfuls, I decide to strike up a conversation. "Is Dad coming home today?"

"I don't know Jacob; you know what he's like with work."

That's true, with Dad being the village leader he must work closely with the guards and always works long hours. He has been known to work for four days straight. As well as that my Dad must often take the three days walk to the Kladoenian city to speak to the King and report how the village is doing.

After our meal, I take the plates and wash them. Looking out the window, dusk is just beginning to fall over the village. Maria stands next to me placing her hand on my shoulder. "We better get some rest."

I nod in agreement and start clearing the table. "What do you think those Chevonic guys were going on about? How we won't be laughing tomorrow?"

"I don't know Jacob, honestly, I have no idea." Maria sighs, "Don't lose any sleep over it. It's probably nothing."

"Then why would they say it?"

"Probably to make you nervous, restless, sort of like you are now."

I am about to say more when I hear an almighty thud. Maria immediately rushes to the door. As she opens it a giant of a man greets us. He has short, dark hair and a kind face which is partially hidden by a long beard. He dwarves Maria and I. Strapped to his back is a wicked battle-axe so big I can't even pick it up.

"Dad!" Maria and I cry. He smothers us with an enormous bear hug. He bundles inside and sits down next to the fire.

Dad puts his feet up and says, "That was great fighting today kids, I couldn't be prouder. They were pretty strong competition, even if they weren't Kladoenian." He smirks to himself, then continues, "I've seen one of them fight before. You know, the small kid? And boy can he fight. Lucky, you caught him with that arrow." He laughs, nudging my shoulder.

I should just be thankful for his compliment but instead, I ask, "Where did you see the little guy fight?"

"His name's Prince Shakra. I saw him fight last time I went to Chevon. His father made him fight these two men. On his horse he went, swinging his sword. Beat the pair of them in under a minute." Dad says.

"Prince?" Maria has a puzzled look on her face, "Why's he over here?"

"From what I've heard his stepmother doesn't appreciate his talents." Dad explains, "Apparently, she wants Chevon to be part of Vlaydom instead of being a lone nation. Under

Shakra's reign that will never happen. From what I've heard he wants to have alliances with Klad, Arabia and Vlaydom. Not just give up his country to Vlaydom."

"So, he is trying to confirm an alliance now before he takes the throne?" Maria questions.

"Not sure," Dad admits. "Maybe, just finding out what Klad is like."

"But everyone knows what we're like," I say. "We are fighters."

Dad smiles. "Are we? I say we are more than just that now. Plus, there hasn't been a war since the Wars of Old."

After a moment, he ruffles my hair with his big meaty hands. "Don't threat Jacob, there's nothing to worry about. He's just passing through on his way to Klad. Probably just entered the tournament for a challenge. Bet he got a shock." Dad chuckles.

"Any idea who the other two are accompanying him?" I ask.

"Er... Not sure. Friends? Bodyguards?" Dad says. I nod. It sounds about right. Our father continues, "The two of you better get to bed, another fight tomorrow." My Dad smiles.

We say our goodnights. I head up to my room and quickly wash before climbing into bed. I look outside my window. The last thing I need is another nightmare I mutter to myself.

In the distance, the Great Woods are silent. I look to the West, over the border, towards the Rocky Pass. I want to get out there, see the world. I wonder what it would be like travelling when and wherever I want to.

I scan the horizon like I've done a million times. Something different appears on the horizon which I don't normally see. I see several small balls of light in the distance, probably just tradesmen sitting around campfires.

I yawn. It's getting late. I have to sleep at some point and face the nightmare again. Lying under the sheets, I can't shake off questioning what the Chevonic guys were on about. What did they mean by *'tomorrow you won't be laughing?'* What were they talking about? Are they going to fight me? Or was it just a bluff like Maria said? She's probably right; again. They are just bluffing. Anyway, what can three Chevonic lads do against a Kladoenian village? It would take a small army to sack it. Tired, I fall to sleep...

Blissfully unaware that my life will never be the same again.

Chapter 2

I have the nightmare. I have it every night. I hate it. It torments me. It always starts the same. I'm deep in the Great Woods; I don't know whereabouts in the woods though. I'm running, trying to chase something, I don't know what. But I need to keep it in sight, I need to follow it.

"Come on Jacob," A sweet voice tells me, "It's getting away."

Then; darkness.

I hear a sickening thud, "H-h-h-h-help-p-p-p," The sweet voice cries. I step out of the darkness. Head spinning, I pull out my knife.

"Hello," I call, but there is no reply as usual. I see a shadow flicker in the treeline.

Then the warrior jumps out. Made from pure shadows, I can't identify his face. The warrior is armed with the usual trident and bossed shield.

A lump forms in my throat. I try to ignore it and act brave. "What do you want?" I ask. My voice quivers with fear.

The warrior says nothing but points his trident at me. I look down at my knife and see that this time it has changed into a battle-axe. I grip the axe a little tighter until my knuckles go white. I am going to have to fight him, again.

I charge and bring my axe downwards at his head. He sidesteps easily. I spin and swing my axe again. He blocks it with his shield. I try for another strike, but the Shadow Warrior catches the blade using his trident. With a simple flick of his weapon, my axe flies out of my hands. I drop to my knees. The damned Shadow Warrior shows no mercy and stabs me in the chest.

I bolt upright, cold sweat dripping down my neck. I sit up in the dark room. It was just a dream, only a dream. I look at my blade. It's my knife, not an axe. I pick it up; just having the leather touching my hand calms me down. What is that nightmare about? It seems so real. Every night I am transported to the Great Woods where I meet an inevitable death.

I put the blade down and try to get back to sleep when there is a knock at my door. I hear my Dad's kind voice, "Jacob... Jacob... Jacob, get up."

Groggily, I moan, "Why?"

Dad rushes in. "Just do as I say, Jacob."

I rub the sleep out of my eyes. It's still dark. What's Dad going on about? It's not more training surely. I change quickly and grab my knife. I rush downstairs. The image I come downstairs to surprises me. A short, skinny lad with closely shaved dark brown hair which had blue beads platted into the back was stood in the kitchen talking in a hushed, worried voice to Dad.

It's Prince Shakra.

As I enter the room he doesn't look up and acknowledge me. He carries on his conversation with my father. I can't quite make out what he is saying as he is talking in hushed tones, but he seems agitated and terrified about something. Something is not right.

"What's wrong?" I ask.

Dad replies calmly, yet his eyes tell a different story, "I need you three to send a message to the King."

Maria walks in, yawning, "Why? Why us? Why not an actual messenger?"

"Shakra will tell you on the way. Hurry up. You are not safe here. Don't turn back, no matter what."

"But..." I plead.

"No buts," Dad interrupts. He crouches down and pulls up a loose floorboard. From the gap, he grabs two packs. He passes me the black one and Maria the white one. The packs are very heavy.

Dad then presents Maria with a ring. I can't see it clearly enough, it's too dark. She examines it and then puts it on. Dad replaces the floorboard and says, "The horses are waiting for you outside."

Confused, I ask, "What horses?"

"Shakra will explain." Then he does something very odd, he breaks down and hugs Maria and me. As I step away, in the faint light I can see a tear glistening on my Dad's cheek. "Go... G-g-g-g-go..." He chokes, pushing us out of the door.

Three horses are tied up outside, including Shakra's giant, magnificent mare. Shakra rushes over and starts untying the knots. "Get on then," he says hurriedly.

"Are you going to tell us what's going on?" I grumble, still rubbing the sleep from my eyes.

"When we stop, I will explain. Now get into the cover of the woods."

The Woods! The Great Woods is a death trap Is he mad? Surely not. I look at Maria, she obviously had heard the same thing but shoots me a glare, telling me to do as Shakra says.

Reluctantly, I saddle up on the nearest horse. Maria jumps on the steed next to me. After a few moments, we set off riding North towards the Great Woods. We ride hard North, trying our best to keep up with Shakra on his incredible horse. After thirty minutes we reach the outskirts of the Great Woods.

Wary not to enter too deep into the woods, we hide in the tree line. The Chevonic Prince then leads us east to the city of Klad. We ride for another two hours before first light appears, but Shakra keeps us moving.

The woods seem strangely comforting and unnerving at the same time. I remember that week Maria and I spent in the woods. It was my Dad's idea. He believes that every person should have knowledge of the wilderness. We spent months in intense training with my Dad. Learning which plants are edible, which plants can kill, how to hunt, how to make shelter and how to swim. I loved it, although I remember constantly having a feeling that someone was watching me.

I hear Shakra muttering to himself which brings my attention back to reality. I stare at him on his horse. I don't trust him. If we needed to, Maria and I could head deep into the woods, live off the land in the sanctuary of the trees. No one could trouble us, hurt us, or kill us there. But Maria wouldn't do it. Firstly, a lot of things could easily slaughter us in the Woods. Secondly, Maria will want to find out the answers and the Great Woods could never provide them. To find out the answers we will have to go to Klad and sort out whatever it is that is so urgent.

After riding for four hours on a horse, at almost full speed, my thighs were in agony. It didn't help that I have rarely been on horseback. Shakra finally suggests stopping for breakfast. From a pack on his horse, he produces six separate rolls of bread. "This is going to have to last us, two days till we reach the city. We don't need to ride as hard now, just a gentle trot. We have half an hour until we set off again; we must keep moving."

"Why?" I ask, "Why do we have to keep on moving and why do we have to go to the King?"

Shakra pauses, then answers, his voice full of pain, "I'm sorry Jacob, but a small Chevonic army is going to attack Rochton..."

"What!" I yell.

"How did you find this out?" Maria asks somewhat accusingly.

"I overheard my two *'friends'* talking about at the attack. They'd kill me in the conflict, and all Chevon would rally and attack Klad, believing I was murdered by a Kladoenian." Shakra explains.

"So where are your two *'friends'* then?" I enquire, "They could be on the way to Chevon, plotting a way to seek revenge for us stealing their horses or running to the Klad."

"I didn't steal the horses," Shakra solemnly says, "My *'friends'* are dead."

Silence falls over the three of us. I've lost the hunger and instead feel sick. The two lads we fought yesterday are dead. Shakra had killed them to save us, or to save himself, I'm not sure.

I look through my pack to take my mind off it. I find a roll of paper with weird drawings on it; five ingots made from the same strange black metal as my knife and finally, two blood-red rubies the size of apples, still not shaped though. I see Maria looking in her pack. She has one of those rolls of paper, four ingots of the same white metal as her knife, two sapphires and a sealed letter addressed to King Edward II of Klad.

How could Dad have afforded this? We manage to stay full and warm, but we have never been able to afford such luxury items. I mean keeping two expensive knives is ok since no one else can use them for some reason. But to have sapphires and rubies lying around under the floorboards, we could sell them and eat like kings for months on end.

I carefully pack my bag as if the rubies may turn to dust in my hand. I will sell these as soon as I've spoken to the King. Surely that is what Dad means for me to do, there wouldn't be any buyers in Rochton, and farmers don't have that amount of money on them.

Shakra wakes me up from my thoughts, "Come on you two, we have to keep moving,"

I take a bite out my bread and jump up on the back of my grey steed. Then I ask, "Shakra, did you hear when Chevon is going to attack Rochton?"

He looks at the ground and mumbles, "Yes,"

"When?"

Shakra's expression saddens, "Now." I turn to see smoke rising in the air.

Maria breaks down crying. Our village is currently under siege. It'll be a massacre. A surprise attack against simple people going about their daily business. Our father sacrificed all their lives to let us three escape. If he had raised the alarm, the Chevon army would know something was wrong. He let the attack be carried out.

I retch. I want to cry, to scream, to fight and run all at the same time. I come to my senses, steering my horse around towards the smoke.

I am about to set off when I see Shakra's sword at my throat. "I can't let you go Jacob; we need to warn Klad about the invasion. Your Dad sacrificed so much to let you two live and you're going to throw it all away by riding into certain death. Queen Antonia wanted you two..." He stops abruptly, knowing he had said too much.

I shake my head, why would the Chevon Queen, Shakra's stepmother, want me and Maria? Can't be for ransom, we aren't worth anything, what else could it be though. Confused, I ask, "What did you say?" Surely, I hadn't heard him correctly.

Shakra sighs and lowers his blade, "They want you alive. I don't why. Bearus, the bigger one of my companions, wanted to kill you in the middle of the war. But the other one, Etin, hit him, and then said that you two were wanted alive by orders of the Queen and that they should focus on killing me. That's when they spotted me, and I finished them off."

Maria finally stops crying, but her eyes are still red and puffy, "What, are we well known?"

Shakra shrugs his shoulders, "No, not to my knowledge. First time I ever heard of you was when we signed up for the competition. The guard said 'Good luck if you're drawn against the Da Nesta's. They fight so well you wouldn't think they were human. Not even a true Kladoenian could beat them.'"

That last comment resonates with me. What did he mean by a true Kladoenian? Did he say that like we weren't from Klad? We've lived in Rochton all our lives, is it because it's on the border? Is it because we cannot use normal weaponry? Is it because of the secret of Maria's knife? Is it because our mother left us? Is it because Maria and I never went to pray? The list of questions goes on and on, it's making my head spin. None of this makes sense.

Forget it. It will torment me if I keep on thinking about things so small, it will drive me mad, like that comment from the big Chevon, Bearus. That's what he meant by we'll sorry by tomorrow. He was talking about the army. Guilt swells up inside. I should have figured it out: the balls of light, the comment, and the arrival of a Chevonic Prince. I want to ask him about his stepmother, but this isn't the time or place. We must get to the safety of the city walls and speak to the King.

"Ok," I agree, "Let's go to the city then," Shakra nods and eventually sheaths his sword. I breathe a sigh of relief. I turn my horse around and head towards the city; Maria and Shakra follow at a distance.

We ride wordlessly until the evening. We stop by a small lake and gulp down the cool, fresh water. On the other side of the lake is a cluster of trees surrounded by bushes, a perfect spot to make camp for the night.

From the packs on the horses, I find four waterskins and fill them up for tomorrow. Shakra is about to collect wood for the fire when Maria stops him and points to the west. "Look towards Rochton." I turn to see two balls of light in the distance. "They may just be guarding Rochton," She carries on, "or they could be looking..."

"For us," Shakra confirms. "No fire tonight. Come on, we better get some rest."

We walk over to a cluster of trees, legs hurting from being on a horse all day. Maria finds a little entrance, hidden from the outside world. Inside the shelter, there is just enough room for the three of us. In the dark, Maria pulls out her knife. She looks at me for confirmation, but I shake my head, I don't trust Shakra enough yet. We each nibble on our bread half-heartedly.

We take everything from the horses that could provide a layer of warmth. Even though it is summer, the nights are still cool. I rest my head on my pack, "You two get some sleep," I mutter, "I'll take first watch."

Neither complains, we are all shattered from a long day's ride. "Wake me up then Jacob when you get tired," Maria says. And with that, the two of them rest their heads and close their eyes.

I quickly mourn over the many faces I've lost forever. I feel sick at the thought of my father fighting alone, trying to hold off the Chevonic invaders. He died defending Klad, there is no greater honour. The priests would tell me that he would live forever in the next life. But I don't believe it. My Dad is dead and I all I've done is run away like a coward. I choke on my tears. I will get my revenge, I promise myself, Chevon will pay.

My eyes start to sting. I wipe away my tears. I can't let Maria and Shakra see me like this, I must stay strong. Taking deep breaths, I calm myself down and focus on keeping watch.

Only an hour has passed when I hear Shakra stir. He gets up and shuffles over. "You all right Jacob?"

I look at him puzzled with his concern, "Yeah, I'm fine. Why?"

"Well, you did lose your father and the rest of the village." He looks at me, puffy-eyed, and softens, "Sorry, I didn't mean it like that."

I sigh, "It's ok. Just been a long day."

Shakra nods his head in agreement, "Rough day indeed," Shakra forces a smile, "Get some rest Jacob, it's going to be another long day tomorrow."

"No, I'm fine."

"No, you're not. I'll wake you if there's any trouble." I don't move, "Come on Jacob, if I was going to kill you, wouldn't I have done it already?" He jokes half-heartedly.

"I suppose." I grab my pack and use it to rest my head. Although Shakra told me that I could trust him, I still sleep with my knife firmly grasped in my hand.

It seemed to take me hours to fall asleep. My dream is the same as always. I'm following the sweet voice again; she is telling me that something is getting away.

Then; darkness.

The sweet voice cries out for help and I escape from the dark. I draw my knife. I see a shadow flicker. "Hello," I call. No answer. Then the Shadow Warrior appears. His trident is pointed at my chest. I look down at my knife, I see this time it has changed into a short sword, a gladius. Instincts take over. I feign an attack to his gut, then strike at his head. He anticipates the attack and easily blocks it with his shield. I duck and attempt to stab his leg, but he is too fast and kicks me in the face. I fall on my back and look up to see the trident enters my stomach.

I sit up, still shaking from my dream. Who is that Shadow Warrior? Never mind. Looking around, I can see Maria, puffy-eyed sitting against a tree. I stretch and say, "Where's Shakra?"

She nods to my right. I turn to see Shakra fast asleep. "Do you trust him yet?" Maria asked.

"No. Why should I?" I complain.

"Jacob, we need him. He knows Chevon. He knows their weakness. And he did save our lives."

"Do you know that?"

She rolls her eyes, "Yes. Blimey, Jacob, he got us out of the battle."

"He didn't get everyone else though,"

"You know that wouldn't work. Chevon would see the mass of people from a mile away, plus the elderly would slow us down."

I hate it when she tells me what I already know. She could just entertain some doubts. "I was just saying." I sigh, "Why do you trust him?"

"His life is in danger; he has no loyalty to Chevon who want him dead. He's helping us, and Dad trusted him."

"But what if he double-crosses us?"

I hear Shakra smirk. He sits up, "Then why would I tell you about the battle and just let you get captured?"

"Fair point Shakra," I mumble, "I'll trust you for now."

"Good," He smirks, "Let's get some breakfast."

We sit down and rip off chunks of bread. I keep eating until I've finished off my first roll. Feeling slightly full, I organise my stuff for the long day ahead. The cool summer breeze brushes past my face. Warm sunshine rains down. This day seems peaceful.

Too peaceful.

Only yesterday Rochton was burnt to the ground and this perfect weather seems to be mocking it. At this time of the morning on a normal day, I would be coming back from a jog, going to the market, training in the arena, or fighting in a tournament.

"What's the royal family like?" Maria asks, trying to make some conversation as we get ready for the day of riding.

Shakra smiles, "King Edward is kind, wise, and a great man. The Queen and her kids are all right once you get to know them but they're a bit snobby." Shakra jumps up on his marvellous horse, Lena, "We're less than a day away from Klad. Not too sure about those lights we saw last night, so we need to keep moving."

I nod and saddle up my horse. Carefully, I jump up on his back and pat his mane. "Let's go then," gestures Maria. We ride in the cover of the trees, constantly looking behind us checking that there is no sign of pursuit.

After an hour or so I'm drenched in sweat from the hot summer's day. My stomach is growling even though I had over half a roll of bread for breakfast. By the time we stop for lunch, I am absolutely famished. Ignoring the looks from Maria and Shakra I scoff down my last roll all in one go. From where we are sat Maria and I could just make out the walls of Klad.

"It's quite beautiful, isn't it?" Maria exclaims.

"Not bad," I lie. It is impressive, not beautiful. The grey stone walls stand tall and firm. Built into the mountain it is only accessible from one side. It was built for one reason only, to withstand a siege. Even from this distance, it seems daunting.

"What's beautiful?" Shakra asks.

"Can't you see it?" Maria questions. "Can't you see the castle of Klad?"

Shakra squints then shakes his head. "Never mind, I've seen it before."

"When will we reach the castle?" I ask Shakra.

Fidgeting with the beads at the back of his hair, he replies, "Not long. With the horses, it should only be a short ride."

"Great," Maria exclaims, "Let's go."

I grab my knife and place it on the back of my belt. The black blade reminds me of the nightmare. I shudder. I hate that dream. Shaking my head, I place the pack on the horse, climb into the saddle and pat his mane once more.

We head to the city of stone, right to the front gate, knowing we have successfully escaped the nation of Chevon. We slipped from their grasp because a rogue Prince had overheard too much. The three of us are free, safe, and away from the harm of Chevon...

For now.

Chapter 3

Enormous wooden doors lined with brass guard the only entrance into Klad. The passage is easily wide enough for five men on horseback to fit through. The grey stone walls are at least three metres high, with patrols of guards pacing the length. We jump off our horses and lead them by the reins. I feel the eyes of archers standing on the wall digging into me. A few have bows in hand and arrow nocked. Five guards stood in front of the gate. Dressed in heavy steel armour, head to toe. They stand like statues, enduring the summer sun.

The guards watch Maria, Shakra and I approach the gates of Klad with scowls stamped upon their faces. Above us, I hear the creaking of bows being drawn. The arrows scrap the shaft as they are being pulled back. I count five different bowmen aiming for our heads. Butterflies dance in the pit of my stomach.

The guards in front of the gates lower their spears and point them towards our chests. We stop still. "What d'ya want?" The guard standing in middle asks in a gruff voice.

"We're here to see the King," Maria answers, eyes glued to the tip of the nearest spear.

"You're 'ere to see t' King, what a surprise," The guard complains, "And who d'ya think ya are?"

Shakra steps forward, "My name is Shakra, son of Markus, Prince of Chevon."

"Yeah," He jokes, "And I'm t' King of Arabia,"

"Well, I'm pretty sure you are not King Tufail," Shakra smirks. "If you don't believe me just take a look at my ring." Shakra raises his hand and the guard examines Shakra's ring. The ring resembles a crowned stallion, proof he is Chevonic royalty.

"Er... Er... Sorry sir, only joking... you better make your way through," The guard answers nervously. He nods. The other guards lift away their spears and rush to open the heavy gate. The archers put their arrows back into their quivers.

Shakra nods, "Thank you," He walks forward, and Maria and I follow the Chevonic Prince through the streets of Klad.

The streets of Klad! I've never seen anything like it. I try to look everywhere at once, attempting to take it all in. The market street was a mix of reds, greens and especially Kladoenian Blue. Imports of silks and spices from Arabia dominate the markets. Just off the main street, there are armouries which are filled with knights and young lads getting their first swords. I glance at Maria who is examining a jewellery stall which I have never known her to be particularly keen on. But now she is wearing the ring Dad gave her it must have sparked an interest.

Shakra acts above it all. He walks in front, head held high, making a path through the people. The citizens part for him; a few cheers ring out. He must be incredibly popular here. People call out his name and waving at the three of us. Klad seems to adore us, or at least Shakra.

Our shadows grow longer and longer. By the time we had reached the castle, the sun has started to set. Waiting at the door are two more guards. They look at me and Maria with the same disgusted looks, then brighten up when they catch a glimpse of Shakra.

The guard on the right smiles, "Ah, Prince Shakra, would you like to seek council, King Edward II?"

Shakra replies in a very royal voice, "Yes, I must speak with him,"

The guard on the left bows and runs inside to inform King Edward. The one on the right looks at Maria and me once more, "Your Highness, what about your servants are they coming in?"

Maria smiles, "We are not servants. Prince Shakra is our friend; we came together from Rochton."

"Is this true Your Highness?"

Shakra nods, "Yes."

"Sorry ma'am, I didn't mean to insult you," The guard apologises with a perfect smile.

"None taken," Maria replies.

"Thank you, ma'am, for your forgiveness."

Maria smiles, "Yes, may we enter?"

"Yes ma'am"

"And give you the horses to take to the stables?"

"Yes, ma'am."

I smirk. Maria seems to enjoy being referred to as ma'am. Shakra steps forward, "Make sure Lena is fine and she is treated properly."

The guard smiles, though seems a little intimidated by the short prince, "Of course, I'll make sure she has the finest stable in all of Klad." He quickly grabs the reins of the three horses and rushes to take them to the stables.

Maria looks at Shakra and me, "Well let's go in then."

The great hall engulfs me with its enormity. The ceiling is as tall as the walls are wide. Down the centre of the hall are open fires. On either side of the fires are two long mahogany tables. Beyond that are people sitting on thrones. A giant stag's head stands proud above the grandest throne. Guards line the walls. Shakra walks ahead, Maria and I follow a few steps behind. Our footsteps echo on the wooden floor. Shakra walks towards the two golden thrones in the centre then kneels. Maria and I copy.

"Ah, Prince Shakra, it is an honour to see you again," King Edward II exclaims in his deep booming voice. "Who are your two companions?"

Shakra stands up with a broad grin, "Your Highness the pleasure is all mine. May I introduce you to Maria and Jacob Da Nesta from Rochton."

"Da Nesta." King Edward pauses, "I've heard that name before. Stand up, let me get a good look at you two."

We stand up; I quickly scan all the royals sat upon the thrones. In the centre are two golden thrones, on the right-hand throne sits a man with short, dark brown hair and a long beard, dressed in ermine fur and velvet in the royal colour of deep, Kladoenian blue. His golden crown is resting on his thinning brown hair but that's not what tells me who he is; leaning on the side of the throne is the sword and shield of Klad. A golden sword and shield encrusted with more jewels than I could possibly name. King Edward II taps the hilt of the sword with his hand.

To the King's left sits Queen Catherine, an elegant lady, with long brown hair with a silver tiara carefully rests upon her head. In her very regal dress of purple and gold, her bright blue eyes look at us with sympathy.

About two metres away from each throne are two smaller thrones. On the king's side is a younger-looking version of the King but aged about nineteen with no beard, long hair, and a scowl on his face: Prince Edward III. Next to him is his sixteen-year-old sister, Princess Silvia. She is the double of her mother except for the expression on her face, that bears her brother's scowl.

On the other hand, on the Queen's side are the identical twins, age thirteen, Princess Elizabeth and Princess Mary. Once again looking like the Queen other than they have their father's brown eyes, not blue. They must be half a foot shorter than their older sister.

King Edward II looks at us quickly then asks, "What business do you seek?"

Maria straightens herself quickly, "My King, I have some grave news from Rochton,"

The Queen leans forward, "What is it, young lady?"

"My Queen," Maria chokes on her own words, "Rochton has been destroyed,"

Silence strangles the court. The hall is in shock. The words seem to echo around the hall. A minute passes before someone speaks. Prince Edward III looks puzzled, "How did you three escape? Who attacked Rochton? And why was Prince Shakra in Rochton in the first place?"

Shakra answers before Maria and I get a chance, "Your Highness, I was in Rochton participating in a tournament. Then on the first night, I awoke hearing voices; voices of my bodyguards plotting. They were hired by my stepmother, Queen Antonia, to kill me during a siege of Rochton. Klad would get the blame for my death giving my stepmother an excuse to wage war on your good nation." Shakra pauses, "They also wanted these two alive," Shakra points at us, "I decided to act and killed my bodyguards. Me and Lena sped to the Da Nesta House knowing their father would want to know about the oncoming attack. I told him, he woke up Maria and Jacob, gave them packs each, as if he had prepared for this moment, and ordered us to ride here. The next morning, we saw Rochton being destroyed. And to make it worse, my lord, I believe that Chevon is going to attack Klad soon."

Once again silence sweeps the great hall.

The King jumps up, "You there," He points at the nearest guard, "Get a messenger over to Arabia, we'll need their help." The guard rushes off. The King points to the next guard, "Prepare the defences, we have about a week before they'll come. And finally, you," He points at a third guard. "Send a small force too clear Rochton of any Chevon scum, check for survivors. Then have a look at the army heading this way." All the guards in the hall leave in a hurry.

The King then reels around to Maria, Shakra and me, and smiles, "Don't worry, when Arabia joins our side, Chevon will run scared. Klad is in your debt. What do you want for a reward?"

Shakra answers first, "If I may sire, I would be honoured to stay here until I am able to take my birthright as King of Chevon."

The King looks shocked expecting more. Then his expression changes onto a smile. "Yes, of course, Prince Shakra. Is that it?"

"Yes, sire,"

"Well, are you sure?"

"Yes, Your Grace" He repeats.

The King sits thinking for a minute. "Very well," He turns to the royals and servants, "Prince Shakra of Chevon I will fight by your side to let you claim your throne. Together we can be strong allies and rule Southern Valouria."

Shakra steps back red-faced. "Thank you, sire, I did not ask for all this."

"Nonsense," the King laughs, "You're loyal and just. All I ask is for you to honour me by marrying my daughter, Silvia."

The room is silent for a third time. Silvia looks shocked, almost giddy. But Shakra doesn't miss a beat and nods, "The honour is all mine. I will wed your beautiful daughter." Mumbles echo throughout the throne room in agreement. Silvia smiles for the first time. Shakra doesn't.

"You shall be married within the month. After we have repelled this attack and your supporters' rally, the Chevon scum that betrayed you won't fight, and I'll sit you on the Chevonic throne. We shall be strong allies. You can even lead the Chevonic supporters into battle yourself. I've seen you fight, and you are amongst the finest I have ever seen."

Shakra smiles, "I may be a good fighter, but I am nothing compared to these two."

The King scratches his beard and examines us, "Maria, my dear, if I may ask: what your father's name was?"

Maria straightens, "Luca; Luca Da Nesta."

The King nods pacing up and down, "Yes he was a good man, a fine warrior..." Then King Edward turns with wide eyes. "Your mother, did you know her, what was her name?"

Startled, Maria answers, "No, we didn't know her, and our father never spoke about her."

The Kings eyes might have grown wider. Behind him, the Queen's blue eyes stare at Maria and me in horror. Shakra has a cocky little grin etched on his face. He knows what the commotion is about.

I step forward, "Our mother. What importance is she?"

The King's warm smile returns, "None child, I did not mean to offend. What do you two want for your rewards?"

"Rewards?" Maria questions, "We had no idea..."

The Queen speaks softly, "Child, I knew your father since were children, we were friends. He would have planned for this, knowing him the items in your packs will explain everything to Edward and I."

Maria and I take off our packs. The King whistles and two servants walk in. "Check the packs." A tall, skinny man with dark hair opens Maria's pack. And to my surprise, a familiar-looking Arabian girl, who is about my age, walks over to my pack. She is different from the other maids and servants I've seen before. She is wearing a simple maid's dress, but she seems too delicate to be a worker. Her small turquoise earrings are visible behind her short, dark hair. A necklace chain is just visible before disappearing behind her dress. She has one ring on her right hand with a small turquoise gem.

As she opens my pack, she smiles at Shakra. Shakra's kind face looks back at her with sadness. He nods ever so slightly towards Princess Silvia. She stops smiling. Confused, I turn to Shakra who looks like he is about to cry. Who is she? Something about her makes me think that I should know her. I want to ask him but now with everyone watching isn't the time.

The King leans forward trying to get a closer look inside the packs. Out of Maria's pack, the tall man pulls out blueprints. "What is it?" asks Prince Edward.

The tall man holds them up to the light and then faces the King. "Some sort of weapon designs Your Grace, more complex than I've ever seen, and the rest of the items must be the things to make it... Other than this," He said holding the sealed scroll addressed to the King.

The King grabs the scroll and quickly reads it. He is expressionless, "Ah, yes... Jacob should also have designs and metal in his bag. Take the designs, metals, and precious stones down to the royal blacksmiths, I want them all working on this. The weapons shall be the Da Nesta's gifts. Tell the blacksmiths if the weapons are ready by the morning, I will pay double, sounds impossible but I'm sure they'll find a way."

Prince Edward's mouth is wide open in shock. "Father! Precious stones! They belong to you, not to these two," He yells pointing at us.

"Why?" The King scorns his son, "They've brought the stones and they've prepared the kingdom from an impending attack. Do you think that a little stone on a weapon will make the world of a difference?" He stands up, "We shall have a banquet to celebrate the engagement of Prince Shakra and my daughter Princess Silvia." He looks at the man holding Maria's bag, "Take the gear down to our blacksmith's, then invite the nobles of Klad. And Yasmin," He turns to the Arabic maid, "Please may you show Prince Shakra, Maria and Jacob to their rooms."

The Arabian maid, Yasmin, curtseys to the royal family before spinning around to face us, "Will you follow me please?"

We are led out of the hall, through a maze of corridors. Shakra walks next to Yasmin, talking in hushed voices; while myself and Maria are a couple of paces behind. The stone walls are lined with wooden doors, lit torches and an array of weapons hanging on the walls.

The first room we reach is mine. Above the doorway is a bow and arrow facing the left, looking ready to fire. I step in. My room is larger than our home in Rochton. In the corner of the room, a fire is going. Opposite that is a double bed with fresh sheets and pillow. Opening the wardrobe, I see a fine selection of clothes. Finally, I see the warm bath. Not your common bucket you bathe in that you pour your kettle into, a proper bath. It is deep enough to stand with only my head above water, long enough for me to swim in and the perfect temperature.

Before I jump in, I shut the door and Yasmin quickly tells me with a sad expression on her face, "The banquet will start in two hours." Once the door has closed, I strip and dive headfirst straight into the bath. I clean all the dirt and grime off my skin. All the pain in my muscles from the last few days oozes out.

After a long soak, I get out of the bath and dry off. I see clothes have been laid out: a long, emerald green tunic with gold thread design and black trousers. I reluctantly dress in the expensive clothes, conscious that someone had entered my room without me noticing.

There's a knock at the door. I open it to find Maria wearing a matching green dress with gold designs. In her hair was gold dust. Around her neck was a long golden chain holding the silver ring Dad gave her. I examine the ring quickly. It is made of a silver metal so reflective it makes a polished mirror look dull, and the gem was the radiant white metal of Maria's knife: the design a winged horse.

"What do you think of the clothes?" Maria asks, "I chose them myself, to bring out the green in our eyes and blonde in hair."

"Bit expensive, different from the brown and greys we wore," I joke. We had only ever had Kladoenian blue ceremonial robes, rest were dull work clothes.

"The fabric came all the way from Arabia." Maria smiles properly for the first time since we left Rochton. "I'm afraid to eat anything; I don't want to spill anything on this dress,"

We laugh for a moment but then it quickly dies. I try and keep the conversation going, "It's a nice ring."

She smiles, "Yeah, it's beautiful."

"Does it..."

She interrupts, "Yeah it does. But it's different, more tiring."

"How long till the banquet?" I ask Maria.

"About five minutes. And don't bring your knife." Maria says firmly.

I pretend to put it away and slip it inside my tunic when Maria isn't looking. We walk towards the great hall as fast as Maria's frock would allow us.

As we walk in, Queen Catherine quickly runs over to position us. To my surprise, we are stood directly opposite the King and Queen who, like the rest of the royal family, are dressed in the Kladoenian colour of deep blue. While Shakra wore a Kladoenian blue and black tunic with jet black beads in his hair to match. He is next to King Edward and gently holding hands with Princess Silvia.

The guests arrive in force. Every one of them bows or curtsies to the King, then kiss the Queen's hand, shake Shakra's hand, kiss Silva's hand, then congratulates them. After that, they walk to the side to collect food which had been put there by the army of servants. In the centre is a ballroom floor with the King's musicians playing a joyous tune.

Once most of the guests have arrived, we are told to mingle with the masses before the dance. Instead of mingling, I walk straight past everyone until I get to the food. I am famished. I fill my plate with bread, meat, cheese, and cakes. The food is fantastic.

After eating my fill, I ignore the guests again and head over to the drinks. Nearly all the drinks are alcoholic. There is an array of ales, meads, and wines. I pour myself a glass of fruity-smelling red wine to try. I take a sip of it and cough and splutter.

"You have to let it breathe," A voice behind me laughs. I turn to face Yasmin. For some reason, she has been allowed to come to the banquet as a guest rather than serving. Wearing a slim turquoise dress that matches her jewels. I can't help but wonder how she has so much money and importance.

"How do you know that?" I ask. "I thought Arabians didn't drink?"

She pauses and smiles, "Most don't, but I do." She pours herself a glass and walks towards the ballroom floor. I smirk and feel compelled to follow. Her eyes are bloodshot, and she still has tear stains on her cheeks. It is something to do with Shakra, I decide not to ask.

Looking around, I can tell that the dance is about to start. In the crowd, I see Maria talking to a lad who looks the same age as her. He wears a long blue tunic, the same colours as Prince Edward. He even looked like the Prince, except he had more muscle, shaved brown hair and a kind face.

I lean over to speak to Yasmin, "Who's that guy talking to Maria?"

She looks around then smiles, "Him? That's Prince Isaac, King Edward's nephew. And that guy next to Prince Edward is his older brother Joshua. The pair of them are the finest fighters in the Kingdom."

I see Joshua drinking ale and laughing with the Prince. He is about two years older than Maria; he looks almost identical to his brother but has a cruel face, stands a few inches taller and has slightly longer hair. "Finest fighters you say?" I say jokingly.

"Do you think you could beat them?" Yasmin smirks. I nod. She smiles and drinks deeply from her cup. Drinking that stuff gives me a headache, so I put it to the side. I take another look at the Joshua and Isaac, the pair of them seem twice the size of me, true Kladoenian warriors. I watch as Prince Edward and Joshua try to seduce some young noblewomen, trying to show off their superior strength. I shake my head, but whatever they were doing seemed to be enamouring the noble ladies, who fawn over the young royals.

Thankfully, the muses strike up a tune, changing the atmosphere of the banquet. A slow and melodic ballad fills the great hall, ready for the first dance of the evening dance.

First, the King walks onto the dancefloor with the Queen and they start to waltz around the floor. After a few bars, Shakra leads his betrothed, Princess Silvia, onto the floor; after them Maria and Prince Edward. The three pairs waltz around the floor with elegance and grace. Where had Maria learnt to dance?

To my surprise, the King and Queen keep on looking over to Yasmin and me. They glide over to us, "You two," King Edward hisses, "Start dancing."

Before I can say no, Yasmin grabs my hand and drags me onto the floor. "Follow my lead," she whispers. I give it my best, but I am hopeless. I've danced once before with Gwen, but I haven't done it since, knowing that the feeling would never be the same. I can feel the eyes of the guests watching me. Poor Yasmin; I must have stood on her feet at least twenty times in the first dance. Yasmin doesn't complain once.

After the first dance, the guests join the floor. Relieved, I slip to the side of the hall as quietly as possible. Yasmin doesn't mind and goes off to find Shakra. I pour myself a drink of icy cold water and gulp it down. Standing at the side, I watch the dance. The bright colours and fine jewellery catch the light as the couples spin around the hall. Over the music, I can hear Maria's laughter as she dances arm in arm with Prince Isaac.

I smile, pouring myself another icy cold goblet of water, the tunic and dancing have caused me to overheat. I head over to a bench in the corner of the room, away from everyone else and continue to watch the dance. To my surprise, someone decides to sit next to me. I am about to tell them to go away when I realise who it is.

Queen Catherine smiles, "How are you finding the banquet?"

I want to lie and say, *"Yeah it's great,"* but I can tell by her expression that she would know I was lying. "It's awful," I admit, "A whole village has been destroyed, a war is coming and we're just celebrating with a banquet that is more drink than food."

The Queen's expression hasn't changed, "I was saddened when you told me about your father."

"You were?"

"Yes," She sounds confused. "Why wouldn't I be?"

"Well... You're the Queen of Klad. My father was just the leader of a tiny village that is on the edge of Klad's territory."

She raises an eyebrow, "You really don't know." She pauses, heartache in her voice, "I come from Rochton,

Jacob. My father was the leader of the village at the time and I was his only child. Your father... well he and I were close; very close." She put a lot of emphasis on *very close,* "But one day the young King paid a visit, and he was dazzling. Then Edward did something unexpected and asked for my hand in marriage. I immediately said yes but my father was not so easily convinced. He told me that a marriage had already been arranged between me and your father, Luca. So, Edward marched over to Luca expecting a challenge and explained what had happened. Luca only sighed and said it was a King's right to take whatever he wants and then simply said that he was happy since he wanted me to have a better life. The young King was so pleased he announced Luca would take over from my father as leader of the village right there on the spot. It allowed my parents to come with me here. Luca claimed he wasn't worthy of the honour. Ever the charmer." The Queen smiles, a reminiscent light glazed over her eyes. "I couldn't believe the news when I heard the rumours of his children. Your mother must be quite a woman." The Queen pauses, realising she may have said too much. Before I can open my mouth, the Queen abruptly ends the conversation, "Well I'd better go. Lots of people to meet." The Queen walks off, hurriedly.

She could've been my mother but left my Dad to be Queen. I wonder why our father never mentioned it, just like how he never mentioned our real mother. I shake my head and decide to leave the banquet and head to bed.

My heavy legs drag me down the hallway to my room. I undress, leaving the expensive tunic in a heap on the floor. Instead of climbing under the covers, I just flop on top of the sheets and fall straight to sleep.

"Jacob," The sweet voice calls. I walk towards it.

Once again, the darkness came.

The sweet voice cries for help and I climb out of the darkness. I draw my knife, awaiting the Shadow Warrior. It steps out of the woods and points the dreaded trident at my chest. I look down at my knife and see it has transformed into a rope dart. I start swinging the rope, yet the warrior remains unfazed. When I unleash the attack at his neck, the shadow catches the dart in his trident and lets it wrap around the weapon. I attempt to pull the dart free but fail. The warrior pulls the trident back, throwing me face-first on the floor. I look up to see him stabbing me in the back.

I jump out of bed screaming and pace around the room, waiting for dawn. Looking out of the window, I faintly see the smoke still rising in the east from the burnt ruins that were once Rochton. If Shakra wasn't here I would have been one of the ashes. But then thinking about it, I wouldn't...

I am wanted alive.

Chapter 4

I wait until Shakra walks past, before rushing into the great hall for something to eat. Other than servants, only me and Shakra are awake. I find it quite humbling that the servants eat at the same table as the royals. I lay a couple of rashers of bacon on my plate and a roll of fresh bread.

Tucking into breakfast, I see an angry-looking Yasmin, storming ahead of the King and Queen. Shakra looks at them, then gives me his I know, and you don't look. I hate that look.

About five minutes later; Maria sits down with a plain bowl of oats. "Urgh," Maria groans, "I drank too much of that wine. I've got such a headache."

Shakra smirks, "Welcome to the world of royalty."

I look around at the royals entering and I immediately see what Shakra means. Nearly all of them stay away from the greasy food and keep on groaning to one another. Chuckling, I ask him, "How come you don't have a headache?"

He smiles, "Everyone wanted to congratulate me, didn't get much of a chance to drink." He starts laughing hysterically, ignoring the looks from hung-over royalty. I can't help but grin. I finish my breakfast in silence and leave to my room. As I'm walking out, I see Isaac sit down next to Maria.

I sit down in my room. Finally, the grief hits and hits me like a tidal wave. I feel sick. All those people needlessly lost. The faces of Rochton locals seem to elude me. I can remember their names, their personality, even how they fought but not their faces. Not even my Dad's face can appear in my mind. I choke back the tears. Shaking my head, I preoccupy myself by sharpening my knife, not that it needed it.

After what seems an age, Maria walks in my room. "The King told me to come here."

"Why?" I ask.

"Not sure," she says blankly. Takes the chair nearby me and stares out of the window. We sit in silence for a few minutes until there is a knock at the door. King Edward II walks in followed two servants carrying our cloaks that we travelled in. For some reason, they have our cloaks wrapped around long thin shapes. We jump out of our chairs and bow. The King smiles gently and gestures for us to rise.

The servant with Maria's cloak steps forward. The King softly announces, "For you, Maria Da Nesta. For valiantly leaving your home and riding here to warn us of the impending attack, I gift to you the freshly forged Dioscuri." He unwraps the cloak to reveal two identical swords in scabbards. I can tell by the shape that they are katanas. At the bottom of each hilt is a shaped and polished sapphire. The grips are made of soft leather. She pulls one of the swords out of its scabbard. The katana is made of the same brilliant white metal as Maria's knife, very thin with a slight curve.

Maria's smile stretches from ear to ear, "Thank you, Your Majesty."

The King turns to me, "And for you Jacob Da Nesta, for aiding Klad, preparing us for the coming war, I gift you Nemesis." He unwraps my cloak. The weapon that he presents me is unlike any I've ever seen. It is two metres long from tip to tip. A wooden staff with two, thirty-centimetre blades at either end made with the unusual black metal. Where the staff meets the blades, there is a blood-red ruby, polished and shaped. On each blade, are two grappling hooks. I notice a thin, red string attached to the lower hooks. It's also a bow. A quiver of arrows is lying in the cloak; red flight, black arrowhead.

I grab Nemesis. Perfectly balanced. I tug at the bowstring. A glaive combined with a bow. The four hooks on the same side as the bowstring, the edged side of the blade on the opposite side. I feel complete. The part of me that was missing is in my grasp. "Thank you, Your Majesty."

The King smiles, "Get yourselves down to the arena and practice. My family will be down in about an hour." And with that he turns and silently walks out the door, his servants following a few paces behind.

We sit in awe for a few minutes. "Come on Jacob, let's go." Maria cries. I put the quiver over my shoulder follow Maria out the door. With Nemesis in my hands, I feel powerful, no one can stop me. I'm so excited; I end up running to the arena. Maria runs just as fast, almost giddy with excitement.

As soon as we get to the arena, I fire an arrow straight through a dummies head, which is standing at the far side.

I practice my shooting for about half an hour; I didn't miss once. Then I start to practice with the blades. I slash at the dummies until they are nothing but straw and rags.

"Not bad Da Nesta's, not bad," I hear a familiar voice shout. I look up to see Shakra in the stands. "Who's the better fighter?" Shakra leans forward, goading us to rise to the challenge. Maria and I look at each other.

"Why not?" Maria says. A broad grin runs across her face. "Be nice for a little duel." She seems very confident. I nod and grab a blunt quiver of arrows. I grasp Nemesis a little tighter. I can win. Maria doesn't have a clue what's coming.

Maria draws the twin swords of Dioscuri. She runs at me. I let loose an arrow, but she ducks. She closes me down too fast for me to fire again. Maria strikes both blades down, I intercept the blow with a parry. I stab towards her guts, but she spins out of it. She swings one sword towards my legs, but I catch the blade in the grapple spikes. Before I have a chance to disarm her, she yanks her katana back. Her radiant swords blind me, she is moving so fast. I've never known anyone to move like that. It takes all my instincts to avoid me getting cut up like confetti. Maria slices at my head but I duck under it. She is too quick. I keep blocking manic. I keep dodging her blades by a hair. No time for a breath.

Then it hits me, a wave of tranquillity. A flurry of attacks continues to barrage me, but I can anticipate everyone. I feel so complete. Nemesis is not a weapon; it is a part of me. I don't have to keep defending. I have control. A feeling of peace. I smile. Maria doesn't seem so fast, she is beatable. I take a deep breath and calm. Wait, I think, wait until she is most vulnerable.

I see the desperation in Maria's face. She rushes into her next attack. I dodge easily and I swipe both her blades to the side. Exposed, I place a kick into her chest. She stumbles backwards. Before she has time to compose herself, I attack again. Stab, slash, feint, roll, parry, kick. Maria is frantic. She somehow stops all the attacks. She desperately lunges but I easily sidestep the blow and sweep her legs with Nemesis. She falls face-first to the floor. Maria sits up to find my blade at her neck. Maria's fear turns to glee and she starts laughing. "You win, finally."

She's right. That's the first time I've ever beaten her. I look up to see Shakra sat up with King Edward II; Queen Catherine; Princess Elizabeth and Mary; and strangely Yasmin. Shakra gives me a smug smile. "Well done Jacob," Shakra shouts down, "Nemesis and Dioscuri are some mighty weapons." There is a nod of approval from the King and Queen. Shakra's somewhat cocky smile returns. Obviously keen to watch some more fights, Shakra calls, "Why don't you fight the royals? It would make a good match." He points at Prince Edward and Princess Silvia who are standing at the side of the arena with their cousins.

"My son and daughter would easily beat them," Queen Catherine scoffs.

Shakra's cocky smile is unmoving. "Your Grace, your children would not beat them. As a pair, they cannot lose when there are equal teams."

I sigh. How can someone so small be so loud and cocky?

The Queen turns to him red-faced, "Shakra, what are you suggesting?"

Before Shakra can answer, the King intervenes, "Catherine, *Prince* Shakra is suggesting that our nephews should also fight. It will be a good fight; the Da Nesta's are formidable opponents. Only Isaac stood to see how they fought; the rest were too ignorant to watch."

I turn to see he is right. It is clear from the ashamed faces of the royal children that they hadn't bothered to watch us other than Isaac. He is still analysing me and Maria intently, he must have been studying us the whole time. He is a true warrior, looking for the strengths and weaknesses of every opponent. I must admit I am surprised he was the one looking; he seems too kind to fight.

Prince Edward steps forward, snarling, "Father, we shall crush these commoners underfoot. But you insist we must fight, then so be it."

The four of them walk over to their personal master-at-arms. They swap their spears for blunt tip ones and they suit up in their expensive plated armour. I turn to face Maria. She nods then walks to the side. A servant offers us a helmet each; we said no, of course, they can't know our secret. We keep our hair down. Maria and I wear light leather armour rather the royal's plated armour. Their spears are much taller than us, their bossed shield cover half of their body and their broadswords can pierce any armour, might as well wear something light.

Maria and I stand at the side, watching the royals get ready. The fight is about to start. I pull an arrow out of the quiver. I rub my thumb over the blunt end. It's not real, just need to make sure I don't kill a royal family member with Nemesis.

The Royals are finally ready. The master-at-arms sounds the bell. I release an arrow, only for Prince Edward's shield to block it. The royals form a small shield wall. My arrows glance harmlessly off their shields. Maria darts to the right. The wall splits up and they throw their spears. I dive to the left, just dodging the javelins. Prince Edward and Joshua run towards me. I quickly jump up and let loose an arrow hitting Prince Edward square in the chest. Joshua swings for my head but I duck. I swipe at his chest, but he blocks it with his shield. Attempting to pull Nemesis back, it throws Joshua forward. I curse. Nemesis' grappling spikes are caught in the shield. Swinging Nemesis around, I pull the shield off his arm. The full weight of the stuck shield throws me off balance long enough for him to stand up. He stabs for my chest, but I jump back and swing Nemesis around, smacking him in the face with his own shield. Joshua crumples to the floor unconscious.

I look around the arena to find Maria. I see Princess Silvia rolling around on the floor groaning. The clang of metal draws my attention. Maria and Isaac are still fighting. The powers of Isaac's attacks are pushing Maria back against the walls. I pull the shield off the spike and ready an arrow. When I let loose the arrow, it hits Isaac in the back with such force that he falls forward.

I walk towards Maria. Maria sits in the corner breathing heavily. She surely can't be that tired. "Are you ok?" I ask.

Maria looks up, watery eyes, "Yeah, I'm fine." She pushes herself up. Behind me, Isaac jumps up with a broad smile.

"Great fight," Isaac booms with a laugh. "Where are the others?" I point them out. Isaac laughs some more. "To think that they were so sure that they would beat you." I can't help but smile until I see the Prince and Princess scowl at the three of us. Unfortunately, Joshua is taken off on a stretcher since he is still unconscious. His nose has been squashed from the blow of the shield. I feel guilty, I'm sure to get a telling off from Maria later.

I turn to go back to training when Shakra comes running in frantically. "You need to get to the palace now. There's some bad news."

*****

Maria and I follow the Princes and Princess as they rush to the castle. We burst into the great hall. The King is sat opposite his younger brother, the General of the Kladoenian army. Between them is a map of Valouria with an army of little figures. Prince Edward rushes to his mother's side and talks in a hushed voice. Slowly his usual arrogant look is wiped off and replaced a look of sheer horror. Shakra leans in to whisper something to the King, pointing at the small figurines on the map. Princess Silvia holds her younger sisters as they shake. The poor twins look on the verge of tears.

The maid, Yasmin, walks towards Maria and I, a scowl stuck on her face. Her footsteps echo in the great hall. In a hushed voice she hisses, "Vlaydom has formed an 'alliance' with Chevon and has ordered the attack on Klad since your foolish King decided not to pay the taxes. The army will reach Rochton in a few days. The King has ordered every man between the age of twenty and fifty to bear arms and ride out. It's not enough men. Vlaydom alone has well over twenty times the numbers of Klad."

I gulp. Those odds don't sound good. Even with the might of the best soldiers, those numbers don't sound good.

"Yasmin," The King calls, "Bring me wine."

"Yes, Your Grace," Yasmin sighs, rolling her eyes.

Wine! Now is the time to concentrate, not drink. Despite my best judgment, I storm forward. "Sire, you cannot drink, not now! We need to retreat to Arabia." Maria tries to pull me back, but I shrug her off. I stare right through the King, determined not to show anyone how petrified I am.

The King ignores me and drinks deeply from his cup that Yasmin has just handed to him. "Leave us," Joshua and Isaac's father gives his older brother a grave nod then leads everyone out of the throne room. I don't budge.

"Silvia," The King calls. His daughter stops and turns around, "Stay." Silvia nods. I sigh and turn to walk away with Maria, my anger building. King Edward snaps me out of my thoughts with his booming voice, "You stay too Jacob." I jump. His voice doesn't seem angry or annoyed, but I could make out a threatening tone. Maria looks confused, but Isaac grabs her hand leads her away. I turn and face the King.

Once the great hall is empty the King makes us look at the map of Valouria. I work out that the figurines represent our troops: blue for Klad, orange of Chevon and scarily a sea of red for Vlaydom. My stomach drops into a hollow pit as I look over the battle plans.

King Edward points at little west of Rochton, "Klad will attack the armies of Vlaydom and Chevon in the Rocky Pass. The army must go through here. Their only other choice is to negotiate the Great Woods which even King Joseph of Vlaydom is not foolish enough to try. In the boulders of the Rocky Pass, an army can hide and ambush the enemy. Chevon's horses will be useless. Their number will not count for much. There is no way they can outflank us. If our line holds, our warriors should overcome all." The King pauses, "But if the worst should happen you may have to defend the city. Silvia, you shall be Queen in mine and your brother's absence." He mutters grimly. He then hands Princess Silvia the sword and shield of Klad. The King continues, "The person who holds these has the divine right to rule all of Klad. Look after them well until I return." Silvia, silent in shock, turns to stone, frozen with the burden her father had just bestowed her. "And Jacob," King Edward says, "You shall be the one to prepare our defences. If you are who I think you are, you and Maria are best suited to defend our home." He takes a deep drink of his wine, "The odds are that most our army won't return but hopefully, neither will theirs once we're done with them. But if you get pushed back to the castle, there's a way to escape."

He walks towards his grand throne. On the wall behind his throne is a giant stag's head. He reaches up to the stag and pulls on the left antler. The golden chair moves forward showing a tunnel in the wall and under the seat. "As you can see the tunnel is big enough for two men at a time, even big enough for a horse the size of Shakra's Lena, if the rider walks. In this tunnel, you shall find packs of supplies and weapons. This tunnel will lead you straight into the Great Woods. Unfortunately, someone will have to stay behind to close the tunnel by repositioning the antler." King Edward repositions the antler to prove his point. The King sighs and drains the last of his wine. Forcing a false smile, the King says his farewells. "Well best of luck, I need to go and see the army."

The King races out of the throne room before we can ask any questions. Silvia and I are left in stunned silence. "I should go and see father off," Silvia mumbles, weighed down by the jewelled sword and shield of Klad. She runs after her father. I sigh. I take another look at the throne that hides the secret tunnel, hopefully, it won't come to a siege.

After a few minutes alone, I come outside to see thousands of men dressed in blue and steel armour. Women and children weep and say farewell to husbands, fathers, brothers, sons, and friends. I look across the faces, the young and the old, wondering how many of those faces will return if any. A soldier's horn blows, and the army saddles their mounts. The greatest warriors in all of humankind trot out to face a foe who outnumber them comfortably. We haven't got a chance, I think.

Isaac walks up beside me, "Joshua will be furious. That nasty knock on the head you gave him means he is still unconscious and unable to ride out with the army."

"Why would he want to ride out to his death?" I mutter under my breath. I turn to face Isaac who obviously hasn't heard me. I look around. I can't see our new Queen; Queen Silvia. "Have you seen Silvia anywhere?" I ask.

Isaac looks at me confused as if what I said has shocked him, "Of course I have. She's over there waving off the army."

I walk through the narrow streets of the market until I reach the city wall. Climbing up the stone steps of the wall, I can still hear the cries of women and children. Looking west, I see the Kladoenian army fade off into the distance. The new Queen stands by her mother and her young sisters, quietly shedding a few tears.

"Silvia,"

She faces me, puffy-eyed. "Yes?"

"We need to start planning the defences, immediately," I tell her. Silva forces out a smile, and we walk slowly to the castle.

By the time we reach the castle, it is starting to get dark. We enter the silent throne room. Sitting down around the table, I see the plan of the King's army. I sweep off the little figures and replace the map of Valouria for the map of the city.

"So, what do we do?" I ask Silvia.

The new Queen looks at me, lost. "I don't know Jacob. What do you think?"

"I have an idea, but we need Shakra to lead a section of the defence." Silvia pulls a shocked face, obviously not enamoured by the idea of her future husband leading the Kladoenian defences. I try to convince her, we need him for my plan to work, "Your Grace, he is no more Chevonic than you or I." I reason.

"Jacob, I don't know... do you trust him?"

I pause. Do I trust him? He has saved my life but at what expense: hundreds died, villages destroyed, and his nation will still be taking my life soon. After Gwen, I had not allowed myself to trust in anyone but my father and Maria. "I trust him with my life." I lie, "He's going to be your husband soon, so you better start trusting him."

Queen Silvia nods, "Ok, what's the plan?"

I pick up a handful of the figurines. "Foot soldiers will be placed on the wall and will be there to repel anyone foolish enough to climb the walls. Archers will be placed on the rooftops of the buildings near the wall, taking out their number and to kill anyone who gets inside the wall. Finally, the horses will be at the top of the market street ready to charge at anyone who enters through the gate. What do you think?"

She agrees silently, hands shaking, "Where do we fall back if we get overwhelmed?"

I point at the castle on the map, "Here."

She breaks down, "We're going to die. Their numbers are too great. We will be slaughtered." Her tears flood down her face. I look sympathetically at her. The burden of leading these people did not suit her. She's looked on the verge of crying ever since we heard of the attack.

I grab her hand and try to console her, "Silvia, we'll survive. Even if our army is defeated, the enemy numbers will be too low to attempt siege. And this city has never been sacked by any man."

"It has been sacked before though, by the Elves in the Wars of Old."

I pause, "Elves are a myth. Even so, humans won the war, Klad was only sacked because it had to be," I shake my head, "Go and get some rest, we need to address the people about how we're going to defend the city."

"Yeah, I'd better go. I'll address the remaining members of the court first thing tomorrow. Goodnight" Silvia looks down awkwardly; we are still holding hands. Quickly, I let go of her hand. Remember what happened with Gwen, I tell myself. Without saying a word, Queen Silvia stands up and tiptoes to her room.

I sigh and tidy up the map. Why do people mention the Wars of Old around me? They are children's stories. Myths about races never exist. Even if there was a shred of truth in these stories, they happened hundreds of years ago.

Knowing that everyone would be asleep, I sneak back to my room. After what seems one of my noisiest ventures, I reach my room and lay down on my bed. For some strange reason, I find myself lying awake, thinking about Mum and how she met Dad. Well, at least the story my father told me.

Dad was out hunting in the treeline of the Great Woods during the winter. A dangerous but necessary task he undertook to provide for the sick and elderly in the harsher months. The story my Dad tells me was that he stumbled across my Mum lying down in a ditch with her leg bent at an abnormal angle. He helped her out of the ditch and tended to her leg. He offered to shelter her in Rochton, but she refused profusely. My Dad built her a fire and a makeshift shelter for her to stay in. After that, my Dad went to the woods every day to check her leg, relight her fire, bring her food and water, and to keep her company.

Then one day she wasn't there.

It was almost a year later when she knocked on his door and presented him with Maria. She lived with my father and sister for almost a year before she left him for a second time. Dad claims that she was not popular with the locals of Rochton and kept on trying to convince him to leave with her.

Once again, she had left Dad, pregnant with his child. And again, a year later my mother returned to Rochton to hand me over to Dad. This time she didn't stay. She left me at the front door with a note and two knives. The knives that Maria and I treasure so much. And that was it, she never returned, never contacted Dad, Maria, or me. I can't help but resent her. Maria always scolds me for speaking ill of her.

Yawning, I place my knife on the bedside table. My mother isn't worth a second thought. I should just forget about her. I glance over at my glaive bow, Nemesis, leaning against the wall in the corner. I fall asleep, having the same nightmare of the Shadow Warrior. Knowing that in a few days...

I'll be dead.

Chapter 5

I threw up this morning; same as yesterday morning and the morning before. My nerves are in shreds. We haven't heard any news from the Kladoenian Army which had left over a week ago. No one knew if the battle had been fought, about to be fought or whether the fighting was currently happening. I hate not knowing.

Queen Silvia is right. We're all going to die. The numbers of Vlaydom and Chevon easily outnumber that of our own, combined the two nations' armies' dwarves Klad's entire population. Even with our superior warriors, the sheer number of enemies will cause the Kladoenians to be overrun and slaughtered. And after our army is destroyed the enemy will advance to siege the castle unfazed.

There is no sign from Arabia. Our only ally is not coming to our aid. It is unclear whether they have received our message or if they have and King Tufail of Arabia has just ignored our plea. Isaac told me that Vlaydom has a garrison called The Outpost which keeps Arabia and Yasu in line. Maybe soldiers from The Outpost had intercepted our messenger.

During these last few days of turmoil, I have felt so alone. I've had no one to talk to. I felt on edge constantly. I can't even find Maria to talk to. The new Queen set up a war council a few days ago which includes Shakra and Maria who would oversee what little cavalry we have. Even

Joshua, who had finally woken full of rage at missing the call for arms, and Isaac are on the council. Only I have been excluded, so much for her father's plan of me leading the defences. All I know is that she is using my plan and that I was in charge of the archers.

I know no one well enough to talk to, not that it matters, everywhere I go in Klad people avoid eye contact with me, walk the other way or go silent. I walk down the busy main street and people parted to let me walk down. I can hear them whisper about me. It isn't doing my nerves any good. Even in the arena where I could normally find someone willing to challenge me, people still avoid me. I just end up training and training until I ache, or the dummy is in tatters. Training with Nemesis is the only thing keeping me going. Nemesis has become a part of me. Normal steel has always felt too heavy and unbalanced whereas Nemesis is light and deadly.

But even as I train, I can feel people's eyes watching me. Whispers echo down the arena. I would hear only fearful tones. The Kladoenian people seemed to fear me more than their impending demise.

After training alone, I walk onto the wall with the lookouts as I do every afternoon and wait until I watch the sunset, expecting to see the colours of an army approaching, silently still hoping that it would be Klad's. The Great Woods loom ominously in North, heckling me with its eery silence. Once the sun begins to hide behind the hills in the distance, I then go and check over what little defences we have as always, knowing deep down if there is an attack our defences would not hold.

But tonight is different.

A lone rider approaches slumped in his saddle. I can just make out the blue armour. "Rider!" I yell, "There's a rider out there," All the lookouts come running over, squinting, trying to make out the rider. I intently point into the distance where the rider is trotting limply over the horizon. Eventually, a handful of the lookouts scream and spot our solider. For a few moments, cheers rang out. Is he a messenger to inform us that our troops have been victorious?

But the fragile hope shattered. In the distance, the rider has fallen off his horse, bloody and weak. I turn and face the newly appointed captain of the guards. "I have to get out there," I tell her. She pauses for a moment then agrees.

I run down the stairs of the wall to the stables and grab the reins of the horse I had ridden into Klad a lifetime ago. "Open the gate." The captain barks. I climb into the saddle and ride out at full speed.

I have been riding for an age and it still feels like I am miles away. I look back and see that the wall of Klad is lined with entire Kladoenian population anxiously watching. Another rider is catching me. I can tell by the magnificence of the horse that it is Shakra riding on Lena. Within five minutes he caught me and rides alongside. He doesn't say a word or even looks at me.

Finally, we reach the soldier, soaked in his own blood with two strange golden arrows sticking out of his back. Cautiously Shakra and I dismount and approach the wounded man. Shakra crouches down next to the soldier. My hand instinctively grabs the hilt of my knife. Shakra cradles the head of the soldier and curses. The wounded soldier is Prince Edward.

The Prince is breathing his last breaths. So much effort is being expended just the fill his lungs. Edward coughs up blood onto Shakra's arm. Shakra seems unfazed, "What happened?"

Edward turns to look him in the eyes. He is struggling to cling onto life. "We... w... were... slaughtered... We... h... h... had... n... no... ch... chance... They... knew... w... w... w... where... w... we... w... w... were... It... It... was... a... t... trap... It... wasn't... j... j... just... Chevon... a... an... and... Vlay..." he is starting to slip away, "Vlay... Vlay..." The Prince draws his last breath and closes his eyes. His body falls limp in Shakra's arms.

Shakra remains calm, turning his head and looks straight at me, "What was he going to say about someone else?"

I stare at Edward's pale face. I thought the sight of a dead body would make me feel sick, but I felt nothing, nothing at all. Though bloodied, Edward looked at peace, almost happy. I face Shakra and shrug my shoulders, "I have no idea what he was going to say."

Shakra grimaces, "We're going to have to go back and tell everyone the bad news." I agree.

I quickly examine the dead Prince's body. There is something peculiar about the two arrows sticking out of his back. I pull out an arrow and wipe off the blood on my sleeve. The arrowhead is a golden metal unlike any I've ever seen. With its indigo flight, the arrow makes me curious. Which kingdom uses that type of arrow and that type of metal? I show Shakra the arrow and he just shrugs his shoulders. He is too busy trying to haul Edward's corpse onto Lena's back. I throw the arrow to the side and help. At twice our size, lifting a limp, lifeless Prince Edward is no easy task. We have to strip him of all his armour just so the two of us can lift him. We work in silence; it takes a long time. Too long.

Eventually, Edward is laid across Lena's back. Shakra climbs on her back and positions himself behind the deceased Prince, I jump onto my steed. We trot back still in silence. It is starting to get dark. By the time we reach the walls of Klad, it is pitch black.

Maria, Yasmin, and the entire royal family are waiting for us inside the gates. Shakra dismounts and passes me Lena's reins. He walks slowly over to Queen Mother Catherine and tells them the bad news. The Queen Mother lowers her head gravely. Queen Silvia and her younger sisters burst into tears, Yasmin quickly comforts them and leads them away, up to the castle.

Catherine drags herself over to see her son and starts muttering to herself. Isaac and Joshua stand in silence trying to take the news in. Shakra takes the reins of Lena and my horse as I dismount and take them to the stables. I feel like I should follow him and help but I just stand and watch him walk off. There is just something about him that I can't trust. I head back to the castle and my room alone, feeling my stomach doing somersaults.

As I climb into bed, I picture the scene tomorrow. Waves of soldiers will come crashing into the Kladoenian walls. We will not hold. The sheer number of Vlaydom and

Chevon will eventually overcome our defences. I would cry if I were not so exhausted.

Unable to sleep, I lie awake all night. Words ringing around my head. *"War is coming."* *"Tomorrow the enemy will be at the city gates."* And most scarily, *"I'm going to die."*

*****

DONG! DONG! DONG!

I sit upright. So today is the day I die, I tell myself. I run to the window and throw open the drapes. Morning has just broken. I see the guards from last night's duty already sprinting to their position at the wall. I cannot hear my own thoughts over the sound of the bells.

I hastily run and change into my fitted, light, leather armour. I tie a belt around my waist which holds my knife in a scabbard at my back. I sling a quiver over my shoulder. I grab Nemesis and sprint out the door. The corridors of the castle are manic as both royals and commoners prepare for the battle. I scramble past them and escape out of the great hall.

As I run down to the city walls, I see everyone panicking to get ready. The bell is still hammering away. Pushing past people suiting up into full plate armour, I head down the main market street at full speed. I pass the little cavalry we have. I run past elderly couples that are being weighed down by their armour. I pass young children who can barely lift a sword. I see mothers whispering to their children as they shove a spear into their arms. I spot a priestess, blessing a mass of soldiers who are kneeling at her feet, relying on some magical, unknown entity to somehow prevent their deaths. I shake my head and continue to bolt down the street.

Three horses almost knock me over as they fly past. Silvia rides down the street, flanked by her cousins Joshua and Isaac. They head for the main gate which is barred shut. I continue to run until I'm at the right house. It is a house right next to the main gate. I go inside and climb the stairs and then climb onto the roof.

I look over the wall for the first time. The army is endless. A sea of Vlaydom Red, Chevonic Orange, and grey steel. The army is a great distance away, but their war drums are already starting to drown out the bells of Klad. More archers rush onto the buildings next to the wall. Kladoenian soldiers climb onto the wall. It is a mismatch army made up of women, the elderly, and children. They all are trained fighters, but, like myself, none are killers. Queen Silvia climbs up the stairs flanked by the heavily armoured Joshua and Isaac. She speaks to each soldier as she climbs, offering words of encouragement and support. She continues to walk until she has made her way to the middle of the battlements, standing above the main gate.

The bells finally stop. Our young Queen turns to address her followers. "Kladoenians, my brothers, my sisters. Today is a day we write ourselves into history. Today we will repel the attack from the cowardice alliance between Chevon and Vlaydom!" There was a meek cheer from the troops. I stay silent. Silvia continues to encourage the troops, but I zone out.

My eyes scan our defences. Silvia stands proud on the wall, directly over the gate. She holds the sword and shield of Klad high above her head. She wears fitted steel plate armour and her helmet is decorated with a gold crown and a blue plume. Either side of her Joshua and Isaac are statues. They had steel plate armour and plumed helmets also. Both carry the same basic weaponry as the rest of the soldiers on the wall. Each soldier is armed with a spear, a shield, and a short sword. The main force of women, children and elderly stand guarding the wall. A smaller force stands behind the great gate. Some of the elderly are having to use their spear to lean on just to stay upright. The young soldiers seem weighed down by their heavy steel armour.

The next line of defence is on the rooftops by the wall. A single road separates the houses from the wall. On each house stood a handful of archers, bows ready to fire. All the archers wear light leather armour and are equipped with longbows and short swords. I look back along the main street. Buildings and flags block my view. Somewhere further along that road are Maria and Shakra, ready and waiting.

I look around my rooftop, there are seven others; a young girl, two old men, an elderly lady and three young women. The young girl stands next to me, shaking with fear. I drop to a crouch, so we are at eye level, "What's your name?"

She looks up at me, her eyes wide with fear and panic. The bow she is holding is the same height as her. The tip of the short sword on her belt is scraping the floor. She must only be eight. "Erika," She replies. The footsteps of the army can now be heard. They are still a few miles away. "Are you Jacob Da Nesta?"

"Yes," I answer confused, "How do you know who I am?"

"People say you're the reason this war started. But they also say you and your sister are the only hope we have left." It feels like a punch in the gut. I try to ignore what she just said. Why are people blaming us for the war? Who do people think Maria and I are? Before I can make up a reply, Erika continues, "Are we going to die?"

I didn't answer her question, instead, I say the only thing I could say, "I'll look after you Erika, don't worry," I couldn't help but put my arm around her for support as we watch the sea of steel get closer and closer. The Kladoenian army stands in silence. Time keeps marching on. Slowly the army that will be our demise comes closer. Still, we stand frozen, watching our deaths approach.

After an hour of waiting, the enemy army is only a few hundred metres from the wall when they stop. Legion after legion stands the red and steel army of Vlaydom. Every so often there are pockets of Chevonic riders clad in orange.

Chevon's Orange banner with a black horse flies next to Vlaydom's Red banner with the image of grey balance scales. On the left of the scale is a steel sword and, on the right, are masses of silver coins balancing the sword perfectly. On our wall are a sword, a spear, and a shield on the blue banner of Klad.

A Vlaydom messenger trots forward until he is forty metres from the gate. "Queen Silvia," He calls, "Tell your people to lay down your arms; open the gates and submit to Vlaydom. None of you need to die. King Joseph of Vlaydom, the King of Kings, and King Markus of Chevon wish you no harm. Pledge loyalty to Vlaydom and we'll turn our army around and return home. Resist us and you will be destroyed."

Silvia doesn't say a word. She's frozen. She is contemplating giving up. My rage builds up. I would not be controlled by Vlaydom. I let go of Erika. I grab an arrow from my quiver. It scrapes as I draw it. Carefully, I nock it on my bow. I can feel the eyes of Klad watching me now. My breathing steadies. I pull back my bowstring to my chin. I carefully adjust my aim.

"Queen Silvia, I must have your answer." The messenger demands. There is a faint whistle through the air, then a thud. The messenger got his reply. My black arrow sticks out of his chest. He falls off his steed. Silvia snaps out of her shock and thrusts her sword in the air. There is a huge roar from the Kladoenian warriors. I should feel ill, I think, I just killed a man. I felt nothing. He may have been the one to kill my father. It was like shooting a deer. No emotions, only duty. I did what I had to.

Horns blow. The soldiers of Vlaydom charge forward to the wall. "Volley," I shout. Arrows rain down upon the enemy. Hundreds of arrows find their mark, but it doesn't seem to make a difference. "Fire at will." I cry. I send my arrows over the wall as quickly as possible. Arrows fly continuously over the heads of our soldiers on the wall. The enemy soldiers fall as arrows hit. But for every enemy that falls, two more seem to take their place.

I hear Joshua shout. "Ladders!" The soldiers lower their spears. All along the wall men in Vlaydom's red armour appear. Chaos follows. Spears thrust and find the gaps in the enemy's armour. Swords clash. The archers continue to fire over the wall. There are few pockets of red on the wall, but our soldiers are repelling the attack well. Any soldier audacious enough to attack the Queen is quickly cut down by either Joshua or Isaac. I spot one of the noblewomen Prince Edward tried to seduce throwing a Vlaydom soldier over the wall, back from where he came. Isaac plants a kick into the chest of one soldier as he tries to crawl over the wall, causing the Vlaydom soldier to lose balance, toppling over his own ladder as he falls.

The dead are slowly piling up. Even though it is not our trained soldiers fighting on the walls, the Kladoenians are much better warriors that the cowards climbing to face them. Each Kladoenian is fighting valiantly. Each Vlaydom soldier that is cut down is immediately replaced by another, but so far, the sheer number is not overwhelming us.

BANG!

The gate shudders. The Vlaydom soldiers are hitting our gate with a battering ram. Our soldiers behind the gate lower their spears.

BANG!

"Aim at the gate," I scream. I nock an arrow and pull back the bowstring. Erika and the rest of the archers copy me.

BANG!

Small cracks appear in the gate. I yell above the noise, "Wait for my command to fire."

BANG!

The cracks become much larger. I slow my breathing down. I faintly hear Maria call out her commands in the distance.

BANG!

The gate flies open. "Fire!" I scream. A wave of death hits the invaders. The Kladoenian soldiers have formed a phalanx, blocking the three roads. The enemy that enter are trapped in a shield and spear wall and are being cut down by arrows.

A horn sounds from deep within the enemy army. I see Vlaydom soldiers move to the side, creating a path straight to the gate. The Chevon riders charge. I turn around to face the castle. I pull back my bowstring and send my arrow high up into the air.

In the distance behind us, I hear Maria yell "Charge!" As our cavalry sound their horns.

Shakra and Maria ride at the front of our makeshift cavalry, charging down the market street straight to the remnants of the gates. The soldiers guarding the main road rush to the sides. As the first few Chevon riders enter through the gate, arrows rain upon them. The two sets of Kladoenian warriors thrust their spears into the sides of the enemy. The Chevon riders keep on charging.

Our cavalry is at full speed. They crash into the Chevon riders that make it past the first defences. I spot Maria who is fighting with both swords of Dioscuri. She uses each sword on a different enemy. Our cavalry is slowly pushing the Chevon army backwards. The Kladoenian defences are standing strong. Ladders are starting to be pushed away from the wall.

The gateway is now sealed with our soldiers. This attack is being repelled successfully. We are slowly clearing our defences; the enemy soldiers can't get a foothold. The Kladoenian army is revitalised. We could win.

Our foolish hope dissipates within moments. A new horn blows. The sound is different. It is not so sharp and raspy; it is pleasant sounding. I look at the soldiers of Vlaydom and Chevon, nothing seems to have changed. Why did they blow the horn? What does it mean?

I look pass the army and into the distance. A gold cloud is approaching and approaching fast. I watch it come closer. It isn't a cloud; it is giant birds. As they come nearer, I realise the full truth. Flying towards Klad is an army of *Gryphons.* The head and front claws of a giant eagle and the rear and back paws of a mighty lion; these magnificent beasts are the stuff of legends. They are meant to be extinct since the Wars of Old. But no, nearly three hundred of the monsters are flying towards Klad at full speed.

The mystical Gryphons are not the things scaring me though. It is who is riding that scares me. On the back of each Gryphon are beings that are also meant to be extinct. The reason that the Kladoenian Army lost becomes clear now. This golden army would've slaughtered them.

I curse under my breath. We are doomed. The Gryphon riders are...

...*Elves!*

Chapter 6

Everyone in Klad froze. They should be extinct. The Elves look like elegant humans with pointed ears. They sit proudly in their gold armour on the back of their regal beasts, Gryphons. The bodies of majestic lions and the head, wings, and front claws of a giant eagle. Each Gryphon carries two Elven riders, an archer, and a melee fighter. These mystical archers are going to slaughter us. My stomach seems to sink into the ground. We're doomed.

Apparently, Humans defeated the Elves hundreds of years ago. They were wiped out. Yet here I am stood watching them fly full speed towards me and my allies. The Vlaydom and Chevon soldiers that had made inside the city walls have retreated to their army and are also watching the hypnotic gold army fly towards the city walls. We watch terrified as the cloud of gold approaches. The Elves in their golden armour are getting closer and closer. I can't help but find the half-lion, half-eagle Gryphons incredible as they soar and dance in the sky. I want to give up, the Elven archers will be able to pick us off from the safety of the sky.

Queen Silvia turns and quickly address our army, snapping me out of my trance-like state. "Archers take out those Gryphons. Everyone else back into formation. There'll be another wave of Vlaydom soldiers soon."

It's hopeless, I think. I nock an arrow and take aim, following the small Elven army as it approaches. The rest of the archers copy. The Gryphons are three hundred metres away, two hundred metres, one hundred. I wait till the first Gryphon flies over the wall, "Fire." All the Kladoenian archers release their arrows. A volley of arrows sails through the sky. The Gryphons are too agile, the Elves knew what was going to happen. The Gryphons soar higher. Our arrows only manage to hit a few Gryphons. One Gryphon that is hit crashes into the wall, knocking a handful of our soldiers off the wall. The Elves return fire. Every arrow seems to hit its mark, finding the tiniest chinks in the armour. One of the women on my roof collapses as an arrow pierces her chest.

The Gryphon army then dives down low. "Fire at will." I cry. My arrow hits one of the Elven riders, square in the chest. Arrows rain down upon Klad. Three soldiers are plucked off the wall by a Gryphon. An archer is knocked off the rooftop by the wing of a Gryphon. One Elf dives off his Gryphon and tries to stab Queen Silvia in the back. Joshua intercepts the strike and throws the Elf off the wall. It is chaos. The archers of the Elves are far more skilled with the bow than any Kladoenian. Our numbers dwindle as the pirouetting Gryphons fly out of our reach, bringing the rain of destruction of the Elves' golden arrows. The Vlaydom and Chevon armies just stand and watch the massacre of the Kladoenian people.

The Gryphon army swoops low for a second time. The second golden, Elven rider on each Gryphon jump off and draws their swords. Arrows continue to rain down. Four Elven soldiers land on my rooftop. I spin around and immediately kill one with an arrow. I pull Erika behind me and attack. Two of the three turn to face me. The first Elf slashes wildly at me towards my head. I sidestep easily and cut through his golden armour as if it's made of paper. The second tries a stab to the gut. With ease, I knock the blade out of his hand. I place a kick to his chest, knocking him onto his back. I stab down. Elves are masters of the bow but useless when it comes to the sword.

The Gryphons and their riders continue to terrorise our army. The Elven archers expertly pick the gap between armour and shields. Gryphons pluck soldiers into the air with their front claws then drop them at a great height. Our archers start to anticipate the flight of the Gryphons. Few Gryphons are shot down, but it is not enough. We are barely making a dent in their numbers.

One giant Gryphon, considerably larger than the rest, nearly twice the size, sets off into a dive. It soars right over my head as it blocks out the sun. A warrior jumps down from her Gryphon's back onto the roof on the opposite side of the road. This warrior is different. She doesn't seem Elven. She wears armour which seems to be an unnatural combination of silver and steel. She seems too short to be an Elf and not as slim. Her frizzy, black hair flows effortlessly from the back of her helmet. Some strange reason I feel a connection with her.

The archers on the rooftops have their swords drawn and look at her warily. She reveals her weapon. It is a short sword unlike any I'd ever seen before. The blade is made from the same silver-steel combination and shines like a polished mirror. One side of the blade is straight-edged whereas the other is extremely jagged. The bottom of the hilt on the sword is a huge emerald. A thin silver-steel chain attaches to the hilt. The chain is about three metres long and attached to another silver hilt which also contains another emerald.

The first Kladoenian that attacks her is disarmed and killed in moments. She throws her sword and impales another. Tugging on the chain, the silver warrior swings her blade around, slicing through a third. She keeps twirling and lets her blade swing round and cut through Kladoenians. It is almost as if she is dancing. It takes the silver warrior less than ten seconds to kill the seven Kladoenian archers on that rooftop.

I am in a daze. I feel like I should know the silver she-warrior as she set about slaughtering another Kladoenian rooftop. Erika clearly did not, sending an arrow flying towards the midriff of the silver soldier. I watch the arrow soar. Without even turning to look the silver warrior knocks the arrow out the air with a swat of her sword, turning to face where the arrow had been fired from. As the silver warrior looks across the street, she locks eyes with me. I swear through her silver helmet there is the slightest a hint of a cruel smile.

Our gaze is broken by an Elven rider flying a bit too close for comfort. I shoot at him, lodging my arrow in the gap in his armour beneath his armpit. He falls off his Gryphon and into the street. Arrows continue to rain down. The majority of our force is cowering underneath the safety of their shields, but it is no use. The Elven archers are too skilled, finding the smallest of gaps and sinking their arrows. Our numbers fall. We're being slaughtered.

I look back across the street. The silver-warrior is too pre-occupied with slaughtering our archers on the other side of the road. Before I can attempt to sink an arrow into her back, a horn blows. The armies of Vlaydom and Chevon have become impatient of watching the Elven archers tear through our defence and decide to join the attack.

"FALL BACK!" Joshua screams, "FALL BACK TO THE CASTLE!"

Panic follows. I grab Erika and climb down quickly from the rooftop onto the main road. Arrows from the Elves continue to rain down on our fleeing forces. Shakra rides pass me with Joshua and Isaac joining him on the back of Lena. I keep hold of Erika tightly with my right hand, my left-hand grasping Nemesis firmly. Poor Erika drops her bow and runs as fast as she can. The Chevon soldiers are hot on our heels. Some brave Kladoenians decide not to run and try to slow the enemy down. The armies of Chevon and Vlaydom crash into them mercilessly. An arrow whistles past my ear and hits the Kladoenian woman in front of me in the back. I sidestep pass her.

Where's Maria I thought. I turn and look. Maria has Queen Silvia holding on desperately as they ride to the castle. They are about fifty metres behind me and Erika. She is riding as fast as she can, but there are too many Kladoenians in her way. On the rooftops above Maria, the silver she-warrior is running parallel to them. Following them. Preparing to attack.

Before I can react; the silver she-warrior leaps off the roof, ready to strike down upon the unsuspecting Maria and Silvia. It all seems to happen in slow motion. A flash of gold appears behind her. The giant Gryphon that had delivered her to battle had wrapped its' talons around the silver warrior, lifting her away just before she can land the killing blow on Maria's exposed neck. I breathe a sigh of relief and continue to run. Maria and Silvia ride pass me unaware of how close they were to death.

The castle isn't far now. Arrows continue raining down on Kladoenians. Everywhere I look a Kladoenian falls with a golden arrow sticking out of them. The soldiers of Chevon have caught up with the slow and weak, cutting them down without mercy. I continue to hold tightly onto Erika's hand as I run through the crowd, clambering over my fallen allies. We are almost there.

We finally reach the castle doors. I turn and look at Erika. Her body is limp with a golden arrow sticking out of her back. She is covered in dirt and blood; I have been dragging her for a while. I scream with rage. My vision goes red. I stand in the doorway of the castle and empty my quiver onto the approaching enemy. Every arrow hits its mark. A young priestess and an elderly man scramble past me into the castle. Before I can recklessly charge; Maria and Isaac grab me, dragging me inside. The doors slam shut behind me.

We barricade the door with everything we have: benches, shelves, tables, we are so desperate even the bodies of those who were shot just inside the castle doors are used. I look around. Only forty of us have made it to the castle. Yasmin, Elizabeth, Mary, and the Queen Mother Catherine meet us there from their sanctuary.

"We need to get the people into the tunnel," Queen Silvia says.

"We won't all make it." The Queen Mother exclaims. She looks around her mind at work. "Save the future. Save the children." She mutters to herself before shouting, "All under the age of twenty follow me,"

"What about the others?" I shout over to her.

The old man that I had saved turns and says, "We'll hold them off lad, give you lot a chance to escape."

I look around helplessly at all those who must stay behind. Prince Isaac grabs my arm, instructing me to run. I sigh and sprint to the other side of the great hall, to the thrones. Shakra gracefully climbs off Lena, Maria does the same with her horse.

BANG!

I pull on the antler. The throne moves to show the hidden tunnel. BANG! Shakra runs in first holding Lena, then a young boy, bow in hand dives in, followed by the young priestess aged about nineteen.

BANG!

A seventeen-year-old lad covered in blood carrying his younger brother aged fifteen, with arrows feathering out of his body, enters the tunnel.

BANG!

The Queen, her sisters and her cousins run in. Yasmin follows.

I turn to the Queen Mother, "Go, Your Grace."

The Queen Mother puts on a fake smile and shakes her head, "Lead them to safety."

BANG!

I nod. Her mind is made up. There is no time to try to convince her otherwise. Maria and I run in the tunnel pulling the reins of Maria's horse. The tunnel entrance closes behind us.

CRASH!

Maria looks at me, "The doors are open."

"We better get out soon," I say. Maria agrees. We sprint down the tunnel until we find a large armoury where everyone is waiting. The walls are lined with packs, weapons, and armour. I see two quivers of my black arrows and I grab them. The others are resupplying. "Take the packs," I say, "and put them on the horses."

I grab two of the packs and put it on Maria's horse. The boy with the golden arrows feathering out of his back can walk, though is bleeding heavily. His older brother is also bleeding heavily behind his armour but is trying to act unfazed.

"We need to travel light and quick. Take all heavy armour off." I command. They do as I say. "Follow me," I grab a torch and start to walk quickly down the dark, damp tunnel.

Yasmin walks alongside me, "Where does this tunnel lead?" She asks.

"The Great Woods, I think."

"The Woods!" Yasmin looks shocked. "How deep are we going in?"

I keep looking ahead, down the murky tunnel, "Straight through the middle and out the other side."

"Jacob, the Great Woods will kill us all." Yasmin pleads.

"Well," I mutter, "We have more chance against the Woods than that army."

"Not much," Yasmin retorts, "What do you know about the Woods?"

"A bit, I have spent time in them,"

"How far in did you go?"

"Not very," I admit. "Felt never-ending though,"

"Exactly," Yasmin points out, "What about the wild animals, bandits, and Elves that live in the Woods?"

"Elves don't live in the Woods," I say.

Yasmin was about to say something smart when we hear the worst. CRASH! The tunnel door has been smashed open.

"Run," I scream. We flee for our lives, but we are moving too slowly. The injured brothers are limping as fast as they can, but it is not enough. I can hear the footsteps of the soldiers running down the tunnel. We have a good head start but they will soon catch us up. I see the brightness of a torch approaching. We are going to die.

Suddenly, the wounded brothers stop still. I turn and face them. "Keep running," The older brother says, "We'll hold them off." I look into his eyes; he knows they are slowing us down and that they are probably going to die anyway.

I put my hand on his shoulder and say a silent thank you. A solitary tear rolls down the cheek of the younger brother. I turn and run. The older brother calls after me, "Keep them safe."

I catch the others and force them to keep on running. Our pace quickens. I can still hear the footsteps of our pursuers. I take Nemesis off my back and into my hands. The enemy soldiers haven't found the brothers yet.

Then we spot it, a narrow rope bridge. The chasm it spans is so deep I can't see the bottom. "No!" I curse. The wounded brothers could have made it. We could have saved them. It's too late. I hear the clang of swords. Then, I hear the screams of pain, echoing down the hall. The brothers die in agony.

We run across the bridge, "Cut the ropes," I say. Isaac and Joshua slash at the bridge with their swords. The bridge falls down. We're safe, for now. I feel sick. Guilt fills my stomach. The rope bridge is gone and so are the brothers; I didn't even know their names.

"Let's keep going," Shakra mutters.

We race through the cold damp tunnel, still hearing the cries of the Kladoenian brothers echo down the tunnel as they are slaughtered. The outrage of the Vlaydom warriors that their way has been cut off, resonates so we can hear. They taunt and curse us.

We slow down to a gentle jog, then eventually a walk. Every inch of me is tired and aching. The tunnel is starting to get wider. Princess Elizabeth and Princess Mary now sit on Lena, while the young archer, Flint, rides Maria's steed. He has a mousy face and wiry hair. Only twelve, fighting in a war at such a young age. I walk next to him in silence until he says, "Are you Jacob Da Nesta?" I nod. Flint smiles, "Nearly everyone in this tunnel is well-known."

I force a smile, "Yes, a few are."

"The Queen, her sisters, her cousins, a Chevonic Prince, the Queen's personal maid who gets treated too well, a wandering priestess and the Da Nesta siblings."

"How did you know about Yasmin, the Queen's handmaiden?" I ask.

"Everyone knows about her." I look at him confused. He carries on not noticing, "And this isn't the first time I've met the royal family."

"You've met them before?" I say curiously, though still not sure why *everybody* would know about Yasmin.

Flint looks around, "A year ago, I was caught stealing a necklace from Queen Catherine's personal jewellery box. A crime like that should have cost me my hand, but the King was forgiving. He asked me why I stole the necklace and I told him about how my father had died, how my mother was sick and me and my sisters were unable to get work. He said I had a talent to sneak past the guards and that I could make a good hunter. He took me to the archery range, and I trained every day. He paid me enough to support my family until my Mum got better. Even after that he still let me train. I owe the royal family more than you can imagine."

"Did you ever get the chance to go hunting?" I ask.

"No," he admits.

"Well, you and I are going to have to do a lot of it once we get to the woods," I tell him. Hearing the sobs of others behind me, I break the silence, trying to drown them out, "Who's she?" I whisper, gesturing at the young priestess.

"Sister Kelley Genesis." Flint explains, "She just returned from wandering all over Valouria to find the light of God," he says in a hushed voice.

"Why did she do that?" I ask, looking at the priestess. She is very tall and slim with long, flowing, brown hair. Her skin is as white as a sheet. The only colour is on her staff and her previously white, bloodstained robes. Her staff is impressive. A two-metre pole which has a religious, jewelled cross which is comprised of four axe blades perpendicular of each other. The opposing end of the staff is a sharpened spearhead.

"I don't know," Flint admits. "Young priests who are strong and brave often make the journey but only few return. She is the only woman I've known to have done it and survived" he whispers.

"How do you know all of this?"

"I just do," He hisses. "Everyone knows everyone in the city." I nod; it was the same at Rochton.

The sobs behind me are turning into tears. I turn to see the Queen, her sisters, and the priestess Kelley all crying their eyes out. We keep on moving forwards. Every so often someone would break down crying and either me, Maria or

Shakra have to pick them up and keep them moving. Even Maria chokes up at one point.

Shakra and I take the lead, dragging the cohort through the tunnel. We are walking slowly. It must be dark by now. Good, I think, it'll be easier to hide if we ever get out of this tunnel. I think about the city and those that stayed behind. They're all dead. They gave their lives up so that we few could escape. The two brothers who'd stopped to bide time, they should be alive, if they only kept on running, we would have reached the bridge with them. I curse, they didn't have to die.

The tunnel starts to slope up. I run ahead and check. There it is; the trap door to the Great Woods. I push it open slowly; making sure no one is nearby. It is clear. Finally, a piece of good luck. I walk out into the forest.

The cool evening is refreshing compared to the stuffy tunnel. The Great Woods are calm and quiet. The door of the tunnel is well concealed into the side of a small hill. Moss has grown on the door blending it into its surroundings. I watch my companions climb out one by one. Covered in blood and weary from the most hellish of days. I quickly scan the surroundings. Not a soul in sight. Just a sea of trees, hiding a countless number of dangers.

I climb to the top of the little hill to take a lookout. Looking south I cry. The city of Klad is on fire. Even in the distance, the blaze is huge. I see the silhouette of the armies; both on the ground and in the air. They are celebrating. I can faintly hear the cheers and songs of victory echo across the night.

Shakra climbs up and stands next to me, eyes fixated at the enormous fire. "Jacob," He says softly, "We should go."

I agree and climb down from my vantage point. Shakra and I pick up the others before silently walking further into the woods. Heading North, away from the great blaze that lights up the night sky. We keep on walking for about three or four miles when Maria forces us to stop and make camp.

Shakra takes first watch. There will be no fire tonight, we must remain invisible. No one speaks. No one makes eye contact. No one has the energy to even shed a tear. We all just sit there, trying to comprehend what has happened. I look around at the faces of my remaining allies, their eyes seem hollow and empty. Maria tries to stay strong for the group. She takes every layer she can find from the packs and hands them out to the group silently. The summer breeze rustles through the trees. Maria thrusts a blanket into my chest. I grab it and thank her. She sits herself down in the middle of the group and gets ready to sleep. The others huddle around her for warmth. They trust her already.

I sit next to Shakra and watch the others fall asleep one by one. After all that has happened, they have earnt this rest. I sit in silence for what must have been an hour before Shakra orders me to go to sleep. Reluctantly, I move and rest up against the trunk of a tree which was about three metres away from the rest of our cohort. I close my eyes. I thought it would be a struggle to get relaxed but sure enough, I drift off with ease to my first ever dreamless sleep. Even though, deep down, I know one thing...

We are going to be hunted.

Chapter 7

I wake up freezing. I look around at the faces of my sleeping comrades, tear-stained and peaceful. Shakra is leaning against the tree, eyes shut; he must have fallen asleep during his watch. I know that I should be angry, but we were so emotionally and physically tired yesterday that it wouldn't matter if something did attack us last night; we wouldn't have had a chance to defend ourselves.

The morning sun is starting to rise and creep through the trees. I stand up, pick up Nemesis and start walking silently. I am tempted just to leave them and make it on my own, but I can't leave Maria and she wouldn't leave the others. I sigh and instead of running I hunt, making sure I don't walk too far away from the group.

Creeping through the woods with bow drawn helps clear my head. I hear the wind whistle amongst the branches. I feel the soft earth under my feet. I see the morning mist starting to clear. The tranquillity of the morning seems to be mocking the horrors of yesterday. I daren't walk too far into the wilderness, so I sneak around the edge of our camp.

Hearing the flutter of wings, I fire. I hit the wood pigeon through the middle. A second rockets out of the nest but gets shot down with one my arrows in its eye. I pick up the birds and retrieve my arrows. Looking up at the nest, I start to scale the tree. I take the two eggs that were there and hurry down.

By the time I reach the bottom of the tree, Isaac is awake. He looks up and smiles. The contents of his pack are sprawled out on the forest floor. The packs contain very few essentials such as waterskins, whetstones, blankets and a flint and steel. Isaac is sat stripping a blackberry bush he has found and filling his pack with the plump fruits.

"What have you got there?" Isaac enquires with a hushed voice, his hands pink with the fruit juice.

"Two fat pigeons and two of their eggs," I whisper.

Isaac smiles as if nothing happened yesterday, "Great, with these blackberries it looks like we'll be having a decent breakfast then. I could do with a few extra hands though."

I nod in agreement, "I'll go and get the others."

Looking over the scarred, peaceful sleepers I feel bad to wake them up. But no doubt Vlaydom, Chevon and the Elves will know about our absence and they will soon be after us. But for now, we're safe. The Great Woods are so vast it will be near impossible to find us. Every part of the forest looks the same, filled with pines, oaks, sycamores and nearly every other type of tree you could name.

Yet I still feel scared. The Great Woods is home to not just wild animals, but: hostile tribes, bounty hunters, sellswords and rumours even say a giant army of bandits, all of whom would love to send our heads to Vlaydom for a handsome cash reward. But the worst thing is, I always feel like someone is watching me while I'm in the Great

Woods. I shake my head. Pull yourself together, I thought, no one is within a mile of us.

I walk over to Shakra who is still asleep. I can't get mad at him; he needed the rest. I nudge Shakra gently. He wakes immediately, eyes full of fear, "S-s-sorry Jacob... I didn't..."

I can't help but smile, "Doesn't matter, the others don't need to know. Just don't let it happen again," He agrees, "Help me wake the rest." I continue. He rises to his feet and walks over to nudge Yasmin awake. She smiles at him and he smiles back. Then next to her is Silvia. Silvia's face beams when she sees Shakra and plants a kiss on his cheek. He accepts it and helps her up.

I get Flint and the priestess Kelley up. Flint's eyes are bloodshot. Kelley just woke up from what seemed the most peaceful sleep. Next person I wake is Maria. Wary of the knife in her hand, I nudge Maria with my foot. She jumps up and swings for me with her knife. I catch her arm. She starts to calm down. "For God sake Jacob, you scared me."

"How do you want me to wake you then?" I ask.

She smiles, "I'll stop sleeping with my knife then."

I chuckle to myself. It was a lie, an obvious lie. Everyone is now awake, and all eyes are glued on me. "Ok..." I say, our makeshift camp falls silent, "Joshua and Shakra collect firewood, we don't need much and make sure it is dry." They nod, "Kelley, take yourself, Flint and the twins over to Isaac and help him pick the berries." Kelley gives me a look of disgust. I try to work out whether she is either not keen on my leadership or not fond of looking after the younger members of the cohort. I expect an argument, but

Kelley turns and takes Flint and the young princesses over to Isaac. I brush it off and continue, "Maria and Silvia..." Silvia coughs. I roll my eyes, "Fine. Maria and Queen Silvia fill up the waterskins at that stream over there and make sure the horses are watered." I say, pointing to a small beck trickling in the distance. Our Queen is about to complain but Maria grabs her arm and leads her to the horses.

"And what about me Jacob?" Yasmin enquires, sharpening her scimitar, "We're the only ones left."

I give Yasmin a small smile, "You're going to help me split these two pigeons and two eggs between eleven people."

Yasmin grabs the larger of the two birds and says, "Before, we sort out that, help me pluck these pigeons,"

I pick one up and start to pull off the bird's feathers. It takes forever. For every feather I pluck, two seem to appear. By the time I have plucked a third of the feathers off my bird, Yasmin has finished. She watches me struggle for a while, then takes the bird off my hands and says, "I'll pluck the pigeon. Clean your knife so you cut the meat off the bone later."

"Sure," I walk down to the stream nearby and wash my knife downstream of Maria and Silvia. I take Nemesis off my shoulder and quickly clean off all the blood and guts. I run my fingers along the icy cold blade of my knife. Still doesn't need sharpening. There is something special about the metal in mine and Maria's knives. I know what is so special about Maria's knife and it scares me. Never mind, I think, I can't get bogged down worrying about that. We've got enough to be worrying about. I pull the bowstring of Nemesis back over my shoulder and place my knife in the scabbard on the back of my hip. I walk back to the camp.

The priestess, Kelley, the twins, and Flint are back from the berry foraging. The pack is about half full of the berries. They split the berries into eleven equal portions. I sit down. Shakra, Joshua and Yasmin are roasting the pigeons on a spit over a small fire. Maria and Queen Silvia are securing the water skins to Maria's horse, poor thing. Maria's horse is dwarfed by Lena, who is carrying packs of firewood with ease. I sit there watching everyone work until Yasmin hands me the birds.

I cut the meat into cubes and say to Yasmin, "We won't eat the meat now." She agrees as she scrambles the tiny eggs over hot stones. We split the tiny portion of eggs and abundance of berries, eating an awaited breakfast in silence.

I hadn't realised how hungry I am. Half a mouthful of scrambled egg is nice, but the sweet and sharp taste of the juicy berries that are perfect. We ate all the berries right then for breakfast. Feeling nowhere near filled, I kick dirt over the embers of the small fire and stand up.

"Get rid of any excess armour now," I say, looking towards Isaac and Joshua, "We need to move light and fast. We'll head north through the forest, then make our way to Arabia."

"Why Arabia?" Kelley asks in a sneering tone.

I turn to face her, it's an obvious answer, "They are our ally, our only ally, they will protect us."

"Then, why are we going all the way through the dangerous woods; when we can head east then walk up the Arabian Pass?" Kelley points out, "It'd be easier, quicker, and safer than travelling through the Great Woods, it is a miracle we weren't killed in our sleep last night." There are a few murmurs of agreement throughout our cohort. Kelley continues, "Also, Arabia didn't come to our aid when we were attacked. What makes you think we'll be safe there at all? We could double back and hide amongst the ruins of Klad, they'll never expect that."

Before I can reply Shakra steps in, "Firstly, doubling back is a stupid idea. There will be scores of men raiding Klad as we speak. Secondly, Jacob is right, Arabia is the right place to go. They didn't aid us in the battle as they will not have known about the coming attack. King Edward's messenger would have ridden down the Arabian Pass, and if Arabia had news of the attack, they would have marched down the Arabian Pass to fight by our side. Vlaydom will have moved their force from the Outpost to the Arabian Pass to prevent any messages getting to Arabia and stop the army if needs be. Now they'll be under the instructions to wait and find us." He looks at Kelley with a look of disappointment, "Surely someone as well travelled and educated as you would have known that."

The colour drains out of Kelley's face. Flint speaks up, "So it looks like we'll be going through the Great Woods then," Kelley's face returns to normal colour. I hear the rattle of armour being taken off by Joshua and Isaac.

"They're going to be after us, aren't they?" Princess Mary anxiously says.

"Yeah," Shakra admits, "They will have sent teams of Chevonic riders to pursue us."

Mary starts to shake, "They've got Gryphons as well. They'll be able to see us from the sky."

I crouch down next to Mary, "Look up," I say pointing at the thick wall of green leaves, "These trees will hide us from above. We just need to be careful. The things we need to worry about are the pursuers on foot, the bandits, wild animals and the weather."

Maria lightly hits me over the back of the head, "Don't scare them, Jacob." She turns to the twin princesses and puts her hands on their shoulders, "We'll be fine. Ignore my brother, we'll be fine." The twins smile.

I grab Nemesis and put it over my shoulder, "Well we better start moving. Mary is right, they will have noticed our absence and will be looking for us."

Shakra gets up and walks over to the horses and leads them back over by the reins. We throw away the heavy armour into the bushes. I adjust Nemesis on my shoulder, grab my waterskin and start walking north. Shakra follows and walks alongside me. Queen Silvia rushes forward to walk with her fiancée. The rest follow with Maria and Isaac walking with Maria's steed at the rear.

*****

After walking for a couple of miles listening to Silvia hide her pain by flirting with Shakra, I decide to drop back and walk with Yasmin. She'd spent the time in silence, glaring at Silvia, then at Shakra. After a mile in silence, watching

Yasmin glare at Shakra, I decide to ask a pretty useless question. "Are you alright?"

Yasmin turns sharply, "Of course I'm not. Do you not remember what happened yesterday?"

I hush my voice, "I meant are you alright with Shakra? You haven't stopped staring daggers at his back for the last half hour."

Yasmin's expression drops. I was expecting some snappy retort or snide remark. But she simply softens and states, "Its complicated, Jacob."

I roll my eyes. It always is. "Simplify it for me,"

She takes in a deep breath and composes herself, "Well, I'm..."

"Sh." I interrupt. I spotted a flash of a silhouette flutter about two hundred metres in front of us.

Everyone stops.

Looking ahead there are two large bushes at either side of the trail we are walking on. There are snapped branches where people have been running. Fresh footprints in the wet mud from the people hiding. The bushes are rustling ever so slightly, but the breeze has stopped. I see a glint of light reflecting off the tip of a spearhead that is peaking out over the bush on the left. The mumbling of whispers ahead travels gently down the trail. And beneath my feet, I see one trodden gold coin from an ambush that had happened before.

I look at Maria to check if I'm right. She nods and pulls out duel katanas of Dioscuri slowly.

"Start walking slowly," I whisper. We start to shuffle forwards. "See those bushes over there," I gesture. "There is an ambush ahead." A few scared looks are exchanged among my allies. I continue, trying to sound brave, "On my mark, we'll attack the bushes."

I slowly ready my bow. The twins and Flint do the same. Isaac and Joshua are poised to throw their spears. The Queen draws her jewel sword and raises her magnificent shield. Kelley is shaking, staff in hand. Shakra and Yasmin jump up on the horses, swords drawn out of their scabbards.

"Steady..." I whisper as we edge forward. "Steady..." We are only five metres away. "Now." I cry. Joshua and Isaac throw their spears into the bushes. We release our arrows. I hear cries from the bushes. The bandits jump out from their hiding. One swings a club towards my head, but I duck and slice his middle. Another tries to stab Princess Elizabeth as she unsheathes her sword. But I parry the strike and pierce his chest. I shout to Kelley, "Get the twins out of here." Kelley doesn't hesitate and grabs the Princesses and runs to the back. A bandit swings his stone axe down towards me. I sidestep and strike at her neck. The limp body collapses.

I end up back to back with Joshua. We work together to fight the bandits that surround the two of us. The twins are now firing arrows upon the bandits, but more keep on coming. Kelley cuts down anyone who tries to get near the twins. Maria, Isaac, and Flint are huddled around Silvia, protecting their Queen. The bandits, hungry eyes, seem desperate for the jewelled sword and shield of Klad.

A bandit boy aged only about twelve hits my ankle with a slingshot. I curse and fire an arrow through his hand. He screams and runs into the forest. Two men charge towards me and Joshua. A spear whistles as it passes my head. One swings a crude wooden club towards my midriff. I dodge the blow and bring Nemesis around towards his head. The bandit dodges my attack at the last second. He's off-balance. A well-placed kick leaves him on his backside. As he sits back up to try and retaliate, my knee meets his face, knocking him out cold. I turn to see Joshua easily disarming a bandit, before thrusting his sword into them.

I look around. We were comfortably superior soldiers than these bandits. Without the element of surprise, the ill-equipped brigands have no chance against highly trained Kladoenians. But they still fight with the same tenacity, not willing to give up.

A horn sounds in the distance. Down the path, I see over a dozen riders lining up. They are led by the second most beautiful girl I'd ever seen. She is stunning. Not quite as beautiful as Gwen but still radiant, as if the whole world stops for her. She must only be seventeen, but the bandits follow her and respect her. Her cinnamon hair flows in the wind. Her dark skin and big brown eyes are breath-taking. Even from a distance, I have to admire how stunning she is. Then I see the deadly khopesh sword she is holding aloft. The sharpened curved steel echoes death. She swings her khopesh down and the bandit cavalry charge.

I am suddenly dragged back into the real world. Without a moment's thought, I draw and release arrows on the oncoming cavalry, bringing down two of their riders. Shakra and Yasmin ride out to meet them. I hear the clang of steel as they pass each other. Two more bandits fall from their steeds. Then the bandit riders meet the rest of our group. I block a sword from taking my head off.

The girl with the cinnamon hair brings her khopesh down across Flint's face. He hits the dirt, dead. They ride straight through us. The bandits on foot scurry back into the brush, disappearing from sight.

The riders regroup after they pass us. The foot soldiers have made their escape, there would be no need to attack us again, their ambush has failed. The girl with the cinnamon hair turns around and meet my eyes, giving me a playful wink. I nock an arrow into my bow and pull back the bowstring. I hold and hold and hold. I can't do it. She shows me her perfect smile and sparkling white teeth, taunting me to release my bowstring. I readjust my aim and let go of the arrow. It whistles through the air. The beautiful girl gasps. The rider next to her falls off his horse, an arrow protruding from his chest. She looks at the fallen man with feigned interest. A broad grin stretches across her face as she looks up and gives me another wink, applauding my shooting. Blowing me a sarcastic kiss, she rides off into the hedges. The remaining riders follow her and disappear into the depths of the Great Woods.

The attack is over. We managed to repel the cowardly ambush.

I turn around to my allies kneeling around the lifeless body of Flint. My stomach churns and seems to climb into my throat. Walking over I see the girls weeping. The cries of horror from the young princesses Elizabeth and Mary resonate amongst the trees. Poor Flint was only twelve. The deep cut across his face is oozing blood and makes him unrecognisable. He is no longer the mousey, joyful lad. He is just another casualty, I tell myself. I reach over and close his eye that isn't cut. Ignoring the looks of horror, I pry the bow out of his hands and then roll Flint over to claim the quiver off his back. I stand up, continuing to ignore my companions' anger and hand the bow to Shakra. Shakra takes the bow and quiver silently, eyes never looking up from the lifeless Flint.

Nobody moves. Our group is frozen by the horror of Flint. How could anyone do something like this? Especially, how could the stunning girl with the cinnamon hair do it? I curse her under my breath. I can't stand just sitting around with the others mourning Flint. I need to do something. I turn away from my group and walk into the hedges, where the bandits had once hidden.

Walking into the bush, I feel sorry for the bandits. There are eight fresh corpses in this bush. My companions are currently mourning over one fallen friend, whereas these bandits have lost eight people in this bush alone. I curse myself under my breath. It's different. We're fleeing a massacre of our people. These bandits are just cowards who tried to ambush a bunch of kids.

Despite my best efforts, I do feel sorry for the bandits as I scavenge their bodies. I find a couple of arrows scattered amongst the bodies. My feeling of sympathy raises for the brigands, the bandits were not well equipped at all. Two had been armed with blunt lumber axes, one with a scythe from the fields; two were armed with sharp stones they must use as daggers and another person held a sharpened wooden rake. They were fools to come after a group of armed Kladoenians. Finally, I find something worthwhile, a longbow and a quiver full of arrows. I walk over to the fallen woman and without thinking I pull of the bow, roll her over and take the quiver.

Then I see what is in her back, a delicate silver arrow is lodged in her. The flights are white feathers which are perfectly shaped. I pull the arrow out carefully. The arrow is made of an unusually light, silver metal with a small arrowhead. Examining the arrow, I can tell that this is the same peculiar silver metal as the ring Maria wears and that decorates the hilts of Dioscuri. I've seen these arrows before, I'm sure of it. I can't remember when, but I've definitely seen them once before.

Confused, I put the arrow in my quiver and carry on searching. I find a spear with a stone head and a second spear which was just a sharpened staff but would work just as well. The man holding this sharpened staff has a silver arrow sticking out of his neck. I look around but see no signs of any movement. Where and who are these archers? I stand up and carrying the weapons out of the first hedgerow.

As I join my allies, I drop the supplies next to Lena. "We need to get moving," I announce, "We must find a place to camp before nightfall."

Maria riles around on the spot. Tears stream down her face. "At least let us bury him," Maria yells. She is livid. Her face is red with either the tears or her insurmountable anger.

I try to stay resolute. We can't stay here too long, "No, we have to get moving, he'd understand." I look at Shakra and Joshua, pleading, "Help me get them up."

Joshua shakes his head, expressing Maria's grief and anger "Who are you to decide if he should be buried or not?"

My frustration boils over. We don't have time for this. The bandits will be back. Plus, Vlaydom and Chevon will have sent men to come and hunt us down. "I made a choice between one being buried and ten of us living." I retort, my hand firmly grasping the hilt of my knife which is resting just behind my back. I try to bite my tongue, but my rage stupidly forces me to continue, "You wouldn't have the brains to work that out."

Joshua's temper reaches new heights, "Why you little... I'm going to kill you!" he attempts to draw his sword but Isaac and Shakra tackle him to the ground.

I guiltily let go of the handle of my knife. My rage dissipates within seconds. I watch the three of them struggle for a moment whilst Joshua calms down. Once he had released his sword, I kneel down next to him and apologise half-heartedly, "I'm sorry Joshua, I didn't mean that."

Joshua grimaces in an attempt to smile, "Yeah, whatever." He shrugs off Shakra and Isaac with ease and stands up. Wordlessly, he turns his back on me and proceeds to sit down next to Queen Silvia, who is still cradling Flint's head.

I shake my head and look at Kelley, "Give Flint his last rights then leave it. We don't have time to bury him." She nods solemnly. Kelley stands up and raises her arms out over Flint's body. Isaac joins his brother and cousins, kneeling and muttering the words of their God. Kelley leads them in prayer, trying to save Flint's soul. Yasmin wraps her arm gently around a sobbing Silvia's shoulders. She caresses her Queen with such care. The two seem to have more of a sisterly bond than that of mistress and servant. To my surprise, Maria stays on her knees, leaning on Isaac as she joins in the prays with Kelley. Maria has never been one for religion but right now she joins in with the blessings over Flint's corpse.

Shakra walks over to me mutters, "Come on; let's leave them to pray." Silently, I turn around and trudge into the second hedgerow. Shakra follows.

Hidden by the canvas of leaves we can hear the gentle hymn of the mourners as they give Flint his last rights. I try to put it out of my mind and focus on scavenging anything I can. This bush has fewer bodies. Shakra finds another silver arrow in the chest of the young boy I had shot in the hand. "Who does this belong to?" He asks rhetorically. Sounding very confused he continues, "It's similar to the metal that decorates Maria's sword." He looks at me and gives me the arrow, expecting an answer. I shrug my shoulders and move on.

I hear a faint moan in the distance. Someone is still alive. Shakra spots her. One of my arrows is lodged in her thigh. Without thinking I rush over and jump over her. I grab my knife and put it against her throat. She breathes a short breath in shock. She is around twenty-five give or take, with pale skin and thick, red, wild hair. She is relatively short and curvy. Her blue eyes scan me intensely. She had a pretty face, covered in freckles but has a scar running down from her top lip and down to her chin.

"What's your name?" I ask.

"What's it to you hun?" The girl retorts.

"Do you want to live or not?" She sees that her woodcutters' axe is just out of reach and she nods. "Well, start talking."

"My name is Laveona," She answers with a scared voice. I slowly take the knife off her throat and sit back a bit. I grab her axe with my free hand.

"Who are these people who attacked us?" I ask with less venom.

Shakra has walked over and I hand him Laveona's axe. Laveona sits up and speaks confidently, "We're the free people of the Great Woods, pet. We were once common people until Vlaydom's laws tightened and left us with nothing. But now we're free, hun. We take from those who had once taken from us. Our leader, the great and wise Carlos taught us how to use to the forest."

"Carlos?" I look at Shakra, the man who knows nearly everyone, but he shrugs his shoulders. I decide not to dwell on it. "Will your *'friends'* be coming back?"

"Yes, but not for another day or so." She answers, "They'll be sending for a large force to clean this up and the nearest camp big enough is over half a day's ride."

Looking at my arrow wedged in her thigh I ask, "Can you walk?" Laveona nods but Shakra shakes his head.

Fiddling with the black beads in his hair, "I may be no healer, but a wound like that will take days to fully heal."

He gives me a mournful look then looks at the knife in my hand. *It's either that or the wolves'* he mouths.

I shake my head, there is a third option. I look her in the eyes, "If you want to live, we're going to have to help each other." Laveona nods vigorously. I don't know what is compelling me to help her, she had just tried to end our lives. But I know we could use her. I continue, "We'll patch you up and you'll come with us. We could use someone like you and if you help us survive, you'll be handsomely rewarded I'm sure." Laveona nods again, but this time looking perplexed. I turn to Shakra, "Help me carry her." Shakra looks shocked but helps obediently. We half carry half hobble the bandit Laveona back to the others.

When we reach the others, they are gearing up to leave the clearing. Everybody gasps when they see Laveona. Joshua draws his sword. My free hand immediately grabbed the hilt of my knife again.

"What is she doing here?" Joshua shouts, waving his sword, gesturing at Laveona.

"She is not our enemy," I try to tell him calmly.

Joshua turns red, "Is that so... Look at what she did to Flint."

Isaac quickly steps in-between his brother and Laveona, Joshua's sword at his chest. "We drew first blood and they struck back."

"They had set up an ambush." Kelley interrupts. Silvia and Joshua mumble in agreement.

Isaac shakes his head, "But they were probably just trying to intimidate us. Get some gold that's all."

"That's right," Laveona speaks up for the first time, "We saw a campfire smoke this morning and the night before we saw a great fire only a few miles behind. The campfire was huge. We were going to surprise the convoy and get their loot."

Joshua lowers his sword, his anger dissipating, "By any chance was that great fire you saw coming from Klad?"

"No," She sounds shocked, "It's impossible to see Klad from that point, hun. It was in the Great Woods. Just a few miles from here. When we saw your convoy, we thought you were only the scouts to a much larger party. Why did you..."

Maria gasps and interrupts Laveona, "We need to go. Now!"

Joshua helps Shakra and I to get Laveona on Lena, an arrow still feathering her thigh. Elizabeth and Mary jump on Maria's horse. Shakra holds Lena's reins and Maria leads her horse. Ignoring the looks from the others I snatch Laveona's axe from Shakra and give it back to her, as well as Flint's longbow and quiver. "Don't do anything stupid, you'd regret it. There's an army looking for us and you're unable to ride alone or fight and they will just kill you." Laveona's eyes widen with fear. She manages a nod.

"Chevon riders will be through here in a matter of hours. You're much safer here with us." Shakra confirms to Laveona. Shakra pulls on the reins and sets off. Queen Silvia takes the other longbow and runs next to Shakra, bow in hand, as a warning for Laveona. I run to the front of the group, leading them deeper into treacherous Great

Woods. Flint's lifeless body grows smaller amongst the piles of bandit dead as we flee further North...

Knowing a couple of miles away an army is hunting us.

Chapter 8

It is pitch black by the time we stop for camp. We risk a fire since it is too dark and cold. We need a hot supper. Isaac, Joshua and Shakra collect the firewood. Maria and Silvia help Kelley tend to Laveona's leg. The twins collect water from the small stream that trickles past where we have set up camp. Yasmin starts working out how it will be best to divide the two small pigeons.

Yasmin instructs me to go hunting. It's pointless. I might as well be blindfolded. Rocks and branches trip me up and it is too dark to see anything to shoot. And even if I could see any game, I am making so much noise by standing on twigs and leaves, alerting any animal within a mile. The animals will have scarpered.

I do quite enjoy a moment on my own. But all I can think about is Flint, Erika, and Dad. We didn't even bury Flint, because of my orders. Who knows whether Dad and Erika have been buried or cremated? A sickening thought of them all being left to rot haunts me. They have all died for nothing. It seems so pointless. I can't shake off the feeling that Maria and I are somewhat to blame for this. I hate it. Everyone in Klad seemed to know something about us, but they all neglected to tell us anything. I kick out at a fern, sending it flying into the pitch black. I take a deep breath and try to calm. There is enough to worry me without me causing any more problems in my head.

I leave the idea of hunting and climb a tree in an attempt to get a vantage of the Great Woods. I see what Laveona was talking about earlier; there are now sixteen large campfires dotted around the forest behind us. They must have split up to cover more ground. The nearest must have been about two miles away but our camp on the other side of a small hill preventing the sight of the fire. They have caught us up by an about a mile in a single day. "Tomorrow I'll make sure we're quicker," I mutter to myself.

I decide to stay hidden away from the group, enjoying the solitude of hiding up in a tree. I watch my somewhat disheartened companions trudge around, trying to keep each other's spirits high. Laveona's leg is all patched up. Maria and Kelley wander around the group, stitching and cleaning up smaller cuts and scrapes.

For some reason, whilst in hidden away in the trees, my path of thought turns to Gwen and the days we had spent together.

Last summer there was a huge celebration held in Klad to mark twenty-five years under King Edward II's reign. People came from all over Valouria make their way to the Kladoenian capital to pay homage. Apart from delegates from Arabia, all the royalty, nobles and delegates had to pass through Rochton on their journey to Klad. Most who passed through stayed for a while, preferring to be rested after weeks on the road.

Then, four days before the celebrations started, Gwen came. She arrived with the Vlaydom convoy. I was standing with my father and Maria greeting royalty when I saw her. She wore an almost see-through white dress and her long soft brown hair that covered her ears and reached her hips, with a small golden tiara. She had sharp features

116

but a constantly, warming smile. Her eyes were ice blue and skin pale. She was tall and slender. She must have been a year or two older than me, it was hard to tell. When King Joseph announced that he and his convoy would be staying with my father my heart leapt.

In the end with our house being quite small, most of the convoy went to the local tavern. But once Dad and I got settled in Maria's room; King Joseph, his Queen Zara, their two infant sons Julius and Augustus, a few guards and to my joy Gwen, all stayed at our house. A few lords were outraged by this arrangement but when they confronted the King; they end up standing opposite Gwen's personal guard: The Behemoth.

The Behemoth is like no other, he must have been over seven-foot-tall with rippling muscles. He carried a heavily jewelled giant gold-steel flanged mace in his right hand with a large diamond in the hilt and a six-foot diameter round golden-steel shield with a boss of giant diamond that was polished so well that you could see your reflection. The metal he wore as armour and weapons were unlike any other, it was the same golden-steel. His shaved hair showed up his scars on his scalp and face. The top of one of his pointed ears had been severed off. He had obviously seen many fights. But this monster of a man would do anything Gwen told him to. He utterly terrified anyone who dared to venture near him.

On the first night, when we sat down for supper, the King of Kings, King Joseph, positioned me and Gwen opposite each other. It was the best meal I had ever tasted; the King had brought his kitchen staff with him. There was such an array of dishes, but I didn't notice any of them. I can't even remember what I ate. I was watching Gwen and she was looking straight back. I couldn't stop smiling. We laughed and joked the entire dinner. The crowded dinner table gave a surprising level of anonymity.

That night after supper we snuck out of the house. We ran out of Rochton and headed west, out to a quiet hill watching the sun go down. The Behemoth didn't follow us and let us have our moment of privacy. It was perfect. We sat hand in hand for hours talking. I have no idea what we spoke about. I think it was the sunset and the beauty of Valouria. Then she got me up and we danced in the meadow. I was hopeless; I must have tripped a hundred times. She laughed, but instead of being annoyed at her, I admit it was quite cute. The moonlight rippled in her luscious brown locks. With the sun set, it was getting dark and cold. That's when it happened: she kissed me. First on the cheek, then on the lips. I melted inside. Before I could say another word and ask for another, she grabbed my hand, and we ran down the hill back to Rochton.

I snap out of my memory. I have to try and forget about her. I'm on the run, hundreds of miles away from her. It will be a miracle if I ever see her again. I feel the warmth in my chest disappear as the hope of being with Gwen dwindles.

Sighing, I jump down from the tree. It had been over an hour since I left the camp, so I decide to return empty-handed. My travelling companions are huddled around a small fire, eating warm pigeon stew with a few roots thrown in that we found on the way. The pigeon stew is more water than pigeon. I am so hungry and exhausted, I don't care. I see that we have sacrificed a spare blanket to use as a bandage for Laveona's leg. The blanket has been dyed red and Laveona's face seems drained. Laveona sits alone, away from the fire, shivering as she sips on her watery stew. No one speaks to her; not even Shakra or Maria. I can't believe them. Laveona doesn't need another reason to hate us. They could have put some effort in with her. I grab my portion of stew and my blanket then head over to sit next to Laveona.

She forces a smile, "Hey, hun,"

"Hey," I reply. We sit in silence for a moment while I eat. Laveona has barely touched her stew. She wipes tear stains off her cheeks. I attempt conversation, "Sorry for what has happened today."

She looks at me and tries to make a joke, "What shooting me or killing everyone?"

I look at the ground ashamed. "Who did we kill?"

She smiles, "No one important, pet" She laughs nervously, "The only other person who actually means anything killed your friend and got away by the looks of it." She must have noticed me sit up and looked intently when she mentioned that she was close to the gorgeous girl with the cinnamon hair. She laughs again, "Don't bother with her hun; she would kill you before you could lay eyes on her."

"Shhhhh!" I look at the others, luckily no one had noticed. They sat close to the fire, talking in hushed tones.

Laveona winks, "Just between you and me kid."

I hate her talking down to me. I'm not a child. I try and ignore it, "How's your leg?" I ask, looking at the bloodied blanket and changing the subject.

"Better now that your damn arrow is out of it," Laveona winces as she moves her leg slightly. "Won't be able to sleep well tonight."

I grin, "Good," Laveona looks at me confused, "We'll talk properly then." I say. Laveona smiles. I look up and see that Elizabeth and Mary are already asleep. Everybody is yawning and settling down for the night. I speak up, "I'll take first watch." Laveona smirks quietly under her breath. Nobody argues and starts to make themselves comfortable near the warm fire.

Shakra gives Lena and Maria's steed water. Then he quickly ties them to a small tree, pats Lena's neck and walks back to the fire. Looking at me, Shakra says, "Wake me up when you get tired." I nod. He lies down and wraps himself in the blanket. It takes only moments before he is sound asleep.

I can tell that I have pushed the group to their limits to try and stay ahead of the Chevonic riders. Even my legs felt a little tired and my eyelids a little heavy. I know that we will not be able to keep this pace up especially with the injured Laveona and the young twins. If we keep on going at this pace, one by one people will drop off and be left to fend for themselves against the wrath of the bloodthirsty army that follows. I shake my head. I'm going to have to think of something.

I sit with my back against the base of a thick tree. I find a few twigs to add to the fire. I find one long enough to stoke the fire with. The flames dance only a few centimetres high.

I shuffle closer to the fire trying to keep warm. My eyelids try to close. I force myself to stand up, I can't fall to sleep. I wait and wait.

After an hour or so Laveona sits up. I whisper, making sure I don't wake the others, "You took your time."

She looks up at me annoyed, "Would you like me to go back to sleep hun, cos' I'm more than happy to."

"Sorry," I apologise as I sit down opposite her.

"Oh, by the way, kid; this is yours." She hands me the bloody arrow that I'd shot her with. I can't help but laugh. She smiles, "So I'm guessing you want me to talk about Rosalyn?"

"Is that the girl with the khopesh?" I ask. I feel it's better to talk about her as a military figure rather than calling her the beautiful girl with cinnamon hair.

"Yes," Laveona answers, "Well as you could probably tell Rosalyn is very important. Her father is Carlos's most trusted advisor and helped Carlos escape Vlaydom. Carlos is a lord's only son and heir to his father's land and titles. But his father despised Carlos because of his..." She pauses, "Deformity. He wanted to get rid of his disabled son when he had a male heir to take his place. When his father's new wife fell pregnant, Carlos knew that it'd be a boy. Carlos raced to the fighting pits where he befriended the arena champion who yearned for his and his daughter's freedom. Carlos provided the brains while Rosalyn's father, Benjamin, had the ability to kill needed for the plan to work. They escaped Vlaydom on the day Carlos' stepmother went into labour with his baby brother. Carlos, Benjamin, and the young Rosalyn fled into the forest after finding a few mercenaries as allies. Word started to spread, and the camp grew and grew."

She looks at my face of false interest and giggles, "Back to Rosalyn, right hun. She is Carlos' heir since Carlos has no children. Rosalyn decided that her suitor would be whoever could beat her in a fair fight. Many have tried... but all have lost. Her father trained her well, while Carlos educated her making her clever and deadly. Me and Rosalyn have been best friends since I joined the camp. And when she comes back to the scene of the fight between us and this lot, she'll bury the dead then she'll start to track you down and hang you from the nearest tree hun."

I couldn't help but laugh. Laveona glares at me. "Sorry," I explain, "A group of vengeful bandits is the least of our problems."

Laveona looks confused; then she hisses, "First of all we're no bandits kid, we're free. Secondly, who are you lot?"

I point at Silvia, "She is Queen Silvia of Klad."

Laveona's mouth drops open. The Queen of Klad had tended to her injured leg. Laveona brushes her bright red hair back when she realises, "What happened to the King and the Prince?"

"They died fighting Chevon's and Vlaydom's armies," I say bluntly. Laveona sits back in stunned silence. I carry on describing who's who, "The two girls next to her are her younger twin sisters Princess Elizabeth and Princess Mary. Over there is her cousin Joshua and next to him is his younger brother Isaac. The Arabian girl is Silvia's personal maid Yasmin. On her own on the other side of the camp is a priestess, Sister Kelley Genesis. And the guy with the beads in his hair is Shakra, Prince of Chevon, engaged to Silvia. And we are the survivors of Klad."

"What happened to Klad?" Laveona asks, she seems in shock by her famous companions.

"It was sacked."

"By whom?"

"Vlaydom, Chevon..." Kind of stating the obvious saying I'd told her they killed the King. Laveona looks at Shakra. I give her the five-second explanation, "His stepmother wants him dead so her son can be King."

"Who else attacked? You sounded like you were going to say some more, kid."

"You wouldn't believe me if I told you."

"Try me hun; I bet I've seen stranger thing than you," Laveona says in a patronising tone.

I sigh, "An army of Elves riding gryphons. They're the real reason we lost."

Laveona sits in silence for a few minutes, looking at the sky as if she were expecting a gryphon to pluck her off the ground and into the air. She then chuckles to herself, nervously, "Elves ain't real kid."

My head drops, "Yes they are."

Laveona can see from my sullen look that I am not lying, "I'm sorry." She sounds full of sympathy. "Anyway, who are you and the blonde girl then hun?" She asks, changing the subject.

Before I answer, a cocky voice speaks up, "That beauty is Maria Da Nesta." Shakra sits up, rubbing the sleep out of his eyes and carries on, "Age eighteen. Acts as the mother of our group. She is one of the greatest fighters known. Very smart and can read the situation in hand. Her twin blades of Dioscuri are made of a strange white metal. Daughter of the great Luca Da Nesta and is the only person Jacob Da Nesta trusts."

He then turns and points at me. "Jacob Da Nesta. Age sixteen. Leader of our company and probably is the greatest warrior I know." Laveona looks surprised. Shakra continues without missing a beat, "He was the one who cut down most of your people today." He grabs Nemesis. "His bow is too light for you or me to handle and the string is almost impossible to pull." To prove his point, he pulls on the bowstring with all his might, but it barely budges. "He isn't as strong as you or me but clever in battle and deadly quick. His blades are made from a strange black metal, the exact opposite of Maria. He's merciless and never trusts anyone but for some reason he let you live." Laveona looks at me. There is an awkward silence.

"How did you know all that about Nemesis?" I ask.

Shakra smiles, "I snuck down to blacksmith's when the weapons were being made and tried a few swings" The little weasel hides a smirk. "Get some sleep Jacob," Shakra orders as he places more wood on the fire, "You need your energy for tomorrow, and we need you at full strength."

I don't argue, grabbing my pack, and using it as a pillow. I wrap myself in a blanket, I lie down and close my eyes. I can still hear Laveona and Shakra talking about me, but I drift off with ease.

The Shadow Warrior did not visit me immediately this time. My dreams show me the last time I saw those silver arrows. Maria and I were exploring the outskirts of the Great Woods as part of our father's training when we stumbled across a grizzly bear lying dead on the trail we were following. We had a look at the body; wondering what had killed such a giant beast when Maria found it. A single silver arrow lodged in the bear's side. Blood still weeping out of the wound. Maria yanked out the arrow and looked at it. She handed it to me and started to search bear.

I scanned the arrow. A small, polished, silver arrowhead; mirror-like with how it reflected the sun. The flights were pure white feathers that were perfectly in place. I didn't admire the arrow for too long since I knew this kill was fresh and whoever killed it was nearby. Looking at the corpse I realise how lucky we were that someone shot them before we'd have to face a fully-grown grizzly bear with just a knife.

We raced away from the Great Woods straight back to Rochton, fearful of the archer who had tackled a fully grown grizzly bear. When Maria and confronted our father about the mysterious arrow, he had reckoned it must have been some lord out hunting and told us to forget about it. It was a lie, an obvious lie.

Unfortunately, before I could get any answers, my dream moved on to the Shadow Warrior.

"Come on Jacob," the sweet voice tells me, "It's getting away." I look to the direction of the sweet voice and see Rosalyn, the bandit with the cinnamon hair. She was holding my hand as we run through the forest. I feel warm inside even though I know it is only a dream. I look ahead to try and see what we're following. All I can see is a blurred green of the forest and a fussy white light in the distance. We keep on running hand in hand.

Then; darkness.

I hear the sickening thud. "H-h-h-h-help-p-p-p." I hear Rosalyn's voice croaks. Climbing out of the darkness, I see Rosalyn lying on the floor with a nasty wound to the head. I grab my knife and gently pull it out of the scabbard. The worn leather helps me to stay calm. The pure black blade poised to kill.

"Hello..." I call. There is no reply. Rosalyn remains unconscious. A warrior of pure shadow steps out. Armed with his trident, bossed shield, and sword; his bright red eyes bore into mine.

"What do you want?" I spit, each word filled with venom.

The wind picks up through the trees. The leaves start to dance. The birds fall silent. He points the black trident at my chest. I feel my knife change. I look down to see the thing I need most... Nemesis. The light but sturdy wood is almost black. The blood-red rubies, below the blades, echo the death and destruction this weapon has brought. The quiver on my back is full of arrows ready to be fired from the bowstring. And the blades are as black as nightmares.

The Shadow Warrior takes a step back. He looks scared but doesn't flinch. He charges at me, shield raised. Without thinking I fire an arrow. It pierces him through his thigh. He stumbles and trips. I jump out of the way before he clatters into me. I get up quickly but so does the Shadow Warrior. He pulls out the arrow from his muscular thigh. He doesn't even wince. His eyes are full of rage and fear. He hasn't realised but he is standing between me and the unconscious Rosalyn. I have to keep his attention on me. I start to fire arrows. This time the warrior blocks them with his shield. He slowly advances. I stop firing. He stabs with his trident, but I quickly sweep it to the side. I swing for his head, but he catches the blow in his trident. It's caught on the grappling spikes of Nemesis. I spin, pulling the trident out of his hands and it flies into the hedges. I turn to face him. He draws his sword. I stab for his stomach; he rolls and bashes me with his shield. I fall back. He stabs down but I dodge and kick him in the face. I jump to my feet.

Baring his ugly yellow fangs at me; I notice a trickle of blood from his nose. In a desperate attempt, the Shadow Warrior throws his shield at me. I hit the deck as it sails over my head. He runs at me. I get up. I dodge his charge. He spins around. He swings at my legs. I jump over the blade and kick him in the chest. The Shadow Warrior stumbles back and falls over. I've beaten him. I've finally beaten him.

Before I take his life, I hear a high-pitched scream, "Jacob!" I turn to see a second Shadow Warrior charges towards me pass the weak heap of Rosalyn. I haven't a chance to react. The second Shadow Warrior has already thrown his trident and it skewers me through the chest. I fall back slowly. Rosalyn cries out but I can't hear her.

Tears roll down her cheeks as the two Shadow Warriors walk towards her swords drawn.

I sit up, drenched in sweat. The campfire is barely embers. I am surprised and somewhat glad to see that Laveona is still with us. Dawn starts to roll over the hills. Maria, who is taking the last watch, raises an eyebrow when she sees me awake. I get up and run to my vantage point, climbing the tree. I can make out the figures of the Chevon riders in the first lights of day, asleep around the smokes of the campfires.

When I get back down to camp, Maria is stood up waiting, "What are you doing?"

"We need to go... Now" I tell her. "Wake them."

"Why?" she asks...

"Because I have a plan."

Chapter 9

It is extremely early, almost two hours earlier than we got up yesterday. Maria and I wake the group carefully as most of our cohort sleep with weapons in hand and wake with rage. Kelley almost cut my throat when I gently shake her awake. The last we wake is Joshua. Isaac has his shield raised and gently taps his brother with the butt of his spear. Joshua jumps up swinging his sword madly; knocking Isaac down with the force when he smashes his sword into Isaac's shield. He eventually calms down and apologises to his shaky brother.

"Grab your stuff," I tell them, "Let's get moving. We'll eat when we stop. We need a few miles between us and those Chevonic riders."

The morning sun is beginning to poke through the trees as Joshua and Isaac pick Laveona up and place her on Lena carefully. Laveona's leg has healed up nicely. She could run with a slight limp, but we need to travel fast. Luckily, she can ride just fine. Elizabeth and Mary are on Maria's steed again. After we tie some of the supplies onto Lena's back and start a light jog.

After only a few minutes of running, I am drenched in sweat. It is another hot summer's day. I can hear the others stumbling over tree roots and rocks that littered the forest floor. Every five minutes is marked by Maria angrily telling me to slow down and wait for the others. I neglect her advice and keep up the pace, forcing the others to try to maintain the speed.

After an hour of running, Maria orders us to stop and tells us that we're taking a breather. Apart from Maria and I, everyone is covered in small scrapes and scratches from running through the forest. Kelley doubles over with exhaustion. I ignore her retching and pull out my knife to remove the bark from a pine tree. I hand out the pine bark to each my companions, "Eat up, we need to keep moving," I tell them. The royal children give me disgruntled looks as they each nibble on their piece of bark. Most cough and choke but all manage to keep their breakfast down. After the ten-minute break, we get up and start running again.

The sun burns through the morning mist and the Great Woods comes alive. The smell of pine fills the forest. It is a little cloudier than the last couple of days but still pleasant. Lucky we're out here in summer, I thought. This terrible situation would be even worse if we had been attacked during winter. At least we won't freeze to death, I think to myself. Seems to be the only good luck we've had so far. Well, maybe whoever the silver arrows belong to. They did help cut down the number of the bandits substantially. Some guardian protected us then. Whoever it was, wasn't kind enough to reveal themselves. Best not to worry about it, especially when thinking about what comes later is making me feel sick in the stomach.

As we run my mind wanders, memories of home fill my head. On a normal day, I would still be asleep; then I would wake for a run followed by breakfast. On a day like this, I would train all morning then grab lunch and walk through the market. Then I would sit in the meadows and look at the clouds or I would find a stream and swim or fish. I would do this alone. It was better that way. If you like someone too much, they'll just end up hurting you.

Afterwards, I'd go home and eat a meal Maria has lovingly prepared. We would sit by the fire and laugh. Finally, I would climb the stairs and find myself beneath my sheets. But today I was up at the break of dawn, running away from men trying to kill or abduct us. I'll be spending most of the day waiting. By evening... well I'm not sure whether I'll make it that far.

I shake my head. Keep running; I tell myself; you can worry later. We needed to find a good spot and get enough distance between us and the Chevonic riders before they wake up and pursue. But the further we run the more fatigued we're going to be, and we will need our energy for later. Plus, we've got to have time to eat as well.

We continue to run for another two hours at a hard pace with few breathers, breaking it up to stop the royals from complaining. The sun is well and truly up now, beating down upon us. The Chevonic cohort will be about to carry on with their pursuit after already having a good rest and a leisurely breakfast. On horseback, they know they are slowly catching us. Even if we woke early and ran every day: we would tire; they would catch us; there is no chance we can reach the end of the Great Woods by outrunning them. With the number of other camps, we can't outsmart one camp by moving too far east or too far west since we'd run straight into another group of pursuing Chevonic soldiers. So, it leaves us no option but defeating the camp directly behind us. Each party will be about thirty strong, well-armed, trained killers on horseback. There are only eleven of us wearing light armour, we're young including two very young girls and one woman who is injured, we only have two horses and all of us are fatigued. The odds are stacked against us.

I sigh. I look over my companions as we take a quick rest. We wait as Kelley catches up, doubling over exhausted. "How much further?" She moans.

I don't answer her. I'm too busy eyeing up our surroundings. Without thinking we have stumbled on the exact thing I have been looking for. A small clearing between thick fauna, a natural tunnel of bushes, leaves and trees. The clearing is wide enough for four horses crammed together. The woods on the left of the clearing are too thick to run or ride through. Whilst on the other side of the bushes right is a stream. The passage is on a slight incline so we can see what is coming. I spy the trees in and next to the bushes were easy to climb and had thick branches leant over the passage with plenty of foliage to hide someone. I spot one tree which looked quite weak as if it only needed a few axe swings to make it fall.

"It's perfect." I grin.

Maria stands next to me and examines the passage, "Yes," She agrees, "This is the place."

Laveona winces as she dismounts Lena awkwardly, "This is the place I would choose kid. This'll work."

"What are you three talking about?" Silvia asks.

I turn to face the group, "Today we're going to get rid of the Chevonic pursuers." Before anyone can protest, I tell them the plan. There are some nervous looks around my allies, but they seem to agree. The plan is high risk, but it may just work. Once everyone is settled and agrees on their roles, I say, "Get your jobs done quickly then relax. I'll get some food and you can help once it's sorted."

Everyone sets off to work. Laveona, Joshua, and Isaac walk over to the limp tree. Laveona uses her axe and starts to hack away. Joshua and Isaac make sure that it doesn't fall just yet. Silvia, Elizabeth, and Mary start to test which trees are climbable and the route on which to take when climbing. Shakra and Maria ride about four hundred metres south of us, scanning for the Chevonic riders from a great lookout spot; nearly invisible for anyone approaching but provides a good vantage point to observe whatever comes riding in. Kelley and Yasmin collect water from the stream and Yasmin informs me it is teeming with freshwater fish.

I take off my boots and wade out slowly into the stream. The water is cool and clear. I can see every rock and fish in detail. Small plants wave as I brush past them. Wading until I'm knee-deep, I stand still, careful not to disturb the fish inhabiting the river. I stand in the middle of the stream enjoying the tranquillity. The warm sun rains down on my back. I listen to the song of the forest for the first time: the gentle trickle of the water; the birds singing a hundred different tunes that harmonised as one; the sound of the soft breeze dancing through the branches and leaves; the calls of various creatures and the buzz of little critters.

I take a deep breath of the fresh air. This was the first time since I left home when I can honestly say I am happy. The happiness won't last long, I thought, blood will be spilt in a few hours but I'm not sure whose blood. Unfortunately, my moment alone ends quickly. Isaac and Joshua have finished their task with Laveona. The two of them dump the contents of their packs and their swords and shield on the bank. They have their spears poised to throw, searching the water for their next meal.

Sighing, I draw an arrow. The fish were no longer bothered with me standing there. The stream is teeming with little trouts and one or two pikes. I nock my arrow and pull back the string. My father taught Maria and me about how the water changes the light to make it look the fish are somewhere else. I find my target, a trout about a foot long. Breathing in deeply, I fire, piercing the fish through the middle. The other fish dart in every direction. I grab the trout, pull out the arrow and place the fish in my pack. I smile, I remember learning to fire a bow into the stream by Rochton. Hunting supper on one of the rare days that Dad wasn't busy.

I think back to Klad, more specifically Rochton. My Dad would be addressing the guards; he knew them all and spoke to them often as equals. Or he would be training youngsters in the arena. He might be on a visit to Klad itself. Now, more than ever, I realise how lost I am without him. I wasn't there to help him. I should have been by his side when the armies of Chevon crashed down on Rochton.

But, despite myself, I can't help but think that he was going to tell me who my mother was and that seemed to matter to me even though I try and hide it. I don't know who she is, but I'm certain that others do. The late King and Queen knew; and Shakra knows, that I'm sure of. I want to ask him, but I've never found the moment. When it was just Maria, Shakra and I; I didn't care to know but now it seems important for some reason.

I snap out of the trail of thought. A plump pheasant is strutting arrogantly by the banks of the stream near Yasmin and Kelley. I pull back the string and release the arrow. It whistles through the air as it flies. It hit the pheasant right in the eye. Yasmin smiles and stands up. She walks over to the bird and picks it up. She holds it up for me to see. I do a sarcastic bow.

Looking to the left of Yasmin; I see Kelley's cold gaze. She hasn't spoken more than ten words to anyone all day. She is the slowest when we run; holding us up and constantly asking to rest. She has half-heartedly done her chores and always is the slowest to get ready.

Kelley has befriended the important members of the group: Queen Silvia; Joshua; Isaac; the young Princesses; and Shakra but has seemed to have ignored the ones she deems unimportant: Maria, Yasmin; Flint and me. I don't trust her, but I can't get rid of her. She has positioned herself perfectly in the group. Plus, her healers' knowledge is much too valuable to lose. I curse Kelley under my breath. She's fine, I tell myself, what has she done to make you doubt her? I go back to my fishing, skewering another trout, turning my back on Kelley and Yasmin.

The fish have scarpered. The day is dragging. The feeling of impending doom causes time to slow dramatically.

Bored, I stare idly at the water. I see the wavy reflection of the bank ahead. To my surprise, I see someone, staring straight at me. In the forest in front of me stands a tall lady wearing a silver gown. Her long blonde hair is similar to Maria's, rippling in the wind. Her pointed ears sticking out of her hair. She wears an elegant silver tiara in her hair.

On her back is a silver hunting bow and a quiver filled with silver arrows. Even from a distance, I could make out her sharp features and bright green eyes.

I've never seen a woman like her before.

She smiles at me. Not a happy smile. She seems neither pleased nor glad, instead, her smile is fake and professional. Her emerald eyes tell the true story. The blonde lady is in limbo between angry, sad, and scared. She is about twenty-five to thirty years old; it is hard to tell; in the reflection of the water, she seems ageless. It is as if a goddess is standing stoically on the embankment; watching over us with her silver arrows. Is she the silver archer that aided us against the bandits? She seems so familiar, even with the flowing stream I feel like I know this reflection.

I look up quickly, to try and catch a better glimpse of the blonde huntress, but the forest is empty. No one is standing in the forest. There is no trace of her. I rub my eyes. I am sure someone was there. I curse, the water must be playing tricks on me.

The sounds of my allies steal away the tranquillity of the forest. Joshua and Isaac are throwing spears into the water. Yasmin is plucking the pheasant I shot. Meanwhile, Kelley, Silvia, Elizabeth, and Mary are stripping a bush of blackberries and picking dandelions. With some more pine bark, we're going to have a decent lunch.

I sigh. I feel like I'm going to lose my mind, I want to scream. My stomach is doing somersaults. All I can do is wait for the Chevonic riders to get here. I'm terrified. When we were ambushed by the bandits, we were against people with hardly any weapons and armour; it was so sudden I had no time to be nervous. When the Vlaydom army was approaching Klad there were thousands of us; we were surrounded by a high wall and I was always kept busy, planning, and sorting out the defences. But now death is riding this way and I must just stay here and hope our ambush works better than the bandit's attempt.

A brave pike swims too close and I shoot it through the eye. I place the giant fish in my bag and walk towards the bank. I place the pack next to Yasmin; she smiles as she examines the fish. I grab Shakra's, Maria's and my lunch that Yasmin had prepared and my waterskin. I leave the riverbank and head south to our lookout spot.

"Any sign of them?" I ask as I approach Maria and Shakra.

"Nothing yet," Shakra whispers.

"Here's lunch." I hand them pine bark, a handful of blackberries and a handful of dandelions each with their water to wash it down.

"Lovely," Shakra comments in a sarcastic voice.

"Well its fish and pheasant for dinner," I tell them, trying to sound upbeat.

"If we make it," Maria adds.

Shakra masks his nerves with his cocky smile, "You two will live. Even if we die and you're surrounded, you will be taken as captors remember." Maria and I glare at him, "Look on the bright side," He continues, "They'll have plenty of food." He forces a smirk as he tries to swallow his lunch.

I want to think of an argument, but I know he's right. "Well none of us are going to die," I say, for my own sake rather than his. I don't believe this for a second.

Shakra softens and says, "You and I both know this is a near-impossible task. If we somehow defeat them there will still be loss of life."

"Why don't we run away then?" I suggest. "We've got the horses and I can go and get Yasmin." Maria and Shakra look at me. "We're probably going to die if not," I add.

"First of all, no," Maria hisses, "And second; why Yasmin?" I throw a look at Shakra. "But he's betrothed to Silvia!" Maria exclaims.

I turn to Shakra, "There's something about you two?"

Shakra sighs, "It is true, and I know Yasmin well but now is not the time to explain. It's truly not a big deal." Maria is stunned, she is about to say something but Shakra changes the subject by catching us off guard with a question. "Your white and black knives intrigue me. I know I can't use either of your blades but are you two able to use each other's?"

Maria and I look at each other. Maria speaks up, "Yeah we can fight with each other's weapons but not as well as we with our own. And Jacob can't use my blade's..."

"Yeah, so we can but not well." I interrupt, desperate for Maria not to confide anything too serious with Shakra. I don't trust anyone in all Valouria enough with that secret.

I try to take Shakra's mind off that last statement, "How come you can't use them, they're just knives?"

Shakra gives me the cocky smile as he plays with the beads in his hair. "I would tell you right now if I could, but you wouldn't believe me. I promise when the time is right, I'll tell you everything I know but not here, not now." He pauses and looks out over the forest. He looks sympathetically at me, "Jacob, I understand your desire to run but we can't leave the others. We've got this far by working together, and we'll make it to Arabia together. Go back to the clearing and we'll let you know if anything happens."

I quickly eat my lunch and walk back to the group. When I arrive at the clearing, everyone is restless. Laveona is swinging her axe fighting imaginary enemies. Her leg seems healed up enough for her to move when being fuelled by nerves. Joshua and Isaac are throwing their spears at the water, getting frustrated, missing the fishes with every hurl. Yasmin and the Queen are in frantic conversation, fidgeting, hands glued onto their sword hilts. Kelley is comforting the twins, whispering religious nonsense into their ears. Fear is taking a stranglehold of my companions. I sigh; I need to take my mind off the attack. I cross the clearing and walk away from my companions who are huddled by the riverbank. I delve into the thicker woods.

It is dark in this part of the forest. I can hear the faint snarls of dogs in the distance. Creaks and cracks echo through the thick brush. There are plenty of animals present in this area of the woods; I just have to take my pick. I keep my head on a swivel as I try to spot my prey. Tracks of hundreds of animals litter the floor. I keep on walking further into the forest following the tracks left by the animals.

I spot very fresh tracks made by something a little bigger. I follow them, savouring the hunt. Allowing it to clear my mind. The large prey will be enough to feed our camp. I thrill as I stalk the beast, savouring the hunt. I tiptoe through the forest, following the tracks. A broken twig, fresh droppings, scuffed mud, and large footprints. I follow the tracks around a large oak tree.

Unfortunately, when I turn the corner, I find the beast that I've been stalking. I muffle my mouth as I let out an inaudible gasp. The juggernaut I've been stalking is a dangerous one: a wild boar digging for truffles. The brute is only twenty-five metres away. He is enormous. He has tusks that can easily rip a man in half; he is pure muscle and scarily close. The creature must weigh close to three hundred kilograms. A bear would scare me less.

Silently, I pull an arrow from my quiver and nock it in my bow. A precautionary measure. There is no way I want to risk my life so needlessly with this brute. Slowly pulling back the bowstring I realise I have one of the silver arrows nocked, that I had found in the dead bandits. I start to back off slowly, the way I came. The last thing I need is to fight this colossus.

I keep on stepping back up until I hear a loud snap. I look down to see a broken stick beneath my feet.

Looking up I see the worst. The boar's ears stand up, hearing the snapped twig. It's too late to change the arrow now. I aim down the shaft of the silver arrow right for its eye, I fire. As soon as I let go of the bowstring, I know the arrow is not flying true. The pig squeals as the arrow lodged in his shoulder. I missed. I curse and draw another arrow, one of my own black arrows. The boar charges at me at a frightening speed, unfazed by the silver arrow. I desperately fire the second arrow.

I dive out of the way at the last second as the boar crashes down next to me. The second shot was lethal. My black arrow pierces the boar through its only weak spot, straight through the eye.

I stand up, attempting to steady my breathing. I walk over to the boar, shaking. After poking it with Nemesis to check that it is dead, I retrieve the arrows. Damn that silver arrow, I thought. It was just as hard to use as one of iron or steel. I snap the silver arrow in my hand and throw it to the side.

I shout for Joshua and Isaac. After about five minutes they arrive soaked from the stream. They stand awkwardly in a shocked silence. After about a minute of the two of them gawping at the boar and myself, Joshua says, "How did you..."

"Doesn't matter," I interrupt, "How are we going to move it and hide it?"

"It's well hidden here." Isaac points out.

Joshua interjects, his eyes wide with a feverish hunger, "I am not leaving this feast for some wild dog to have. I'm already sick of pine bark and berries." He walks around the carcass quickly, analysing it, "We could drag it," Joshua suggests.

"No." I say firmly, "It'd be hard and take too long. Even you two giants wouldn't be able to move this. Plus, we won't be able to hide a full boar when Chevon attack and I don't want to ruin the surprise." I pause. "How about we just take its legs?"

The brothers look at each other and shrug their shoulders. Joshua draws his sword and started to hack at the hog's legs. He still has a lump on his head from when I hit him with his shield. I fill with guilt at my mistake that had ultimately saved Joshua's life. The swelling has come down somewhat at least.

Joshua makes short work of cutting the pig's legs off. Joshua grabs his two front legs, holding them over his shoulders while Isaac and I carry a back leg each. We leave the rest. We can't carry it and can't hide it when the Chevonic soldiers ride in. It seems a waste but I'm sure something else will devour it.

The midday sun is starting to hide behind the clouds when we arrived back at the stream. Yasmin smiles when she sees the boar's legs. She takes his legs and looks at me. "We'll have to cook it later." I tell her, "We don't have time now, keep it cool and safe until tonight." She nods. I give her the other silver arrows I have found in my quiver, "Put this in my pack as well please." Yasmin doesn't say a word but grabs the meat and arrow and heads over to place them in a pack.

It is starting to get cold out of the sun. Time seems to drag. I walk down the bank to the stream and sit on my own. I pick up a handful of stones and start to throw them in the water. I am feeling sick. Every minute brings what is probably going to be our death closer. Will this ambush work? It didn't work for the bandits and they do this all the time. And they didn't do it against thirty or so armoured riders.

I look at my usually steady hands, quivering like leaves in the wind. My stomach feels like a hollow pit. I feel like I am about to throw up. I look at the others. Yasmin is back from hiding the boar legs with our packs. She is sharpening her scimitar with Laveona who is doing the same to her woodcutter's axe. Queen Silvia is knelt praying with her sisters, her cousins and Kelley.

I pull out my knife. The worn leather of its handle on my skin calms me down. My stomach stops doing somersaults. I feel the light breeze through my hair. I breathe in the fresh air deeply. I am finally getting control after a day of nerves.

'Maria, Jacob listen to me.' A soft woman's voice spoke in my head. I jump up with shock. What is this? Who is this? I grip the handle of my knife tightly. The soft, melodic voice continues, *'You are about to be betrayed. Someone has been planning this betrayal for a while. I do not know who this traitor is or what they plan to do but I know that innocent blood shall be spilt by their hands. Our people will be unable to help you this time. You must fight this battle alone my dears. Trust no one and watch each other's back. You are who Chevon want. The others are not deemed important to them. Please remember I will always love you no matter how far away you think I am, I've always been watching over you. I am sorry about leaving you with your father; he shouldn't have been left to look after you alone. We will meet someday my children and we will be reunited as a family. Good luck my dears, the Chevonic riders will here soon.'*

I look around for the woman. No one is there. Silvia and the others are acting as if nothing has happened. That was my Mum speaking to me, it must be. No. It must have been my imagination. If it were real, I would see Maria and Shakra any minute informing me that Chevon's riders are approaching. I turn to face the direction where they are at lookout.

I look to their direction. Nothing. I breathe a sigh of relief. It was just my imagination. I turn away and crack a smile. It was just my imagination. I chuckle. I'm losing the plot in the Great Woods.

Then my stomach drops. I hear the sound of frantic riding. Two horses riding hard. I turn back and sure enough, Maria and Shakra are riding towards us at full speed. The look from Maria tells me she has been told the same thing by the mysterious voice. I run to join up with the others. Shakra rides up to me and says only two words...

"They're coming."

Chapter 10

Everyone panics. We run to the clearing where the ambush will take place. Shakra gives Yasmin his short bow and quiver and then rides south-east with Maria. Anything we didn't need to fight with we hide in the bushes.

Laveona and Isaac sprint to the limp tree. Silvia, Yasmin, and I scuttle up strong trees, choosing those with big overhanging branches with lots of leaves. Below us, Joshua stands stoically guarding Elizabeth, Mary, and Kelley, hidden amongst the fauna. We are invisible to the outside thanks to a wall of green.

We wait in silence. My nerves claw around my stomach. I look south and see nothing. I crouch on my branch, trying not to shift my weight. Slowly, I grab Nemesis off my back and grab her firmly in my hand. The leather grip relaxed me. I concentrate on breathing slowly, taking deep breaths of air. Inhale; exhale. Inhale; exhale.

In the branches beside me, Queen Silvia gives me a nervous look. The colour has drained from her already pale face. Yasmin tries to reach over to calm Silvia but shakes and stumbles. A few green leaves drop from her branch.

"Shhhh!" Joshua hisses down from the brush. "Try and stay calm," He whispers, "Jacob's plan will work." He gives me a reassuring nod. I smile through my nerves; he may not always agree with my leadership but deep down he is a good man. I watch as Joshua whispers encouragement to his young cousins. Elizabeth and Mary's bows tremble in their hands. I sympathise with them, they are only thirteen, have barely lived at all. But they put on brave faces.

I cannot help but think back to the woman's words that spoke in my head. "*I do not know who this traitor is or what they plan to do but I know that innocent blood shall be spilt by their hands.*" I feel like I know who the traitor is, it must be Laveona. Laveona will be using this ambush as a chance to escape us. Why should she risk her life fighting our battles? It is all my fault. I kept her alive, I should have just gotten rid of her when I had the chance. It is simple, I tell myself, I will just have to make sure Laveona has an unfortunate accident during the upcoming conflict. I fill with a sense of dread. Am I so cold-hearted?

As I struggle with an internal conflict, the wind starts to pick up, rustling the leaves of the bushes. The early afternoon sun remains hidden behind the light grey clouds. There are no bird songs, only silence. In the distance, I faintly hear hoofs. They are becoming louder and louder. My hands are shaking. I still can't see them.

Panic begins to set in. Will the ambush work? Is the plan good enough? Are there enough of us? Will we live another day? The questions circle around my head, making me feel dizzy. The sound of death is galloping closer. Then the riders appear climbing the hill. Thirty armoured knights on horseback riding towards us.

I signal to the others from my branch. Silently, I pull an arrow from the quiver and nock it. I draw back the bowstring and wait. Looking around I see Yasmin do the same. I follow the Chevonic riders with my arrow. The group narrows to three riders wide as they ride down the thin path.

Time seems to slow down as they trot down the path. They casually prance underneath where I am crouching. I silently inhale deep breaths. They keep on trotting towards the limp tree Laveona and Isaac are hiding behind. I count the riders. Thirty-two mounted soldiers are stretched out along our thin path. As the first riders reach the limp tree, there are still plenty of riders beneath me, unaware of our trap.

CRACK!

The limp tree fell in front of the first row of riders. The horses rear as the men draw their swords. "Ambush!" They shout as they see the tree has been hacked down. From the south, cries of approaching warriors charging forward can be heard throughout the forest. Shakra and Maria charge towards the back of the Chevonic cohort fearlessly, swords raised.

The Chevonic soldiers try to turn their steeds around and prepare to charge.

"FIRE!" I scream.

Arrows rain down on the riders at the front. A couple of riders fall. The riders stop. They try to work out where the archers are hiding. We keep firing. More fall. I look and see Maria and Shakra about to crash against the Chevon forces and into our fire.

We stop firing just as Maria and Shakra strike. I jump down from the tree and kill the Chevon rider below. He falls off his horse with my strike. I land in his saddle. The others attack from the trees and the bushes. A rider to my left swings his sword at my chest. He hits me with the flat of his sword, knocking me off the horse. I feel all the air leave my body as I hit the ground hard. I jump up quickly and cut the rider down.

I spin and draw my bow. I fire my arrow, killing a rider who had just grabbed Silvia. One rider throws a spear at me. It sails past my head, missing by only millimetres. I charge at him and stab him before he can draw his sword. Yasmin's arrow pierces a Chevon's chest. Over half of the riders have been unhorsed or have decided to carry out the rest of the attack on foot.

It is very claustrophobic in this narrow clearing. Horse rear and bolt in every direction. Two heavily armoured Chevonic soldiers walk slowly towards me, shields raise, swords pointed at my chest, crouching behind their shields with only their eyes and helms peeking above. I quickly nock an arrow. There is no shot. They keep getting closer. I start to back up slowly. They are getting quicker. Then I see the shot and fire. My arrow pierces the ankle of the guard on the right. He screams in pain. He stands up leaving his chest open. My second arrow goes straight through his heart. The other Chevon seems unfazed and carries on advancing, crouching even lower so his shield hides his feet. I point the tip of Nemesis toward his chest. He gets closer and closer. He lunges for me with his swords. I sidestep and slice, but he manages to raise his shield just in time. My blow smashes against his shield; the power knocks him onto one knee. I bring Nemesis down onto his unguarded head. I see the fear in his eyes before my blade enters his skull, straight through his helmet.

I spin around, looking for Maria. She is still on her horse riding through swinging her swords at anyone who dares to come close. Thinking of the warning the soft woman's voice had said earlier, I run to help her. I ignore the others and jump on the back of her horse. She looks at me and nods. I start to shoot as she rides. I hit one Chevon in the hip just before he cut Yasmin's throat. The second arrow goes through his back. He falls without a scream. I feel someone grab my shoulder. Turning, I see a Chevon rider trying to pull me off the horse. I elbow him in the stomach. He doubles over winded. I quickly draw my knife and slash. He falls off his horse, dead.

Maria and I keep fighting, chasing the Chevonic riders, driving them south. I rain arrows upon soldiers. Maria's dual swords of Dioscuri are white flashes of death.

Where is Laveona?

The last I saw of her; she had parried a strike that was intended to skewer Shakra's horse Lena. I don't have time to think as I nock another arrow and hit a swordsman who was trying to pursue Maria and me.

The battle is starting to end. A few riders scarper south, seven riders had survived the ambush and now escaping. My arrow lodges in the back of one of the last Chevonic soldiers who stayed and fought. He screams in pain before Isaac puts him out of his misery.

I jump off the back of Maria's horse, bow drawn. Maria stops when she spots a friendly face. She grabs Isaac and rides off to find the rest of our cohort. I keep walking around, looking for loot and survivors. There are plenty of good horses left without their riders. I grab the reins and round them all up.

"Jacob..." I hear a voice. I look around. Queen Silvia is trapped under a heavily armoured corpse. I help her push him off. She pulls the jewelled sword of Klad out of his chest. She cleans the blade with her sleeve. "Where's everyone else?" She asks.

"Not sure." I admit, "Maria and Isaac are ok." Silvia gives me a panicked look. I quickly add, "I'm sure your sisters will be fine, I made sure Joshua was looking after them. No Chevon coward would dare try to attack him."

Silvia forces a smile and takes a couple of the horses' reins. "Let's go and find them." I nod and follow my Queen.

We walk to where most of the fight took place; past the fallen tree. The ground is littered with Chevonic dead. Arrows cover the ground and decorate the bodies. I sling Nemesis over my shoulder but still have my knife in my hand, as a precaution.

We hear hooves approaching. Silvia and I ready ourselves to strike. A Chevon rides at full speed towards me.

Shakra.

Sitting upon Lena, he rides in haste. Blood has dried on his face and hair. His hands are coated with the stuff. The blood on his hands is still wet. He looks worried. "Jacob. Silvia. Come quick." He turns sharply and rides off in the direction he came. We run after him. Even though we ran for a couple of minutes it seems like a lifetime.

Is he the betrayer? I can't stop thinking about it. Would a squadron of Chevonic soldiers be waiting for us when we got there? No... No. I tell myself. Shakra is our friend and the rest would be putting up a fight that I would hear from a mile away. Shakra is now more Chevonic than Maria or me.

I curse. It must be Laveona. What has she done? I try not to be sick. I should have killed that ginger bandit the moment I set my eyes on her. Silvia grabs my hand as she pulls me to speed up. I keep running knife in hand. I can't believe I've let Laveona do this. She is a cutthroat; she has betrayed us. I curse again and again. Silvia desperately keeps us running, following the route Shakra had taken, until we hear the desperation and tears.

Shakra, Maria, Isaac and Yasmin are crouched down together in a group. Someone is lying down in the middle of them. To my shock and awe, Laveona also crouches by the wounded soldier, trying to stem the bleeding. My five companions are pushing down on a pierced stomach. The blood is pouring out of the stab wound, no matter how hard they try to stop it. I run over as quickly as possible. Joshua lies on his back, pale. Tears roll down his face. I kneel and cradle his head on my lap while the others try to stop the bleeding. It's hopeless. Joshua knows it. More and more blood gushes out of the wound.

"Stop..." Joshua croaks. I look up at Yasmin and she nods. She sits back. The rest slowly copy Yasmin's example. Maria drags Isaac off his brother and comforts him.

"Who did this?" I ask.

Joshua looks up, "Kelley. She took the girls. Elizabeth and Mary. She hit them over the head and handed them to the Chevonic soldiers. I couldn't stop her. She stabbed me before I could do anything. I swore to protect those girls and I failed. They were heading for you Jacob, but you jumped up on Maria's steed and rode off. But they got the girls and Kelley went off with them."

Joshua starts shaking. "I don't want to die... I don't... I want my mother..." He chokes. The brown eyes of the boy are overflowing with fear.

The wound is too great for him to carry on. I look around at the others. Maria catches my look then at the knife, still in my hand. She nods. She knows what is best. Taking Isaac's hand, she stands up and leads him away from his brother, wrapping her arms around him. The others understand. Joshua looks at me and whispers one thing. "Do it..."

Yasmin holds his hand, "Look up at the sky, at the clouds; beautiful, aren't they?" He looks up, revealing his neck. Tears roll down his face. A faint smile appears as he catches a glimpse of the sky between the trees. I slowly bring up my knife. My hand is shaking. "Listen to the birds," Yasmin whispers to him, her voice breaking, "And the wind through the trees." He smiles. My knife is just above his neck. I take a deep breath. Life pours out of his eyes as I open his throat. He is still smiling as I close his eyes.

Shakra puts his arm around the crying Silvia and leads her away from her lifeless cousin. Laveona follows them in silence. I wipe my knife on the grass. I rest Joshua's head and stand up. Yasmin lets go of his hand. I look at the dead boy and curse Kelley with every curse I know. Of course, she was the betrayer. She was always so self-centred. She has been slowing us down all day. Kelley had travelled all of Valouria, she must have spent plenty of time in Chevon and Vlaydom. I should have never trusted her.

Yasmin tries to stand up. She cries out and stumbles onto the floor. I quickly run over. "What's wrong?"

She grabs the side of her right thigh. There is a deep cut, bleeding heavily. I quickly rip off a sleeve of my shirt and tie it tightly around her leg to stop the bleeding. She winces but doesn't complain. I pull her up. With her scimitar, she is too heavy for me to carry. We hobble to the others as quickly as she can.

When we reach the others, Maria rushes over and immediately starts attending to Yasmin's leg. "It's not too bad," Maria tells her, "It'll be fine if you rest it."

"Rest it!" I shout in shock. We need to get away from here. A silence falls over the rest of the group. They stare at us, almost looking frightened. Maria stands up and storms off. She glares at me, beckoning me over. I follow her in a fit of fury.

When the others are out of sight Maria spins around and slaps me in the face. "What's wrong with you Jacob? We need to protect these people. We've lost four people from our cohort already today and I'm not about to let it be five. The Chevon riders are going the other way. We can rest just one night. They need this. They've lost their home, their family, their friends and might even lose hope."

"Lose hope?" I ask confused, "Maria, we've lost our home, our Dad is dead. Only two of them are Kladoenian and all of them are slowing us down."

Maria slaps me for a second time. My left cheek is glowing red hot with pain, but I try not to show it. Maria hisses at me, "We can't leave them, Jacob. They need us. Silvia is our Queen. We need to protect her. Her sisters have been kidnapped and her cousin has just been stabbed by someone who she thought was a friend. She needs time. We'll bury Joshua. Gather the stuff. Leave the Chevon dead and it'll slow any riders that follow. We'll ride out tonight for a little while. Get dinner and rest for a day. We'll still reach Arabia and the Chevonic soldiers will be miles away."

I pause for a moment, "Those bandits will be after us. We don't have the numbers to defend an attack and Laveona isn't going to help."

Maria's head drops. "I believe she has proven herself today. But we can never be sure of anything. We'll make sure the camp is well guarded and if there is any trouble, shoot her straight away. So, let us have one day's rest."

"Ok," I agree. "One day." The corners of Maria's mouth turn up. Normally she would be grinning ear to ear with a victory over me but not today. She turns around and walks back to the others. I sigh and follow slowly.

The scene Maria and I arrive at is manic. Isaac is beating a wounded Chevon soldier. Shakra and Silvia are trying to hold him back, but neither of them are desperate to get in the way of Isaac's fist. Yasmin is sat down with her leg, attempting to calm him down. Whilst Laveona is sitting on a rock as if nothing is happening. I have never seen Isaac lose control like this.

Maria dives between Isaac and the Chevon who is sprawled helplessly on the ground. Isaac stops immediately. I run over to the dying Chevon whilst Maria and Silvia lead Isaac away. Shakra kneels next to me and the Chevon. "Who sent you?" He asks.

The wounded man spits out a mouthful of blood. His face is completely bashed in. His broken nose gushes blood. The Chevonic soldier looks up at Shakra with his non-swollen eye, "Your stepmother, Queen Antonia."

Shakra bites his lip. "What did she want?" He spits.

He pauses, spitting out more blood, as well as two of his teeth, "Your head..." Shakra sits back and curses. The Chevon soldier coughs and chokes on his own blood, "There's more." I lean forward, "The Lady of Ismai wants some people called Da Nesta, and she wanted them alive and well."

Laveona pipes up from behind and shoots me a confused look. "Who is this Lady and where is Ismai?"

The dying Chevonic man replies, "I don't know her name, all I know is she is the Queen of the Elves. The Elves live in a hidden mountain paradise behind Vlay's Retreat in Vlaydom. They're the ones with the long brown hair, riding gryphons and wearing golden armour. They're the best archers in Valouria."

Shakra sees that the wounded man does not have long left, "What did this Elf Queen want with the Da Nesta's?"

"I don't know. I only got the orders to bring them to her." The Chevonic man's eyelids are getting heavier as his life is slipping away. "She claims they are... they are..." His non-swollen eye closes, and his body becomes limp.

I shake my head. If Isaac hadn't beaten him to a pulp, he would have been able to finish what he was going to say. Laveona is still looking at me confused, as is Yasmin. I walk away with their eyes following me.

I find Isaac in tears with Maria comforting him. Silvia is attempting to help but is breaking down herself. When she sees me, she hugs me and cries. I awkwardly return the hug. Her dark brown hair is getting in my face, but I don't complain. She needs this. Holding it in would just break her, letting it out now will do her the world of good. Maria looks at the two of us and raises an eyebrow. I scowl. Maria turns back to Isaac.

I slowly pull away from Silvia. She's still in floods of tears. I walk over to Isaac who is sitting on a boulder. I crouch down so we are at eye level and say, "Why did you attack that wounded Chevon?"

"He killed my brother." Isaac spits.

Maria turns to me with a steely expression, "Jacob; now isn't the best time."

I ignore her and carry on, "That man did not kill your brother. Kelley did. She has betrayed us all. When the time comes, no one will stop you from getting your justice, but save it for her. That boy would have given us useful information. Don't kill the wounded, they might tell us why they are after us." Isaac sniffles and nods. "Come on," I tell him, "Let's bury Joshua, grab the stuff and get away from here."

I give Isaac a hand up and embrace him with a hug. The four of us walk over to the others who are looting the dead. Yasmin has already skinned the boar's legs and is rubbing in salt, that Laveona had found, to preserve it.

I grab the reins of the horses, there is enough for one each and two spares as pack horses. I walk them over to the stream to make sure they've drank while the others give Joshua his last rights. When I get back, I help Isaac and Shakra with the digging with the small shovels we found in the Chevonic packs.

By the time we are ready to leave it is already late afternoon. We gently trot north. Yasmin is unable to ride so she sits side-straddle with Shakra; Lena is so strong that she doesn't seem to notice the extra weight. I lead the way. Nobody utters a word as we ride. The gentle breeze is whistling through the forest. Every minute seems an hour. We keep on riding until the sun is starting to set.

We stop and make camp on a small hill which flattens out at the top. A small beck trickles over the rocks. There is no need to hunt or forage tonight with the boar, the pheasant and all the fish. Yasmin has already rubbed salt into all the food and decides we should have fish and I mouthful of pheasant each. No one argues. This meal is going to be the biggest we had since we left Klad. Laveona and Maria fill up the waterskins and tie the horses with long rope so they could graze and drink.

Isaac and Silvia just sit crying. It must seem like the whole world is against them. Joshua is dead; Elizabeth and Mary have been kidnapped and they have been betrayed by a friend. They had been crying the whole time whilst we were riding. The tears have stained on their cheeks. Every time you think they're getting better the more tears flow.

Shakra and I walk off to collect the firewood out of the sight of the others. "How are you fairing?" Shakra asks.

"Fine." I look at him puzzled, "Why?"

He turns and forces smiles, "You always are."

I raise my eyebrow. What's that meant to mean? I ignore it. "Are you ok?" I ask.

He fiddles with the beads in the back of his hair. He does that when he's nervous, "I'm not going to lie, Jacob, I'm scared. We're dropping like flies. I'm not sure whether we'll make it to Arabia. The Vlaydom soldiers of the Outpost will be waiting for us even if we make it out of this damned forest. If Chevon or the Elves don't catch us Laveona's bandits will."

I look at him in the eyes, they are bloodshot and filling up with water. "We'll be ok, we'll rest for a day and after that, we'll ride off to Arabia." He nods in agreement and puts on a brave face. I can tell he is just burying his fears for my sake.

He tries to act his usual confident self. "Yeah, we'll be fine." He continues to nervously fiddle with his beads in his hair, "You still don't trust Laveona though?"

"Of course, I don't," I admit.

"Why didn't you just take care of her in the first place?"

I turn to face him, "Don't know... If she weren't around those riders would have probably killed us all. She was pretty handy with that axe. But unless we're careful she may be the death of us."

Shakra looks me in the eyes, "Should we get rid of her?"

"No. Not yet at least. Your fiancée, Silvia, has lost too much already, and she still may come in handy. But when it's her watch at night either you, Yasmin or I will stay awake and keep an eye on her. And if we're chased by anyone, knock her off her horse; she'll slow down any pursuers."

Shakra nods in agreement, "Grim thought, but we need to look after ourselves." We stand in silence at the grim prospect of leaving Laveona for death. We collect the firewood in further silence. The sky is turning from orange to purple. "We need to be getting back."

"Yeah." I agree. We slowly walk back to camp.

By the time Yasmin has finished making supper, it is dark. The cool evening air flows between the trees. Although the meal should have been the best since we escaped the war; with all the misery of the day it tasted bitter and flavourless. There is no conversation. Only the crackle of the fire and the rustle of leaves in the wind breaks the silence. The others sit in one big group, huddling for the extra warmth, whilst I sit on the other side of the fire on my own.

I look around the group, apart from myself and Maria the others are covered in scars, cuts, and bruises. The group is in no shape to fight or flee any pursuers. Even a small group of untrained, poorly armed bandits would probably finish us off. But we are being pursued by a massive bandit clan, the Chevonic army, the Vlaydom army and worst of all we were being chased by Elves, a race until recently only lived in the myths of the Wars of Old. But the thing that slaughtered the Kladoenian army is no myth.

I shudder at the thought. Unless we make it to Arabia quickly, we will be killed. By what, I don't know but I'm certain the longer we wait the more likely our doom is. I curse. We are about to waste a day tomorrow, allowing anything that is chasing us to get closer.

After we finish the fish and pheasant, Maria announces to the group that she will take first watch. I volunteer for the second. The others settle down and try to get comfortable. After a day of so much loss, sleep will not come to many in our group. I sit and listen as one by one people rest their heads and sob. Tears flow as each member of our cohort lets out their pent-up emotions.

Once everyone settles, Maria instructs me to sleep. I groan; sleeping means dreaming and dreaming means nightmares. I find a spot to rest my head, then I shut my eyes, knowing that there is no immediate threat...

Or so I thought.

Chapter 11

For the first time since Gwen left, I didn't dream about the Shadow Warrior. Instead, I am sitting next to a large campfire deep within the woods. The warmth of the fire fills me and makes me feel a hundred times better.

Looking around, I jump up terrified and grab Nemesis, readying for a fight. Twenty Chevonic soldiers surround me. The group are sat, eating their supper. I quickly draw my bow and let loose an arrow. It harmlessly passes straight through the head of the nearest Chevon. Ok, I think, just a dream. It seems so real. I feel a gentle breeze float through the Great Woods and can smell the charred wood on the fire.

I look at my arm and panic. I am made of black smoke. I am partially see-through, as the jet-black smoke wisps about and dances in the breeze. I can make out the outlines of my limbs and torso but there is no detail. I try to calm down, this is just a dream. I must be invisible to the Chevonic soldiers as they ignore me completely.

I scan the area quickly. There is another fire about thirty metres away with two small silhouettes sitting next to it. I glide over in this dream state. It is hard to get used to it; I am still holding Nemesis which is also purely made out of black smoke. I sling Nemesis over my shoulder; it's no use in this dream.

The silhouettes sat by the fire are gaining colour. It is Princess Elizabeth and Princess Mary. I move close enough to examine their faces. They seem fine... No bruises, no cuts, not even a scratch. They sit, warm and comfortable next to the fire, eating large bowls of hot stew and bread. I look at them again. No chains, no ropes, they had even given them a knife each for their meal. The twins could go free, attack their captors.

I glide back over to the main fire. There is some sort of argument going on. The Chevon, who is obviously in charge, is yelling, "Why the hell did you bring those girls? What use are they?"

A familiar female voice screams in retort, "Sorry I didn't have time to grab everyone, Claudius. You should be glad I got you those girls. And if they're not important, kill them and be done with it."

The Chevon captain, who must be Claudius, slaps the traitorous Kelley in the face, "You Kladoenian idiot. The Chevonic people do not harm prisoners, especially little girls." He growls, "Kelley, your job was so easy. All you had to do was either lead them to the Arabian Pass where the Vlaydom soldiers are waiting or when we caught up with them, you would make them yield. Yet you let them ambush us. I lost twenty-five good men and horses in that ambush. Some spy you are."

A tear rolls down Kelley's bruised face, still with a red hand mark from where the Chevon had slapped her. "Well, are we going to pursue? We can still reach them before they got to Arabia."

Claudius turns to his men, "No, we're going home. We had sixteen teams of about thirty in this damned forest, but now there are only twenty of us riders. Those bandits and the runaways from Klad. We have entire cohorts missing. We've found others dead, littered with silver arrows. We'll send a bird to the Outpost to let them know that the Kladoenians are heading towards them. We are going home," Claudius' men mumble in approval. "Now eat up, get some rest, it'll be a long ride back to Chevon."

The Chevon leader stands up and walks over to the twins. I follow. Kelley walks straight through me to get to her steed, cursing the Chevonic soldiers under her breath. I'm sure her God wouldn't appreciate that language.

The leader, Claudius, carries on walking to Princess Elizabeth's and Princess Mary's little fire. He crouches down next to the girls and asks in a kind voice, "How was your stew?"

"Lovely, thank you," Elizabeth admits cautiously.

"Good," Claudius sounds genuinely pleased, "Would you like anymore?"

"No, thank you," Mary replies.

The Chevonic captain quickly grabs a couple of blankets from the nearest packhorse and hands them to the girls, "Get some rest, it'll be an early start and a long ride."

The girls throw the blanket over themselves then Mary turns and asks, "Why are you being so good to us? Kelley's right we're worth nothing."

"You heard that?" Claudius' eyes fill with sympathy. He sits down and smiles, "Although my men may seem rough and scary, we're all human. I have a son who is about your age. Killing someone so young, and innocent would be one of the greatest shames I could imagine. Plus, you're good riders, not slowing the group down, not eating all our food and handy with your bows which is what we need against those bandits. You may think its madness for us allowing you to have the weapons but if you try to escape where would you go? If you stay with us you will be fed, kept warm and safe. Then when we get to Chevon, after a few days of rest, we'll escort you two to Vlaydom where you'll be treated correctly and where me and my men get a nice little cash reward. Now it's getting late, get some rest Your Highnesses" And with that Claudius stands up and walks off.

The girls look at each other. Then after some silent agreement, they settle down and shut their eyes.

Behind me a deep rich voice speaks, "You see Jacob, they're safe." I jump and turn to see a tall, muscular man with dark skin and dreadlocks. Even though he seems only in his late twenties, his dreadlocks are starting to grey. He stands arms folded, eyes studying me. He is wearing full bronze armour. He has a bronze net thrown over his shoulder and a bronze quindent, a spear with five points, is stuck in the ground next to him. In his hand is a knife identical in shape to mine and Maria's, except this one is bronze and has an amber gemstone. The blade is gently glowing orange.

I go to open my mouth and ask him a thousand questions, but he speaks first, in a rich, warm voice, "Now's not the time Jacob, it's time for you to wake." He flicks his knife, and an orange glow surrounds me, and the dream disappears.

*****

"Jacob... Jacob... Get up, Jacob."

I open my eyes. I see Maria sitting over me, gently trying to get me up. She sits me up. It is pitch black apart from the campfire. I can barely see Maria never mind the others. She hands me my waterskin. I take it and drink some. "Thanks."

Maria smiles. A proper smile. The first proper smile since we left Rochton. But then, as quickly as it had appeared in vanishes into the night. She replaces her smile immediately with an emotionless frown. A one moment of happiness gone, just like that.

I obviously have a frown on my face as well since Maria asks, "What's wrong? Another bad dream of that Shadow Warrior again?"

"No," I admit. Maria raises an eyebrow, "It was about Elizabeth and Mary." I say.

Maria brushes her long, blonde hair from her face, "I know you're worried about them and probably blame yourself. Don't worry we all do." Maria says, trying to reassure me.

I shake my head, "No it wasn't a dream like that." I tell her about the dream: how it was more of a vision, how Kelley was there, then how Mary and Elizabeth were being treated well and finally how I was made purely out of shadow just like the Shadow Warrior. I don't mention to Maria about the man in the bronze armour. I need time to figure that part out myself first.

Maria doesn't seem surprised, doesn't mock me at all, and just listens intently. Then after about five minutes she finally speaks, "I've had a few weird dreams since we fled Rochton." Maria admits, "Just like your dream you just had. The first night we left I was standing amongst the Chevonic and dead Kladoenians in Rochton. A few days later I was standing in the smoking ruins of Klad itself at the aftermath of the war. Then yesterday I was stood once again in Rochton watching the armies of Vlaydom march past on their way back home, leaving Klad as a smoking ruin, none stayed behind to claim it, and they just left it. Each time I was invisible to others but instead of being made from black, smoky shadow I was made purely out of brilliant, white light."

"White light?" I ask.

"Yeah, don't know why," Maria admits, playing with the ring Dad gave her.

"Do you think these visions are real?" I ask.

Maria sighs, "It's not the first time we have had visions or dreams. You knew when the livestock were under attack by bandits back in Rochton. I dreamt about you and Gwen over a year in advance."

I look around at our sleeping allies, "Mention nothing of the dreams to the others please."

"Yeah," Maria agrees, "We won't mention the dreams."

166

We sit in silence for a moment before I move the conversation on. "Why do we have to stay here another day? We should be riding to Arabia, not waiting to be attacked."

Maria shakes her head, disappointed with me, "Jacob, the others need the rest, they've been through a lot. And according to your dream, the Chevonic hunting parties are riding in the wrong direction."

"Yeah, but the bandits are still out there, plus there are wild animals and by now there are probably bounties for us." I stress, "Why can't you and I just saddle up to horses and leave them? We wouldn't be stopping all the time, slowing down with injuries. We can even leave the others our food and I can hunt on the way."

Maria shoots me an annoyed glare, her green eyes piercing straight through me, "We can't Jacob. And even if we did where would we go? Half of Valouria is looking for us and the other half is in fear of those who are looking for us. Arabia won't open their gates for us without Silvia, Shakra and Yasmin. They're royalty or an Arabian; people who will always get help from Arabia. We're just two teenagers with large bounties. If the two of us went to Arabia alone they would probably cart us off to the Outpost. We need them and they need us. Plus, Silvia is our Queen; it is our duty to make sure she is safe."

I groan, "Our home is gone. Silvia is Queen of the ruins. She has Isaac, and Shakra, and Yasmin, and even Laveona to protect her."

"Yasmin has a bad leg. Laveona is still slightly injured and isn't exactly the most trustworthy of people." Maria pauses and then suggests, "How about we stick with them till we get to Arabia? Then we can decide what to do later."

"Maria..." I plead, whining like a child, "It's not that they're not good people but with this group with all the stops and wounds, we're wasting time. We should be on our way to Arabia. That attack from the bandits won't be the last attempt and now that the Chevonic riders might have gone home, someone else will pick up the trail. We may get cut off by soldiers from the Outpost."

"Ok forget it. I can't argue with you when you're like this." Maria says waving her arms at me, "We're staying, that's it. Let's move on the conversation or I'll go to sleep."

"Fine." I give up. We sit in silence again, listening to the breeze through the forest, the trickle of the river, and the deep breaths of our fellow runaways. Compared to all the fighting and war the world seems at peace, if only for a moment. "The fire's dying," I comment, still annoyed at Maria.

"I got it," Maria mutters. Instead of reaching for the small pile a twigs and sticks Shakra and I had gathered, she did something I've only seen her do a couple of times before. She pulls out her knife gently from its scabbard. Maria closes her eyes and concentrates. The white knife slowly starts to glow. Her blade glows brighter and brighter. Then, in one swift movement, Maria flicks her knife towards the direction of the fire. A radiant ball of white light shoots toward the fire. When the ball of light hits, the fire gets brighter, making it bigger and hotter. Maria turns, obviously impressed with herself and looks at me, "What do you think?"

"I think you need to work on your aim," I say holding up a twig which was lying about a metre away from the fire. One end of the twig is on fire like a candle.

"Well I managed to sustain the glow," She says, wearing a huge grin, "And it actually worked properly."

"Yeah, it was good." I smile. Ever since Maria first got her knife to glow, I had spent months trying to replicate what she had done with my knife. But I have never managed it, not even a shimmer. I had even taken Maria's knife to see if it worked but it seems to get duller than brighter. I still didn't understand it fully, "So, what does it actually do when it glows?"

Maria chucks a couple more twigs onto the roaring fire, "Well it gets brighter when I want it to, all I need to do is think of happy thoughts. But it seems to take up some of my energy, making me tired. I've managed to brighten things such as lamps, torches and fires." Maria explains, "Here, look, this is cool."

Maria's knife starts to glow again. She then forms another orb of light and flicks it towards me. This time it is much bigger and slower, floating in my direction. I start to back up when Maria says calmly, "Its fine Jacob, trust me." I sit still. Maria shuffles closer, the orb slowly comes to a halt. I move forward towards the light. Maria reaches around the orb and places her hands on the back of mine, slowly lifting my hands to the orb.

When I start to hold the orb, I expect my hands to burn with pain. Instead, it just has a gentle, warming effect throughout my body. All the fatigue, pain and misery are flushed away and replaced with good memories. Memories of Maria and me playing in the river as children, being taught to ride a horse by my father and the bandit Rosalyn with her cinnamon hair smiling at me. But the most vivid vision is of two blonde women carrying me to my Dad's house, but I am only a baby. The one who isn't holding me is smiling intently, whereas the woman who is carrying me just scowls at me. I feel like I should know their faces, but I can't place the names of either of them.

It feels as if all the bad things that have happened have all been undone. I see images of Rochton as it was with people in the market, children running around with wooden swords and the general happiness of the arena. I feel my father's pat on the back he used to give me when I did something well. The sun rains down and brightens the town. I am home. Nothing can go wrong.

I look at the orb. It is getting smaller by the second. I only have a couple of seconds left. My best memory then appears. The memory of Gwen and I sitting in the meadow watching the red, setting sun. Her hand is holding mine ever so gently. The memory is so real I can feel her hand brushing against mine. Then after the sun sets, Gwen pulls me up to dance. But the dream is fading. "NO!" I scream as Gwen starts to float away.

Suddenly I am back in reality. The orb is gone. All the happiness, warmth and good memories are drained from me. My muscles feel tired again. The campfire isn't as warm anymore. When I try and visualise a happy memory it is replaced with the image of Klad burning. I curse silently.

Maria is sat in the exact same spot, watching me. "Good, isn't it?"

"Do it again," I beg.

"Jacob, it's not real and it doesn't last for long at all. It's not worth it. It makes you feel bad afterwards." Maria explains.

"I don't care. It was worth it." I retort.

Maria raises an eyebrow, "You were with Gwen weren't you."

"I might have been."

Maria scowls, "You have to forget about her Jacob. She's miles and miles away. She never replied to a single of your letters."

"Shut up," I tell her.

"Ok, ok," Maria utters on the defence. "Sorry, but you know I'm right. No more of the orb, forget about Gwen."

I hold back my anger and take a deep breath. "Yeah, you're right." She is right, I know it. I should have forgotten about Gwen, but I just can't. I change the subject, "Do your swords and ring do the same as your knife?"

"Dioscuri does the same as the knife except for the orb. I can brighten fires and create radiant light, but I can't create the ball of light that you just held. The ring... The ring..." She starts to fiddle again with the white and silver ring Dad gave her.

"What about the ring?" I ask.

"It's different." She says bluntly.

I don't bother asking how; I know I'll get the same answer. Maria flicks her knife at the fire one last time. No orb this time. The fire got hit by some invisible force and got brighter and much bigger. "We're definitely not going to tell the others about this," I tell Maria.

"No. Not yet. There will be a right time when we tell them." Maria yawns, "I'm going to go to sleep. Wake Laveona later, it's her turn to watch."

"What?" I reply in shock, "Do we trust Laveona enough not to slit our throats during the night?"

Maria pauses, "Well yeah. You're the one who let her live. She's still injured and would be alone in the Great Woods." Maria says as she lies down next to where I am sitting. She leans against me and shuts her eyes. It takes under a minute for Maria's breathing to turn heavy and she is sound asleep. I smile; it seems as if her glowing orb came to her when she is sleeping. She is happy in her sleep. I wonder what she is dreaming about.

I stand up, carefully placing Maria so she is leaning against my pack and the tree. I am cold and stiff from sitting on the ground. Thanking Maria silently, I walk to the large warm fire. Although it is late summer in Valouria, the nights are a few degrees above freezing, or at least that's how it feels.

I pace around the fire trying to stay awake, alert, and warm. I pull out my black knife. Knowing that nothing will happen, I start to try and get my knife to glow. Nothing. I concentrate even harder. Happy thoughts. I struggle to find any happy memories without the assistance of the radiant orb of light. Beads of sweat trickle down my forehead. Still nothing. No glow; no brightness; the fire didn't get bigger; if anything, it is dying down. I curse. How does Maria do it? I throw some firewood onto the fire to get it back up to size.

Silently I sit down next to Maria again, letting her head rest against me. I start to think about my father. I couldn't help but think that he knew that Maria and I would be fleeing Rochton and Klad and heading to the Great Woods. He had taught us how to ride, even though neither of us wanted to be part of the cavalry. My Dad spent hours teaching us what was edible in the woods and what wasn't. He had taught Maria and I: first aid, how to fish, how to hunt, how to build fires, how to set traps, how to camouflage ourselves so we could hide, how to set an ambush, how to always know which direction we were going just by looking at the sun or the stars, everything we needed to know on the map of Valouria and made us remember every detail about it.

Unlike most he wasn't afraid of the Great Woods, he seemed happier when he was in them. He would stroll in with us any moment he managed to get a break from work. Helping us track animals that we'd hunt. Then he would make us build a fire, collect edible roots and berries. In the evening, he would watch us cook and prepare the meal. After he had finished, he'd always congratulate Maria and make the same comment that it was the best meal he had ever tasted.

Our father had even written a letter to the King explaining everything years in advance then hid it under the floorboard waiting for the day Shakra knocked on our door in the middle of the night. He knew that we would see the King and he knew that he would want to reward us. He'd sorted everything out, so the blacksmiths knew exactly what to do. He even watched Shakra at a tournament, so he knew who he was. Most of all he had stayed behind to slow down the Chevonic scout army, stopping any pursuit as we fled to Klad. I owe my Dad so much and I have no way to repay him. I never realised until now how much my father did for us. After long days at work, he always made time for us.

I sigh. It is still pitch black apart from the fire. How long have I been awake? One, maybe two or even three hours. I sit for another hour before waking Laveona. When I go to wake her, I can't help but notice she has gotten rid of the bow but now instead of her woodcutter's axe she has picked up a double-edged battle-axe and two one-handed axes from the Chevonic dead. The axe blades catch the light of the dying campfire, filling me with dread.

"Morning already?" She asks as I woke her.

"It's your turn to watch," I tell her.

She smiles, "You're finally starting to like me, hun."

"It was Maria's idea."

"Ah." Laveona grins. "You just do whatever she tells you to, don't you?"

"I wouldn't put it that way," I mutter, annoyed.

"What way would you put it, kid?" She knows she has gotten under my skin. Her freckled smile unashamedly grows.

I have to pause and think. Do I always do what Maria tells me to do? I slowed down when I ran ahead after she shouted at me. I didn't ride off to Arabia alone when Maria told me not to. And we're resting for a day when I wanted to keep moving. "I listen to Maria's advice and make my own decisions."

Laveona laughs, "Ok hun. So, tell me why we are staying here for a day?"

"I... I... Err... Maria thinks it'd be best." I admit.

Laveona laughs at my expense, "Don't always do what she tells you to do hun," Laveona says softly. She then moves closer and looks me in the eyes. I try to back up, but I had a tree behind me. Laveona's voice mellows into a soft whisper, "You don't want to stick around here another day hun. How about you and I saddle up a couple of horses and leave now? Keep riding till we get to the nearest village. Lay low for a while, then live quiet lives away from all this war and violence."

It sounds like a good idea. No more waiting for others. No more fear. No more death. All I had to do was saddle up a horse and start riding north. I was about to take her up on the deal until I saw the others. They desperately need my help. "Sorry, Laveona. I'd love to but I can't. I can't leave Maria and I don't fancy your axe sticking out of my back."

The smile is immediately wiped from Laveona's face. She sits back a bit, "Hun, forget about Maria. She's the one who bosses you around all day. And if you still don't trust me, I'll leave my axe here."

I curse, "Laveona you have no idea how badly I want to say yes. But I don't trust you and I can't leave without Maria. Maria won't leave the others. Nothing is stopping you from saddling a horse yourself and leaving tonight."

"Kid, you're making the wrong choice."

"I know but I can't leave."

"If you stay here for a day, something or someone will pick up the trail and will attack you." The former bandit advises.

We sit in silence. Laveona is right and she knows I know it. "I need to get some sleep," I tell her. "I hope to see you tomorrow." I lie down, desperate to end the conversation.

Laveona doesn't look at me, huffing in disapproval. I close my eyes, drifting off to a sleep filled with the dream of the Shadow Warrior; unaware that Laveona is right...

We are about to be attacked.

Chapter 12

I awake to Isaac nudging me. I tap Maria to wake her and get her off me. Rubbing the sleep out of my eyes I stand up. It is a beautiful, warm morning. Blue sky with a few wisps of white cloud. The cool gentle breeze passes through the trees. Birds are singing. All this made me wonder why Isaac is as white as a sheet.

His eyes are still red and bloodshot after crying about the loss of his brother and the kidnapping of his cousins but that doesn't explain why he looks so worried. "What's wrong?" I ask. But looking around the camp I immediately know the answer.

Laveona is gone.

Laveona has taken a horse (thankfully not Lena), her water skin and her axes. She hasn't taken any food. The others are already awake, looking for any signs of where she has gone. By the looks of it, they realised what had happened, woke each other up to try and find her and when they failed to do so they wake Maria and I as a last resort. Do we intimidate them? Never mind, I think. There's a more urgent matter.

I take Isaac's hand and he pulls me up. Maria gives me a look. She knows what to do. We set off in different directions analysing at the ground, looking for any signs of Laveona. The others watch in silence. After a little over five minutes Maria announces in a curious voice, "She headed east towards the Arabian Pass."

I walk over to where Maria is standing. She is right, Laveona did ride through here. "But she turned and came out here and headed west, deeper into the woods." I point to a gap in the trees. "Ok. She hasn't been gone long, plus she is currently wounded, so she won't be riding too quickly. Maria and I will ride west and see if we can find her or catch her. Yasmin rests the leg, you're on breakfast duties. Silvia collects water. Shakra tends to the horses. And Isaac, keep your eyes peeled." Our comrades instantly agree and rush to work. Shakra hands the reins of Lena to Maria and then gives me the second fastest horse, a smoke black stallion. Maria and I climb into our saddles.

"We won't be long," Maria announces to the group, "But if we're not back by tomorrow morning just leave without us and head north." With that, we set off west in single file, Maria at the lead with me following.

After about an hour of a light trot, the trail gets steeper. Even though the ground is hard, it is easy enough to see where Laveona had ridden. The incline continues to increase. Laveona must have dismounted looking at the prints and the broken twigs which they've stood on. She isn't a confident rider. Luckily, this hill is no problem for Lena who bounds up the trail. My back stallion struggles slightly but manages to climb to the top of the hill.

When we reach the summit of the hill, the tracks have stopped. We can see a vast area of forest. Passing Maria, the reins to my horse, I dismount and climb a tall, sturdy tree for a better look. From this altitude, I can make out the eastern edge of the forest where the Arabian Pass is. There are several plumes of smoke, curling up from the pass. Well; I am right about an army being placed there. I guess it's the soldiers from the Outpost, Vlaydom's garrison. They must have sent a legion out to guard the pass. I look north. A sea of trees lies between us and sanctuary. I squint and try to spot the northern border of the Great Woods. My eyes may be deceiving me, but I might be able to see it. I smile. Who knows, we may survive this damned forest.

But we might not make it thanks to my stupidity. I shouldn't have encouraged Laveona to leave last night. It was idiotic of me. She may have reached her fellow bandits and then she could have launched an attack, taken our allies as hostages for a reward and are just waiting for us. Maria and I should get back and get the others to leave.

I climb down and turn to Maria, "Maria, we need to head back. I have no idea which way she went. Laveona may have reached a bandit camp by now." I plead.

"You're right," Maria says solemnly, "The others could be in danger."

Maria turns Lena around and flies down the hill at full speed. I jump onto my horse and follow, but my steed can't keep up with the raw power of Lena. By the time I reach the bottom of the hill I have lost Maria and Lena. I keep on riding hard hoping to catch a glimpse of them.

I curse. I must have made a wrong turn. The trail is gone. I push my steed, making the poor thing race at full speed. I'm well and truly lost.

I am about to stop and climb another tree to see which direction I was riding in when a woman's voice spoke in my head. Not the same voice that spoke to me before we fought the Chevon, but a different lady. This voice is soft but not as soft as the other voice that had spoken in my head yesterday.

'Jacob, I shouldn't talk to you. My sister has forbidden us to speak to either of you, especially you, but this is an emergency. The others are in trouble, including your sister. They are under attack. I'm meant to let you find your own fate, but my sister broke the rule she created. Keep riding down this path. You'll stop when you're in the right place. Good luck.'

From nowhere my horse gets a sudden burst of speed. He turns and avoids trees without my control. It gives me time to think as my horse zooms through the forest. Who do these voices belong to? Why do they keep talking to us? How are they able to talk to us in this way? And how do they know what was going to happen? I had almost forgotten about the first voice. I need to talk to Maria about it, but if the voice is right, she is in trouble. Laveona's bandits must have reached the others and Maria before I can. I should have just cut her throat when I first found her. Why did I let her live? I knew this would happen. This is all my fault.

By now I should be near the camp, I think, grabbing Nemesis off my back. But the horse has not slowed down at all. I am still waiting for this voice to magically let me know when to stop. Looking around I see no bandits meaning they must have already attacked or about to attack. I am hoping for the latter. I turn to look forward again.

SMACK!

I yell with pain. My steed had ridden under a low, thick branch of a tree. It caught me square in the chest and knocked me off my dumb horse, onto the flat of my back. I lay there trying to overcome the pain. The wind has been knocked out of me. I roll around trying to recover. I feel like I am about to cough up blood. Luckily, I took Nemesis off my back, I think, wouldn't be ideal to have one of the spikes impaling me. Nemesis is lying a few feet from where I am sprawled out.

I am too exposed here. Slowly I roll onto my front. I grit my teeth through the pain as I inch towards Nemesis. I clutch onto Nemesis. Think, I tell myself, I need to hide. Desperately I look around. About three metres to my left there is thick foliage. I begin to drag myself to the bushes, pulling on tree roots and small plants. I keep a tight hold of Nemesis in my left hand as I edge closer to the bush. Pain sears through my chest and back.

Once under the cover of the bushes, I quickly check my body. No broken bones, well, that is a good sign. I take deep breaths. The pain is slowly dying down as I cowardly lie, hiding. I twist, cracking my back. Pain dances up my spine. It takes time but I slowly sit up, pulling myself up with the help of the branches about me. Calm down, I tell myself, I'm ok. I've got Nemesis, my knife, and a full quiver of arrows. I'm fully armed.

I slowly make it to my feet. I groan as my body cracks. Pain flickers as I stand. My first couple of steps are a bit shaky but after a few more, I am standing normally enough. Apart from a sore chest and back, I am relatively ok seeing as I just fell off a horse. Good thing I wasn't riding Lena, I chuckle to myself, I would have hit the branch a lot harder and had a further fall to the ground. I see the stupid beast that made me crash into that tree. I walk over to it, cursing the dumb animal. My steed seems relaxed and watches me as I approach. I put Nemesis over my shoulder. "Let's go find the others," I say to the stallion, a little panicked at all the time I've wasted.

Just before I climb into the saddle, I feel something cold against my neck. Careful not to move, I see that the cold thing pressed against my neck is a sword. I curse loudly.

"Get away from that 'orse." A gruff voice behind me says. Slowly I raise my hands and take a couple of steps back. There must be two of them since one of them grabs my arms and ties them behind my back whilst the sword is still being pressed under my chin.

Whatever knot is tied, it isn't a strong one. I move my arms slightly and the rope loosens. Annoyingly they have the brains to take Nemesis and the quiver of arrows off my back. But luckily, they haven't noticed my knife which is in its scabbard down the back of my trousers and the hilt is covered by my top. I smile. Wait, I think, don't attack yet.

"Turn 'round," The gruff voice barks at me.

What I turn to see shocks me. The sword pressed against my neck belonged to a short, stocky, bald, middle-aged man with a squashed nose. He is wearing boiled leather armour. He has black tattoos covering all of his face, his bald head, and every other morsel of skin visible. Tattoos of snakes, eagles, wolves, bears and weapons, lots, and lots of weapons. The sword he is holding is slightly rusted but is still sharp enough to cut my neck open with a quick flick.

Where is the second person? I look down to find the second tying my ankles together with the same pathetic knot. It is a woman, with the same short, stocky build as the man. Same age, also having similar tattoos that cover her face and body but instead of tattoos on the top of her head, she has a dirty brown, greying ponytail, which seemed to shimmer with grease. Once she has finished her attempt at a knot, she stands up next to the man.

The tattooed woman pulls a piece of paper out of her pocket then takes a step closer and grabs my face. Her breath stinks of rot. I gag with the smell. She begins to inspect my face and compares it to the paper. "It's him," She declares, almost giddily, "Its Jacob Da Nesta." A huge toothless grin appears on her face. She turns to the man, "We can leave the others and just take him. That'd be ten thousand gold pieces. We'd be like lord and lady."

Slowly, I grip the hilt of my knife and loosen the rope around my wrists.

"What 'bout Christian?" The tattooed man asks.

"Who cares about Christian? He'll be dead before sundown. Borge, no one knows that we got Jacob Da Nesta." The woman tells the man who must be Borge.

"You're right Rhoda." Borge grins as he lowers his rusty sword away from my neck.

Rhoda looks at him with disgust, "Of course I'm right." I slowly draw my knife out of its scabbard, careful not to let it scrape. Rhoda starts muttering to herself, "I'm going to be rich. Finally, someone worth hunting."

Borge seems concerned. His ears have pricked up. He's heard someone or something. "Rhoda shush." His knuckles are white as he grips his rust sword tighter,

Rhoda whirls around in anger, "How dare you tell me to shut up!" She smacks his arm, "You're a blithering idiot. This is my moment. I caught Jacob Da Nesta."

Borge takes no notice of her. His head is swivelling, frantically looking for something or someone. "Who's 'dere?" He calls. He unconsciously moves his rusted blade further away from me. There is no reply, just the carefree whistle of the trees.

Rhoda turns on Borge, "See you buffoon, there's no one there. Now stop being an idiot and help me carry this cretin out of here." Borge ignores her. Rhoda raises her raspy voice, "Borge, you slimy git, listen to me."

Borge is snapped back into reality. He screws up his face thinking. Eventually, Borge opens his mouth to say something in retort when his body suddenly goes rigid. He falls forward. There is a one-handed axe sticking out the middle of his back.

Rhoda screams in despair and draws her sword. "Where are you? Who did that?"

From a bush in the distance, a second axe flies through the air towards Rhoda. Rhoda dives out of the way, hitting the deck. On instinct, I throw the rope off my wrist and ankles. Knife in hand, I run over to Rhoda and stab her in the back.

"How... How did you..." Rhoda utters.

"Learn how to tie a damn knot," I tell her before she becomes limp. I quickly grab Nemesis and an arrow. I draw the arrow and aim for a thick, bush where the axe was thrown from.

"You're not going to shoot me again are you hun?" A familiar voice calls from the bush.

I pause and look at the axes. I lower my aim, "Laveona?"

A freckled lady with wild curly, red locks stands up and walks out the bush carrying a two-handed battle-axe. She wears a huge grin as she walks over. "Did you miss me, kid?" Laveona says, winking.

"Hmmm... No."

Laveona picks up her axes and pulls a face, "Well I could have left you for Rhoda and Borge, hun."

"I had it under control."

"I could see that." Laveona smiles.

I decide to keep my mouth shut. Goodness knows what would have happened if Laveona hadn't turned up. But one thing is bugging me, "Why did you come back?"

Laveona shrugs her shoulders, "As soon as I left, I wanted to turn around and come back. When I reached the top of the hill I stopped. As I looked back, I saw a group of bounty hunters run towards the camp. I knew I had to ride back and help. By the time I got to the camp Yasmin, Silvia and Shakra were tied up while Isaac was surrounded. I hid behind trees, waiting for an opportunity to help. Maria rode in and was caught off guard by the fighting and the leader of the bounty hunters, Christian. He knocked her off Lena with the butt of his spear. Isaac was also taken hostage after cutting down two of their men. Then we heard a thud and a yell. Christian immediately told two to find out what it was going on. He knew who Maria was and sensed you must be near. I followed the Rhoda and Borge at a distance making sure I wasn't noticed when I found you, kid."

We stand in silence. I crouch down and pick up the papers that the lifeless body of Rhoda is still holding. Quickly, I start reading them. Maria and I have a bounty of ten thousand gold pieces, alive only. Shakra is only worth one thousand gold pieces alive and half of that if he was dead. Silvia is five hundred alive, three hundred dead. Yasmin is the same as Silvia. What is so valuable about Yasmin? Isaac is worth only a hundred gold pieces alive or fifty dead. I also find the bounties for the twin princesses and Joshua. No mention of poor Flint. I scrunch up the paper into a ball and throw it away.

"What are we going to do?" Laveona asks.

I sit down and think, "Did Rhoda tie anyone up?"

Laveona pauses to think, "Isaac. I think their leader, Christian, tied everyone else up. Why?"

I smile, "Her knots were rubbish; Isaac could slip them. They don't know you exist." Laveona eyes widen. I grab my quiver of arrows off the floor, "Ok, here's the plan."

186

*****

About fifteen minutes later Laveona and I are ready. Hiding just outside the camp my stomach is full of butterflies. I grip on to Nemesis to stop my hands from shaking. Taking a deep breath, I stroll into the camp alone. I spot my friends sat in a circle talking in hushed voices near the edge of the camp, both their hands and feet are bound. Their weapons are scattered about ten feet to their left. Isaac's face is cut, bloodied, and bruised; the rest seem unharmed thankfully. There are two heavily tattooed bodies piled to one side. The bounty hunters are cooking the boar I had slain yesterday, whilst eating bread as they wait. All of them are covered in the same tattoos that decorated Borge and Rhoda, apart from one. There are eight of them in total, three women and five men. All the men have shaved heads apart from the one without the tattoos and the women all have their hair in the same greasy ponytails. They all have the same stocky build as Rhoda and Borge had except the one without the tattoos.

I look at the man without any tattoos. He has scruffy brown hair. He is tall and lean rather than short and stocky like his friends. He carried a polished spear and a small dirk at his waist. He must only be in his mid-twenties, but he carries a quiet confidence about him; although he is skinny, he is muscular. The slim, young man stands whilst his friends sit. He doesn't eat, instead, he paces around the camp smugly, showing off and twirling his spear in his hands. The biggest of the tattooed men keeps on looking at him with evil eyes.

The slim man without the tattoos spots me and turns around, opened arms, "Ah, Jacob, we've been waiting for you." The other bounty hunters stand up and smirk, swords in hands.

I grip Nemesis tighter. Good, I thought, they're all looking at me rather than at Maria and the others. I have to keep their attention, "You know my name, what's yours?"

The tall man smiles, "I'm Christian Foxson, the greatest bounty hunter in all of Valouria. And you Jacob are going to make me rich." He claims, pointing the tip of his spear towards my chest.

I draw my bow. The tattooed bounty hunters laugh. Christian gives me a wink, "I wouldn't do that if I were you."

Why did he wink? He caught me off guard. "What?" I ask, confused.

Christian doesn't answer. Instead of an answer, chaos breaks loose.

Christian spins and stabs the biggest of the tattooed bounty hunters through the chest with his spear. Maria and the others have slipped out of the ropes, picked up their weapons and charged at the tattooed bounty hunters.

I stand still in shock. Laveona steps out of the bushes near where our friends had been tied up. She is wearing the same shocked expression I must be wearing. We just stand watching the massacre of the bounty hunters unfold. Maria is an angel of death. The two blades of Dioscuri cut through the tattooed bounty hunter like they are made of paper.

After thirty seconds, all the tattooed bounty hunters are dead. I am still standing in shock while Maria and Silvia start thanking Christian like he was some hero. Isaac slaps Christian on the back. Christian walks over to me with a huge smile on his face. "You ok Jacob?" He smirks as he dismissively chucks his spear to the side.

"What happened? Why did you help?" I manage to ask.

Christian shrugs his shoulders, "My mother was Kladoenian. I've never captured or killed a fellow countryman. Don't know why. Must be the last scrap of honour I have."

"What about your *friends*?" I ask, still in a stunned shock.

Christian smiles again, "Before last year I had always captured bounties alone. But then I got more ambitious wanted to go after bigger bounties and gangs but that meant I need helpers. I befriended the mercenary group called the Tattooed Men. They forced me to go after you. If I hadn't agreed they would've killed me for weakness. They needed me since I'm the best tracker, but after they found you all there was no need for me. They were sick of being ordered around by someone so scrawny and the man I stabbed was planning to kill me as soon as we captured you. I devised a plan; either Rhoda or I tied the people up. I tied weak knots on purpose and Rhoda..." He pauses with a smile, "That wretch could only tie terrible knots that anyone could slip. Then I whispered a plan of attack into Maria's ear. We knew when you appeared that you would be the perfect distraction. The Tattooed Men would forget about their prisoners, giving the others the chance to break free."

Maria catches my eye and nods, letting me know that Christian's story is true. "How long will you stay with us?" I say.

Christian scratches his chin as he thinks, "I'll lead you to Stonemarsh, my home, it's a nice village and it'll be on your way to Arabia. I assume you're heading that way."

"What will you do then?"

"When you're safe I'll go west to the hideout the Tattooed Men had. I'll collect the gold and retire. Might buy myself a little farm in the middle of nowhere and live on my terms. No more travelling. No more violence. I'd only have to work when I wanted to, be my own boss. Finally, I'd be at peace." Christian says wistfully.

I smile, with all the madness and violence living peacefully away from everything sounds incredible to me. Christian walks off towards Silvia, wanting to pay homage to his Queen. Maria starts up a conversation with Isaac in a hushed tone. Knowing I wasn't wanted in that conversation, I wander over to Yasmin who is still sat on the same rock as she was when Maria and I rode off to catch Laveona.

"You ok?" I ask her.

She shakes her head.

"What's wrong?"

She sighs, "Flint and Joshua are dead. Elizabeth and Mary are hostages. We've been betrayed by Kelley. We were taken hostage ourselves after being captured easily. And I'm currently helpless and slow with this leg." She points at her thigh with the huge cut.

I put my arm around her shoulders, "Yasmin, we'll be fine. In a day or so we'll be out of this damned forest."

"Yes, but then we'll be out in the open, stuck between Vlaydom's Outpost and the small army they place down the Arabian Pass. We'll be out of the frying pan and into the fire." She has a single tear rolling down her cheek.

I wipe the tear off her face gently, "We've made it this far, only a little further to Arabia."

Yasmin looks at me directly in the eyes, "You do understand that Vlaydom won't give up their hunt just because we're in Arabia. We're going to put everyone in Arabia in terrible danger."

"I know Yasmin but there's nowhere else to go." I look at her with sympathy. Yasmin always acts so strong in front of Silvia, trying to be her strength. It seems easy to forget that she is struggling like the rest of us.

"We could leave Valouria, climb over the mountains." Yasmin suggests, "No one would follow us."

Yasmin is right about that. No one would follow us over the mountains. It is pure madness. Suicide. The mountains that surround Valouria make the Great Woods sound like a picnic. No one would follow us because no one ever returns from the mountains that, according to the legends of the War of Old, men climb over the mountains into Valouria. But other than those from legends of old, no one has left Valouria and no one has entered. It is believed the mountains mark the edge of the world.

"Yasmin, you know we can't go over the mountains. And this war won't stop if we leave. Vlaydom has a taste of blood and it won't be long until they turn their attention to Yasu then Arabia."

Yasmin nods, tears glisten in the corner of her eyes, "You're right. Of course, you're right." We sit awkwardly for a couple of minutes until Yasmin says, "Get that boar off the fire and hand it out, we'll eat it now."

I stand up and walk over to the fire. Looking at the fire it reminds of the night before with the light of her knife. I need to talk to Maria about that and about the voices that keep speaking to us in our head. I pull the boar off the fire and pass it around the group.

The mood of the camp is lifted. There aren't a lot of meals nicer than salted pork. For a moment, it felt like being at home. Everyone is in good spirit. We joke around the campfire. It is as if nothing had happened. There is even a bit of a singsong which I politely refuse to join in with. They are all hopeless apart from Maria. She has such a soft, sweet, gentle singing voice. I did have to question myself how we are related. Eventually, I have to get Maria to calm down and relax since her knife is starting to shimmer and gently glow. Thankfully, no one else spots this.

After an hour, the boar is gone, and the fire is dying down. It is as if everyone had held Maria's orb and now it has just vanished. Everyone looks deflated, even Christian who has only been with us for a few hours. People just mope around the camp, killing time before we all sleep.

Once darkness begins to set in, Christian volunteers himself for the first watch. Yasmin meets my eyes and takes first watch, with the excuse that her leg was sore even with stitches Maria put in. It is too early to trust someone who has just killed his *friends* to gain our allegiance; especially a bounty hunter.

I place my head on my backpack. I stare through the canopy of leaves that block the night sky. The fire gently crackles as I shut my eyes. For the first time in the Great Woods, I feel truly relaxed. But one thought echoes around my head: it's not long till we are out of the woods. But Yasmin is right, "Out of the frying pan..."

"And into the fire."

Chapter 13

I hate sleeping.

Getting to sleep isn't a problem. Neither is waking up. It's the dreams that come with sleeping that I hate.

"Come on Jacob," Rosalyn's sweet voice tells me, "It's getting away." She is holding my hand as we run through the forest, her cinnamon hair floats in the wind. I look ahead; the thing we are following is some sort of bright light, the same kind of light that Maria can form with her knife. But this time it isn't an orb, it is moving like a bird.

Then; darkness.

For once it isn't completely pitch black. I had fallen into some kind of hole in the ground. Rosalyn stands up and brushes the dust off herself, "What's this?" She pulls me to my feet. Rosalyn continues fiercely, "We need to get out or we'll lose it." I smile and give her a foot up out of the hole. She climbs up using me to get to the top.

She gasps. I hear a scrape of metal as she draws her khopesh. There is the clang of metal as if there's a sword fight. In a panic, I try and climb up the hole. I stumble and land flat on my back. It knocks the wind out of me.

I hear a sickening thud. "H-h-h-h-help-p-p-p." I hear Rosalyn's voice croak.

Desperately I climb out of the hole and see Rosalyn lying on the floor with a nasty wound to the head. I go to grab my knife as I always do in this dream. But this time I notice Nemesis is on my back. Taking Nemesis off my shoulder I am ready for him.

"Hello..." I call. There is no reply as usual. Rosalyn lies unconscious behind me. A warrior of pure shadow steps out of the bushes. The Shadow Warrior is armed with his trident, bossed shield, and sword. His bright red eyes spot Nemesis; they widen with fear. He starts to back up. I didn't bother asking him what he wanted, this time I just attack.

All the hate and anger I have built up over the last couple of days comes crashing down onto the Shadow Warrior. He manages to parry the blow with his trident, but the force of my attack is so strong it snaps his weapon in two. I keep on attacking. The Shadow Warrior cowers behind his shield. My attack is relentless. Swipe, jab, smash, stab; but somehow, he keeps on blocking the attacks. His shield is in tatters. Dents decorate his broken shield; it seems as if the next strike would just cut through it and into him.

Somehow after the onslaught, he manages to roll out of the way. I take a step back making sure I am still standing between him and Rosalyn. Finally, she is starting to come around. The Shadow Warrior is breathing deeply; he looks at his shield with disgust. It is dented so badly it looks like it is limply hanging off his arm. In desperation, he throws his shield at me. I sidestep easily.

The Shadow Warrior looks beaten. He only has a sword. I have beaten him. The torment is over. No more treacherous nights without rest. I am going to end this nightmare here and now. I am about to attack when I notice the Shadow Warrior smile.

I hear Rosalyn's high-pitched scream, "Jacob!" I turn to see a second Shadow Warrior charge towards me pass the weak heap of Rosalyn. He throws his trident towards my head.

I am expecting it this time. I drop to the floor watching it sail over my head. I was half hoping it would skewer Shadow Warrior number one but of course, I am not that lucky. With cat-like reflexes, he catches the trident. Now Shadow Warrior number one has a sword in his right hand and a trident in his left. While Shadow Warrior number two has a sword and shield.

The Shadow Warriors are standing either side of me slowing advancing. I need to try and fight them one at a time.

As quick as a flash, I draw an arrow and shoot the first Shadow Warrior in the foot. He roars in pain and takes a couple of paces backwards. I spin and kick the shield of the second Shadow Warrior, he stumbles backwards and trips. I run towards the first Shadow Warrior who has just pulled the arrow out of his foot. He manages to find his feet just before I reach him.

I swipe at his head; he ducks and smacks me in the stomach with the butt of his sword. I double over, coughing. He tries to stab me, but I drop to my knees and punch his injured foot. He roars again. I scramble away as he is hopping around.

I turn to see the second Shadow Warrior charging towards me. I jump up and catch his blow in the grappling spikes of Nemesis. I twist Nemesis and his sword flies out of his hands. Unfazed, he smacks me in the face with his bossed shield. I spit blood as I back up. My nose, broken, has blood streaming out of it. Shadow Warrior number two ignores me and walks towards his sword, that is lying on the floor. I turn, a little dizzy, to see Shadow Warrior number one limping in my direction. He throws his trident. I swat it to the side with Nemesis.

My arms feel like lead. Breathing deeply, I grab the trident from the ground and throw it at the second Shadow Warrior's back. It misses him by a hair but manages to knock his sword further away. I draw my bow and fire at the first Shadow Warrior. He deflects the arrow with his blade. I glance over my shoulder; once again that trident has been thrown by the second Shadow Warrior. It misses me by a fraction. It skids off into the brush.

Rosalyn is now attempting to stand. Blood continues to pour out of my nose. I am still disoriented from the shield to the face. I have no time to breathe as the first Shadow Warrior attacks again. I parry his strike and kick him in the chest. I turn and fire an arrow at the second Shadow Warrior. He blocks it with his shield. He stays hidden behind his shield. Warrior one swipes at me. I duck then roll out of the way of his jab. I feint then slash. The move was perfect but the Shadow Warrior number one moves with incredible speed and knocks Nemesis out of my hands. He pushes me and I stumble to the floor. He strikes down, I roll over. The attack is so close it cut the quiver off my back. Before he can attack again, I sweep his legs and get up. I take several paces away and slowly draw my knife.

The Shadow Warriors are smiling, slowly circling me, and sensing my likely defeat. I thought this time I would beat them. I look over to Rosalyn in despair hoping she is ok enough to come to my aid. But the second Shadow Warrior has mercilessly drawn a red smile across her neck, keeping her down permanently.

My vision goes red. I am angry. I am bloodthirsty. But I don't have the energy to attack. Despite myself, I drop to my knees. Both Shadow Warriors rush in and stab me in the chest and neck with their swords. Warm blood soaks my shirt. My body turns limp and I fall to the side.

*****

Even though I had been killed in a dream, I didn't wake. My dream has shifted. Something tells me I am in a similar area of the forest to where the Shadow Warrior dream takes place. It is morning, I walk through the woods. I am unarmed, only wearing a simple shirt and trousers. The clothes are silvery, baggy, and unnaturally light, flapping around in the gentle breeze that passes through the forest. I wander through the forest barefoot. Somehow, I know which direction to head.

After what seems a quarter of an hour, it is hard to tell in a dream, I have reached a clearing. In the middle of the clearing sits a woman crossed legged. The first thing I notice is her bow, a quiver of arrows and sword are leaning against a tree; all of which are made entirely of some kind of silver. The same polished silver that decorates Maria's weapons.

Next to the lady sits a muscular black man I have seen before. He was the man I saw in the dream with the Chevonic soldiers. He sits eyes closed, meditating, with dreadlocks and a small, well-groomed beard. His dark hair has hints of grey which seems strange seeing as he only looks like he is in his late twenties. He has bronze-steel armour, a weighted fisherman's net and what looked like a trident, except it had five points instead of three, one longer one in the centre with four shorter blades perpendicular from each other. The quindent has a giant amber stone in the hilt.

I turn to look at the woman. She must be about thirty. Her long blonde hair reaches the floor when she sits. Her hair is light blonde, almost white, much lighter than Maria's or mine. She has sharp features; pretty in an impish way. She is tall and slim, wearing a long dress made from the same silvery material as my shirt and trousers. She has big, intelligent, green eyes that examine me as I approach.

"Hello Jacob," She speaks softly. It is the same voice that spoke in my head the second time, the one who warned me about the bounty hunters. "Come sit with me." She invites me, patting the ground next to her.

Cautiously, I walk over and sit next to her. I recognise her from somewhere, "Who are you?"

The woman smiles, "One day you'll find out on your own but that's not important at the moment. Just call me Kyra."

"Who's that?" I say, gesturing to the meditating man.

"His name is Elijah, he is the reason I am able to talk to you now, you'll meet him eventually."

"Where am I?" I ask.

"The Great Woods."

"But where about in the Great Woods?" I mutter.

"Once again, you'll find this place again later then all will be explained." Kyra comments.

"Is there anything you can actually tell me about?" I growl. I'm starting to get annoyed.

Kyra grins, "I'm sorry, but now is not the right time."

I sigh. I hate all this mysterious rubbish. "Ok, you're the woman who spoke to me, warning me about the bounty hunters." Kyra nods, I continue, "How? Why?"

"To answer 'how', Elijah allows me to speak to you," Kyra explains as if it was obvious. "But for 'why', now is not the right time."

I roll my eyes. "Can you at least tell me why I am here in this dream?"

Kyra nods, "Yes. You are here Jacob to talk to me."

I finally remember where I have seen this lady before. It was from a memory; from when I looked into the orb. "You were one of the blonde women who carried me to my father's house when I was a baby. You weren't holding me, the other one was. But you smiled while the other scowled."

"I'm surprised you remember." Kyra pauses, "Ah, Maria must have worked out the power of her knife already. Do the others know?"

"No," I answer stunned. "How do you know about Maria's knife? And if you were there carrying me when I was a baby to my father's house, you're either my Mum or someone close to her."

"You're a clever one, Jacob." Kyra's smile grows, "I am not your mother, but I guess you could say I'm *close* to your mother. And I know about the knife since I'm *close* to your mother." For some reason, Kyra put a lot of emphasis on the word close.

"What's my mother like?" I sound like a little kid.

Kyra shakes her head, "You'll find out for yourself soon enough."

"When?"

"Now," Kyra says with a mischievous grin.

From behind Kyra's right shoulder, three people crash into the clearing and storm past Elijah. There are two guards dressed in silver armour, both have long blond hair. Standing between the two guards is the woman who scowled at me as she carried me to my father's house in the vision. She wears a similar gown to Kyra but also wears an elegant silver tiara in her blonde hair. She is a little older than Kyra, but it is hard to tell, their faces seem ageless. She looks very alike to Kyra. It is as if they are related.

"How dare you bring him here, Kyra. You disobeyed a direct order." The woman with the tiara yells, pointing at me.

Kyra sighs with an amused grin, "Tatiana, I was just having a chat. You're the one who spoke to them first, warning him and Maria about the betrayal."

Tatiana turns red, I am not sure if it is embarrassment or anger, "Guards, get rid of him."

Tatiana's bodyguards race over to me and grab both my arms before I have time to react. The two of them start to drag me away. I struggle but it is no use. Kyra and Tatiana are still arguing. Kyra looks on the brink of laughter, as if Tatiana's rage is a great victory. Tatiana explodes at Kyra. "Kyra, I forbid you to speak to him again."

Kyra turns and winks at me, "Sis, why do you hate him so much? He's your _son_."

I feel like I have just been punched in the gut. The words echo in my head. '_He's your son_'

Tatiana is my Mum, making Kyra my aunt. Tatiana glares at Kyra and then slaps her in the face. My mother turns to face the guards, "Wake him up." Her words are empty as if she is asking her guards to get rid of some diseased animal. She storms off back to where she came, not even looking at me. The guard to my left draws his silver dagger and stabs me in the heart.

*****

I wake up drenched in sweat, screaming, and waving my knife wildly. The others are already awake and are sitting in silence watching me. Their eyes are full of concern. Maria moves carefully to sit next to me, "Drink," She tells me, handing me my waterskin. I take small sips, wary of all the eyes on me. I notice Isaac has three rabbits on his belt.

"You hunted?" I ask.

Isaac nods, still looking petrified, "Yeah, Christian and I. They ran straight in front of us. We couldn't miss."

I drink some more water, I am parched. Within a minute or so I've drained my waterskin and starting on Maria's. I stare at Maria. I desperately want to tell her what I have just seen, but not in front of the others. I put on a fake smile, "Well let's get some breakfast and ride off."

Maria looks at me sympathetically, "Jacob, we've all had breakfast. It's midday."

I frown. It surely can't be midday. I look up at the sun, it is directly overhead. They are right, it's the early afternoon of another warm summer's day. "Why didn't one of you wake me?" I ask.

Shakra kneels so he is at my eye level. He has a cut on his cheek which is weeping blood. "We tried to wake you, but you were thrashing about with your knife. When we grabbed your arms and shook you, you wouldn't wake up."

I look around noticing a few people are brandishing cuts and scratches. I apologise to everyone. I have even caught Maria. She has a tiny cut on her arm and part of her sleeve is shredded. I accept Shakra's hand and he pulls me up. I stand a little jelly legged, conscious of the others staring at me.

"Come on," Shakra smiles with his annoyingly cocky grin, "Let's get moving."

The others walk off and get ready for the ride ahead. After silently filling my waterskin and eating the last bread roll Christian had, I climb into the saddle of my smoke black horse.

Before we start to ride Maria walks over, "Are you ok, Jacob?"

Looking around making sure no one is eavesdropping, "No. We need to talk later."

Maria steps even closer and whispers, "You had another vision, didn't you? What did you see?"

"I'll tell you later." I hiss through gritted teeth. Maria agrees and heads off to saddle her horse.

Five minutes later, we set off at a gentle canter. Christian takes the lead with Laveona riding beside him. Yasmin is still unable with her injured leg to ride on her own, so she sits side-saddle on Lena with Shakra sitting behind, taking the reins. Next in our little convoy are the three smallest horses we use as pack horses. Shakra somehow manages to get the three packhorses to follow him in formation without holding onto any reins. Following the packhorses are Maria and Isaac who are deep in conversation. Bringing up the rear, I am stuck with Queen Silvia.

Apart from Christian, Silvia must have been the person that I have spoken to the least. And the first hour of riding is completely silent; I have nothing to talk to her about. She just stares ahead at Yasmin and Shakra.

At first, I welcome the silence because it allows me to think about the vision. My mother seems to hate me, whereas Kyra likes me. She probably only likes me because my Mum doesn't. It annoys me. Tatiana, my mother, hates me for no reason I can think of. Whilst Kyra just used me and won't give me any useful information apart from who my Mum is. But I still can't see either of them in person, only in stupid dreams, courtesy of Elijah, whoever he is.

Thankfully, Silvia eventually spoke to me; I am going mad with my own thoughts.

"Jacob," Silvia says gently, "What's wrong?" I pretend I didn't hear her. Silvia sighs, "I knew you wouldn't tell me. You don't trust me yet. You don't trust anyone apart from Maria."

I shrug my shoulders. It is true. It may have been meant as an insult; I didn't think of it as that way. The more people you trust the more people can stab you in the back. "It's not like I don't like you or wouldn't trust you with most things." I lie, "I just try not to allow myself to get too close."

Silvia shares a flicker of a smile. The answer I gave her must have been better than she expected, "Well unlike you I do trust the people here." Silvia says firmly. "I never expected to be Queen. I didn't want to be. All I hoped for was a marriage to someone like Shakra, move to a different land and be Queen, whose husband ruled. But now I am the Queen of Klad, and I've let my people die just so I could get away." I thought she was going to break down, but she manages to keep it together. "My parents are dead; my brother is dead and since we have been in these damned woods, I've lost a cousin and I'm not sure about my sisters..."

"They're fine," I interrupt. Silvia raises an eyebrow. I quickly backtrack, I can't tell her about the dream, "Just believe me," I tell her. "They're not going to harm two young girls."

Silvia looks at me curiously. She can tell that I am speaking the truth. Silvia continues whinging, "Maybe you're right. But it seems everything is going wrong. I finally got the engagement I wanted with Shakra and now I'm stuck in this forest fleeing for my life. And I doubt Shakra will ever marry me." A tear rolls down her cheek.

"What makes you say that?" I ask, feigning interest.

Silvia sobs as she points a shaky finger at Yasmin and Shakra. They are laughing amongst themselves ahead of us. Shakra's arms are wrapped around Yasmin as he holds onto the reins. Silvia brushes tears off her cheeks, "He loves her, and she loves him back."

"How do you know that?" I say, trying to comfort Silvia somewhat. I feel bad saying those words. It is obvious that Shakra and Yasmin like each other. And what is even more obvious is that they have seen each other before Shakra arrived in Klad's lands with Maria and me. Before Silvia has time to answer the question I say, "Yasmin is just a handmaiden, you're the Queen. Shakra's just being friendly. You just need to talk to Shakra more. Everything will be fine."

Silvia relaxes a little. I told her exactly what she wanted to hear, not what she needed to. It seems stupid that she is so worried about her engagement whilst we are in the

Great Woods fleeing bandits, bounty hunters, Vlaydom, Chevon and Elves. Luckily, Silvia decides to drop the subject. Unfortunately, though it means we ran out of conversation again.

Our silence is broken by the sounds of Maria and Isaac howling with laughter. It is unnerving me how much time those two spent together. They are always in good spirit when together. Isaac's brother is dead, and his cousins have been taken prisoners, but when he is with Maria it is as if nothing has happened. It seems that Maria doesn't have to use her orb to make Isaac happy.

As we continue to trot north, the sun slowly sets behind a wall of clouds. I smile; at least it'll be a warmer night. We keep on following Christian north. And then, before it turns dark, we finally reach it: the end of the Great Woods. I should feel elated, we had passed through the unsurpassable, but all I feel is dread. We are still in danger.

We all climb off our horses, sore from riding all afternoon. "We'll make camp a couple of hundred metres inside the forest," I suggest, "That way anyone who passes by won't see us." It makes sense but everyone knows that no one would be walking so close to the forest. Nobody seems that keen to spend one more night in the Great Woods, but no one complains. We trudge back to a nearby stream, collecting firewood on the way. We are so used to our duties that we have a fire cooking a meal of rabbit and some roots, that Maria had found, within minutes. I promise everyone I will hunt in the morning before we leave the forest and head for Stonemarsh.

I also volunteer to take first watch. There are a few half-hearted arguments about how I had taken the watch the night before, but they all agree. I want to delay any dreams and talk to Maria in private. After the meal, I watch the others fall to sleep one, by one. I can't help but smirk when I see that Silvia has positioned herself between Yasmin and Shakra. Isaac takes the horses to the water then fastens them to a tree to make sure they don't run off. He lies down and within a couple of minutes is snoring. I sit with my back to an old oak. Maria sits close and leans gently against me. I chuck a couple of twigs onto the fire and wrap myself up for the night...

Completely oblivious to the dangers that lie ahead.

Chapter 14

When I am certain everyone is asleep, I nudge Maria. Without any complaints, she sits up a little groggily. Rubbing her eyes, she says, "Ok, what have you woken me for?"

"Er, well, last night... I had another vision, dream, thingy." I say nervously, struggling to get the words out.

"What was it about then?" She asks sleepily.

I take a deep breath, composing myself, "I met our mother."

Maria sits up straight and looks me in the eyes to make sure I am not just making it up. Then after what seems an age, she says, "What happened? Tell me everything." I thought she would be livid or jealous, yet she seems calm.

I spend the next ten minutes describing the dream. About how I found Kyra in the clearing, sat with the mysterious Elijah. How Kyra talked to me but wouldn't explain anything. I tell Maria about how Kyra had spoken to me in my head before we ran into Christian's former bounty hunter allies. Then I explain about Tatiana, our mother, and her two guards crashing into the clearing. How Tatiana seemed to hate me and was yelling at Kyra that she had disobeyed her orders. Finally, I tell Maria how

Kyra let me know Tatiana was our mother and Kyra was our aunt.

The whole-time Maria just sits and listens in silence. She seems particularly interested when I mention Elijah. I would feel better if she just calls me a liar or questions everything I have said; that is what I would be doing if it was the other way around. After five minutes of an awkward silence Maria speaks, "Well, I guess you met our mother."

"It was just a dream," I say trying to convince myself as much as Maria.

"No," She says. She freezes, looking past me as if I am not there. Her eyes glaze over, her blonde hair ripples in the gentle breeze. A minute passes. Then another. I sit awkwardly as she looks into the distance. Eventually, she speaks, "It wasn't a dream you were there with our Mum."

Raising an eyebrow, I ask, "How do you know?"

"Tatiana..." She pauses, "Our mother just told me. She said that she'd speak to me tonight."

What! That isn't fair. Our delightful mother had me woken up by a couple of guards without even regarding me as her son, while she decides to spend quality time with Maria. What makes Maria so special? I try to shrug it off, "So what does our beloved mother want?"

Maria sighs, "She told us we were in danger."

"Really." I interrupt, "I hadn't noticed."

Maria smiles. A sad, sympathetic smile, "She said that your dream was a vision. That you and I are far more important than we have ever imagined. That we have a great role to play in the future. And that many want to prevent that future from happening and will stop at nothing to see us dead. She says that you and I should trust no one from now on apart from each other."

After Maria finishes, we sit in an awkward silence. I am still annoyed at our mother's preferential treatment of Maria over me. But I am glad that she agrees with me that no one here should be trusted.

The gentle wind continues to whistle through the trees. There is a chorus of soft breathing coming from our sleeping allies. It is so quiet that I can hear the scuttling of insects, moving through the night. I need to tell Maria what I really think. I look at the faces of our companions, they seem content and are resting easy. They are as safe as they are ever going to be.

Finally, I pluck up the courage to tell Maria what I want to say, "We should leave Maria, now. Take two horses, our own packs and waterskins, leave them the rest. They have Christian, who has promised to lead them to Stonemarsh. We can ride west in the safety of the Woods. Then leave to find a sleepy village or a farm in the middle of nowhere, change our names and live our lives."

Maria sighs fed up with this conversation, "Jacob listen, we both want to run, hide, try and be someone else but we can't leave them. They need us and we need them. We'll be safe when we get to Arabia."

"We don't need them. They slow us down." I protest. "We'll be safe when we get to Arabia you say, we were going to be safe in Klad and look how well that turned out."

Maria looks deflated, "Jacob, we both know that Vlaydom can't afford to destroy Arabia, its trade is much too valuable. When we get to Arabia we can start over and hope no one tries to sell us out. If we go alone, we'll be caught."

I nod grimly. I know she is right, but I don't have to like it. The first request didn't sway Maria as expected so hopefully, she'll soften for the second. "Maria, can you create that ball of light again?"

Maria shakes her head firmly, "No."

"Please," I beg, ashamed of how pathetic I sound.

Maria tries to stare me out but gives up too easily, "Fine. You need to forget about Gwen but if you're that desperate I'll do it." She draws the short white blade of her knife and closes her eyes. The blade starts glowing brighter and brighter. A ball of light slowly starts to grow at the tip of the knife.

Eventually, when the orb is large enough and Maria flicks her wrist, causing the orb to gently float towards me. I put my hands on either side of the orb. Happiness floods over me. This time I know to focus on just one memory. I am transported to the only memory worth seeing. I am sat in the meadow with Gwen holding my hand, watching the sunset.

"It's beautiful, isn't it?" Gwen gasps.

"Yeah, it is," I reply. I wasn't even looking at the sun or the sky or the forest or the meadows, just staring at Gwen.

Her ice-blue eyes light up in the setting sun. Her luscious brown hair floats gently in the breeze.

Gwen shakes her head, "The Behemoth and I are only going to be staying here for two weeks while the rest of the convoy heads off to Klad." My heart skips a beat. She will be here for two whole weeks! I only expected her to only stay one night. My pulse races as I excitedly imagine how amazing these two weeks will be. I pluck up my courage and move my hand closer to hers, hoping she'll hold it.

The memory fades into another. Once again, Gwen and I are sat on the meadow but facing the other way. Gwen is leaning in against my chest and I have my arm wrapped around her. Our two weeks are up. The best moment of my life has passed so quickly. We watch as the King of Kings' chariot rolls into Rochton. Gwen has a single tear rolling down her cheek and to be honest so do I.

"We should do it," Gwen says, "Just run away and live our lives together. We can go anywhere we like, free from responsibility. We could live on a small patch of land or be lord and lady in some kingdom. I don't care where, but we have to leave now."

It sounds great; perfect in fact. But I can't leave yet, I am only fourteen. According to the Laws of Klad, I am not a man till I am eighteen. If I left now it would bring great shame to my father and my sister. I can't leave like my mother did. "Could you just stay?" I plead.

Gwen solemnly shakes her head, "The people of Klad have little love for me and my people. I had to stay here instead of going to the city of Klad itself. I fear I have outstayed my welcome, if it weren't for The Behemoth, I would have been run out of the town already."

It is true; everyone has acted hostilely towards Gwen for no reason and seem to shake their heads when they walk past the two of us walking hand in hand. "So, is this it, is this goodbye?" I ask.

Gwen spins around to face me, "Let's not call it goodbye but 'I'll see you later'. Four years will pass soon enough. If you still love me follow the sunset west until you reach the mountains, then go north until you're in Vlaydom. Tell a guard in golden armour you are looking for Gwen, he'll send you straight to me. I'll be waiting." She stands up and gives me a hand up. "I will wait for you." She tells me. I nod in agreement. Gwen starts to shed tears, "Hopefully I'll visit here again before your eighteenth birthday." She gives me one last kiss and runs off down the hill.

I am left standing on the hill, heartbroken. Then a voice which isn't a part of the memory pipes up and says, "So that's why you still love her." I jump. Slowly I turn to see Maria. Not the memory of Maria but the one currently sat in the Great Woods. She sits a few feet away on the hilltop, looking at me disapprovingly.

"How did you enter this memory?" I demand furiously.

Maria shrugs her shoulder, "I just held the orb."

"Why?"

"I needed to see this, why you're so desperate to go west, why you keep wanting to see these memories... why you still love her. I always thought she did you some wrong and just left you broken-hearted." Maria explains.

How dare she? I have never been so angry with Maria. This is my memory, not hers.

Maria continues "Jacob, you can't go and find her. We're wanted fugitives and you want to walk through the main gates of the kingdom that wants you arrested."

I turn my back on her in disgust, "How much longer is the orb going to last for?"

"It's finished," Maria says. I look up at the night sky through the trees and leaves. I sigh, I hate this forest. "You ok Jacob?" Maria asks. I ignore Maria, what right does she have to enter my personal memories? "Get some rest," Maria tells me, "You took first shift last night." I'll wake someone up in a minute.

Wordlessly, I lie down on my side, my back to Maria. I fall straight to sleep, angry and ready to fight the cursed Shadow Warriors.

*****

I wake up feeling surprisingly refreshed, even after being slaughtered by those damned Shadow Warriors again.

It is considerably colder this morning. Sitting up, I look around and see Christian on the other side of the camp. He sits methodically sharpening the point of his spear and then his knife. Slowly, I stand up, trying not to wake Maria who is lying only inches to the right of me. I tiptoe across to where Christian is sat.

"Morning," He says without even lifting his eyes off his blade.

"Morning," I reply as I sit next to him. We sit awkwardly in silence for a few minutes. "How far away is Stonemarsh?" I ask.

"Not far." Christian shrugs, "We should arrive there well before nightfall. There's a new tavern in town, small, quiet. The innkeeper's wife is my sister so they should let us rest up there; maybe lay low for a couple of days." He pauses, "But we won't be able to just walk through the front gate on horseback dressed like this. They'll be a small garrison of Vlaydom guards, but other than that the town is fairly independent. The guards are all local men, untrained but are loyal to Vlaydom who pay them handsomely. We'll need to sneak you lot in."

"How long do you think we could hide there?" I think wistfully of the opportunity of a warm room and featherbed.

"About a week if my sister is feeling kind. But I wouldn't stay too long."

I nod, it is what I expected. "And how far is it from Arabia?"

"Not certain," Christian admits, "I've never gone that far north. But at a guess, you'll reach the desert in less than two days."

I smile, "You're a good man, helping us like this."

Christian blushes, "I needed to do one decent thing in my life before I passed, so I guess this is it."

I pat him on the back in approval. I understand where he is coming from; I have my own demons to shake off. I stand up, "I'll get breakfast." Taking Nemesis off my back, I wander deeper into the forest looking for something to eat.

Half-heartedly I creep through the forest knowing we are going to have a hot meal tonight. A small lone fawn stumbles past about fifteen metres away. Easy pickings, as I put an arrow in her neck.

The animals here act as if they never had been hunted before, it was too easy. It must have lost its mother. I pull out the arrow from her neck and sling the deer over my shoulder. I gut her and carry the poor thing back to camp.

Even though the young doe is only little, it takes me an age to carry the carcass back to my allies. Everyone in our makeshift camp is awake by the time I stagger into the clearing. I am covered in a film of sweat. Yasmin smiles as she hobbles over and takes the fawn, hacking the petite deer to pieces. Within an hour, we are sat by the remnants of the fire, eating our breakfast heartily.

We saddle up quickly, excited to finally leave this damned forest. Yasmin is now able to ride on her own, even though she winces as she climbs into her saddle. "Watch the skies." Shakra announces, "I don't fancy a skirmish with any of the Gryphons." We all agree as we set off in convoy, Christian and Laveona at the front; followed by Shakra and Queen Silvia, who looks elated to have Shakra at arm's length; then Isaac and Maria, leaving Yasmin and I stuck at the rear.

It must have been an hour before anyone utters a word to me. Yasmin breaks our silence, "So... How do we get into Stonemarsh?"

I shrug my shoulders, "I'm still thinking." No point in lying.

"So much for the man with the plan," Yasmin mutters under her breath, not expecting me to hear. I ignore her comment. She doesn't seem pleased to be riding next to me, "May I make a suggestion?"

"Please do," I grumble.

"Well, we obviously can't go as ourselves; we'll be arrested before we make a hundred metres," She explains, "So why don't we go as them?"

I look at her confused, "As who?"

"Look east,"

I squint and see two small trade caravans on the horizon heading west, towards us. "You want us to kill them?"

Yasmin smirks a little, "No. Don't be stupid."

"How then?"

"Those are Arabian caravans. We Arabians will always trade and will always accept a good deal."

"A good deal..." I scratch my head, "We have little to trade with and lots to buy."

"We'll send a small party, just you and me," Yasmin says begrudgingly, obviously not keen on her own plan. "I am a fellow countryman in need; they should give us a better deal."

"Why should I go?" I ask.

"Well firstly, I may be wrong, and the caravan may not belong to an Arabian. Then yes, we would have to fight." Yasmin smiles somewhat bemused, "But if they are Arabians it does not guarantee us safe passage. If the deal goes sour, you're my protection. At least keep me alive until back up arrives; if you need it."

I nod. It's not a great plan but those caravans may be the only way we get into Stonemarsh undetected. Yasmin calls the others to halt. She tells them the plan. The others agree reluctantly. We dismount our horses and sit on the grass, watching the two Arabians creep closer.

An hour passes before the traders are close enough. Yasmin and I jump onto our horses and trot over. The Arabians smile as we approach. Their smiles are not warm. This isn't going to be friendly; just professional. As we approach, the traders study us and the horses we ride. Three Arabians dismount the first caravan in unison. Two of the three Arabians stay next to the first caravan, hands resting on the hilts of their scimitars. The tallest of the three approaches slowly. He strolls confidently towards Yasmin and I. Yasmin jumps off her horse, handing me the reins and walks forward to the lead trader.

The lead Arabian trader is a tall, slightly crooked man, hair starting to grey and even has flecks of white tips at the end of his beard. He adjusts his purple and gold headscarf then bows extravagantly. "My Lady, my name is

Razak, a humble trader from the golden sands of Arabia. What do I owe the pleasure of greeting such a beauty?" His voices oozes confidence and suave.

Yasmin does all she can to prevent blushing. She curtsies politely, "Razak, I'd like to thank you for your kind words. I come on behalf of my companions. If possible, we would like to trade with you. We require the larger of your caravans and the goods inside."

Razak scratches his beard slowly, contemplating the potential deal, "My dear this would cost a great price, one which you may not be able to afford. The goods we carry are some of the finest silks in Valouria."

"We do not have gold," Yasmin admits, "But we do have goods to trade."

"Goods that match the quality of our silk?" Razak enquires.

Yasmin pauses. She turns around desperately. We have no goods. Yasmin knows this. Yasmin continues to fumble with her words, "We, we er have..."

"What do you have?" The trader calmly demands. Yasmin is becoming flustered. Razak is getting impatient. "You have some fine horses," Razak observes, "I've always wanted to breed horses." He pauses and thinks. "How about I give you the larger caravan and we take the horses except two of your choice to pull it."

Yasmin takes a step back, "My lord, is that not a bit steep."

Razak twists his gnarled fingers through his beard and sneers, "My dear. I don't think you are in the position to bargain."

Yasmin turns redder, "I don't know what you mean."

Razak's cruel smile widens, "I know exactly who *you* are. *All of you.* You need my caravan to hide from Vlaydom patrols. I'm in half a mind just taking you for ourselves and collecting the exceptionally large reward."

In a flash I have Nemesis gripped firmly in my hand an arrow pointing at Razak's chest. "You'll be dead before you finish giving the order." The Arabian's guarding the caravans draw their scimitars.

Razak keeps his cool, he seems to be enjoying the rising tempers, "Put away your blades child. As you can see, I have taken no such action, and neither should you."

Yasmin turns to me, "Do as he says, lower your bow" Reluctantly, I follow Yasmin's order and return my arrow to its quiver.

Razak's smile is unwavering, "Good man. If any harm should come to me, there would be no one to call off the attack. You were too arrogant to notice but I have a score of men surrounding your friends awaiting my order."

I turn to see and my stomach drops. He was right. There are twenty Arabian's hidden in the long grass around our cohort who are blissfully unaware, sat chatting amongst themselves. Razak continues gleefully, "I have no doubt, should it come to a fight you and your friends will be far superior in fighting ability to my men. But we will win. We outnumber you comfortably and have the element of surprise." Razak pauses and smiles again. He locks eyes with Yasmin, "Now my dear, you and I both know that if me and my men collected your bounties, whether you be dead or alive, will be much more of a reward than the price of a few Chevonic steeds."

"You're right. So why not fight?" Yasmin venomously retorts.

Razak looks delighted, "Well my dear I am a gambler. I believe if you receive my caravan you will make it to Arabia safely. You'll have to cross the desert but I'm sure _you_ will be able to navigate it. And when you do, King Tufail will want to hear your tale. When you and your friends of high importance reach Arabia, you will tell King Tufail of how I, Razak, was paramount in your safe passage through Stonemarsh to the Arabian Desert."

I shake my head, "Why would we do that?"

Razak chuckles, "Because your friend will swear on her father's honour. If she doesn't, well I give the order and you all die." Razak grins. He knows he has bested us.

Yasmin looks up at Razak, fighting back tears. Razak has clearly got under her skin. "I swear on my father's honour."

Razak claps his hands, "Wonderful..."

Yasmin interrupts him, "Let us keep four horses, not two."

Razak's smile is finally wiped off his face, "My lady, I'm not sure you are in a position to make the demand."

Yasmin musters up courage from seemingly nowhere. Her hands balled into fists and her face as red as the evening sun, "You will let us keep four horses, or with the Gods as my witness there will be no place on heaven or earth that my father's wrath won't find you."

Razak's eyes are drowning with fear, but he manages to find his tradesmen smile, "My lady, pick the four finest steeds to pull your caravan and I'll bid you a good day." The snake holds out his hand and Yasmin shakes it without hesitation.

Who on earth is Yasmin's father?

Yasmin marches towards me and leaps onto her horse, "Stay here Jacob," She demands in an authoritative voice. She doesn't even look at me, she just locks eyes with Razak, "If anything happens or it takes even a fraction of a second too long; kill him." She points directly at Razak's throat. Without another word, Yasmin turns and rides back to the camp.

I smile and nock an arrow. Razak tries to stand confidently but I can tell that Yasmin has gotten to him. He looks like a wounded animal.

A few minutes later, my friends ride in, led by Yasmin who looks ready for blood. But somehow everyone keeps their cool. I see Razak's men rush behind them on foot.

Yasmin dismounts and the rest copy. Shakra quickly grabs the reins of all but four horses and hands them to Razak. Yasmin looks straight through the tradesman when she spat, "Now leave."

Razak bows nervously. He and his men saddle up on the horses and take the smaller caravan east. We watch them slowly disappear over the rolling, green hills.

Once the Arabian traders are out of sight, I take a look at the caravan we have just purchased. It is just a plain wooden cart with a white canvas roof. Looking in the back I understand how crooked Razak is. Razak's *finest silks* are nothing but peasant's clothing.

I look down at what I am wearing. My clothes are still the same rags I was wearing the day we escaped the war at Klad. They stink, are ripped, and are covered blood and goodness knows what else. I'm still missing a sleeve that I had used as a bandage for Yasmin's leg. Although the clothes in the caravan are not what the weasel promised, they are clean, fresh clothes. I keep searching through the caravan. Apart from the clothes, there isn't much except for a little wash bag with a used bar of soap. Looking at myself I admit a good clean wouldn't go amiss.

When I climb out of the caravan, I find the group waiting for me. They stand in silence, all eyes glued on me. I tell them about the clothes and that we should all wash. They agree. Everyone feels grotty and grimy. We climb into the back, whilst Shakra and Maria sit at the front, steering the caravan. We trudge north, with Lena and the three other horses pulling the cart.

Maria spots a small stream ahead. The girls wash up first with the guys keeping guard at a distance, then when the girls are done and clothed the four lads wash up. The water is cold and shallow; there hasn't been any proper rain in weeks, but by the looks of the sky we may get some soon. Thick, black thunder clouds are rolling in. By the time we have all washed the river is brown with mud. I get changed into baggy trousers and top. Razak's 'silks' are itchy but better than the rags we had been wearing.

We keep on moving north. The sun is starting to set behind the storm clouds by the time Stonemarsh appears on the horizon. A warm room, a comfy bed and a hot meal are waiting for us there. A whole night without danger or threat...

Or so I thought.

Chapter 15

Sitting in the back of the caravan is awful. Yasmin, Shakra, Silvia, Isaac, Maria, and I are all crammed at the back of the cart. The rest of Razak's *'finest silks'* are hanging from the door of the cart, hiding us from the outside world. The caravan is cramped. Each bump in the road throws us about like rag dolls. The air is hot and stale. I feel like I'm suffocating.

But it could be worse. The grey clouds I spotted earlier were in fact storm clouds. The rain is lashing down, beating the caravan. Christian and Laveona are sitting in the uncovered driving seat being soaked by the torrential storm. It is impossible to talk over the sound of the wind and rain. We sit in silence, nervously fidgeting. Shakra is nervously playing with the beads in the back of his braided hair, Isaac is biting his nails, whilst Maria is running her fingers along the flat of her knife. The tension is unbearable. Our lives hang in the balance with the two least trusted members of our group. These outsiders would determine our fate in the coming moments.

The caravan keeps on creaking slowly towards Stonemarsh. The cart rocks and bounces on the dirt track. The six of us in the back of the caravan are thrown again as we hit another mound in the road. Shakra mutters to himself under his breath, cursing Christian's ability to steer the horses. Silvia grabs Yasmin's hand and starts to pray. Isaac closes his eyes and joins in, whispering silent prayers to himself. I shake my head, after all, they've been through, they still have faith.

I turn to peep through my little lookout spot. Through a small tear in the canvas, I can see the backs of Christian and Laveona. A flash of lightning illuminates the small village of Stonemarsh. We creep closer and closer, undeterred. I can make out the guards at the gates. The red uniform of Vlaydom is proud and clear. Both guards are heavily armoured and holding pikes, two metres tall.

A sudden panic hit me. We are approaching a garrison of our enemy and all our hopes are on a thief we kidnapped and a bounty hunter who had attacked us. My hands start shaking. After all the trauma and hardship, we had been through, it has all come down to this. I want to run but we are too close. There is no way to escape. We are four hundred metres away, three hundred metres, two hundred...

The cart halts and the guards at the gates approach pikes in hand. I look at Maria, with a panicked expression. I can tell she understands what I am thinking. She pulls a face, telling me to calm down. I go back to looking through my peephole in the canvas. Christian is talking to the guards. Slowly I unsheathe my knife. I silently hope I don't have to use it. I don't fancy our odds if a fight breaks out in the caravan. I try to focus on what Christian is saying. I can barely make out a word as the storm lashes down. There are a lot of hand gestures and what looks like one of the guards laughing. One of the guard's points at Laveona, Christian seems to blush and says something. The guards look stunned then there is a lot of handshaking. Christian makes a gesture to the caravan and jumps off his perch and walks around to the back of the cart, the guards follow.

This is it. After everything we've been through, we are going to be caught. I brace myself. I feel the storm rush into caravan as the back is opened. All Christian has to do was pull away the clothes and they'll see us. I have my knife in my hand and get ready to strike. Isaac and Yasmin also have their weapons ready.

Then I hear Christian's confident voice, "... So I get the wife and a job at her father's tailors."

"You're a lucky man Christian," A guard says, "Go on then, get inside and tell your sister the good news."

The canvas closes. I can still hear fragments of their muffled conversation as they walk to the front of the cart. There is a collective sigh of relief from our cohort. We sit back. The rain continues to lash down upon the canvas. Christian's lie had obviously fooled the guards. I relax, I should have trusted him. Twice now he has saved our skin.

The caravan creaks and starts moving again, through the small wooden gates into Stonemarsh. I turn back to the small tear in the canvas watching our caravan roll along through the main street which is a little more than a mud path. The horse hooves squelch as they trot through the rain and the mud. We pass small homes and a few stalls as we roll down the street. Looking ahead I spot the tavern: *"The Humble Hearth"*.

The Humble Hearth looks cosy and warm, sitting at the end of the small street, facing any coming traveller. The ground floor of the inn is a combination of stone and deep, red wood. Whereas the first floor is all wooden panels. A large window faces out from upstairs, straight down the street, watching us as we approach. Smoke floats out of the chimney. I smile, at least it will be nice and warm.

Christian steers the cart around the back of The Humble Hearth to a small stable that is attached to the side. Once under the small shelter, the cart stops and Christian jumps down and heads around the back. "Ok," He says, water dripping from his soaked brow, "It's safe to get out."

We climb out of the caravan. The small stable is empty except for a few goats tied to a post, sheltering from the storm. Christian runs out from the stables and pounds on the back door. The others follow him to the door; I stay warily by the caravan. Silently I take Nemesis off my back and nock an arrow. I don't feel safe. There is no answer. Why don't I feel safe? I feel like something is going to happen. Something isn't right. Christian knocks again, much louder. This time the door creaks open. From behind the door, a woman pokes her head out. She is a few years older than Christian. Her hair is a shade darker than Christian's. She is about half a foot shorter than Christian and has darker eyes but the same steely expression that tells me this is his sister.

Christian smiles, "Ah, Joan, good to see you." He places a kiss on her cheek. "May we come inside?"

Joan opens the door fully revealing her bump. I curse; she's pregnant. Christian has just brought the most wanted people in Valouria into his pregnant sister's inn, endangering not only her life but also the life of her unborn child. Joan silently gestures for us to come in. Christian smiles and strides through the doorway. After a brief hesitation, the others follow one by one. I put the arrow back in the quiver before anyone could notice. I sling Nemesis over my shoulder and follow the others inside.

The Humble Hearth reminds me of home. My old home. It is warm, comfortable and most of all cosy. The bar and kitchen take up one side of the room. In the centre of the room, there is an ever-present fire giving light and warmth to all the tables surrounding it. Paintings, antlers, and candles decorate the wooden walls. Thankfully, the inn is currently empty.

Joan sits us down on a table near the kitchen. Joan and Christian walked into the kitchen. I can hear them argue in hushed voices. A third voice speaks; much deeper and gruffer. We sit silently. Five minutes pass, then ten minutes. I catch Maria's eye; her look again tells me to relax. The hushed voices sound more in agreement, finally.

After an age Christian, Joan and a young, large, ginger, bearded man walks out of the kitchen. They stand awkwardly until Christian speaks up, "This is my big sister Joan and her husband Hugo. They're going to let us stay for one night. We're staying in the four guest rooms. I had to say I was engaged to Laveona to make it past the guards. They know me here and know I only visit when there is a reason to. I expect it may be busy tonight, many people will want to congratulate myself and Laveona. Stay calm and keep a low profile and it should be fine." The group nods with approval. If I were put in Joan and Hugo's situation, I would have kicked us out, one night in a feather bed is a blessing.

Joan nervously steps forward, trying to act brave, "Christian told us who you all are. Hugo and I are honoured to have you as our guests."

Silvia stands up and does her Queen impression. "You have done us a great kindness and put yourself at great risk. One day we shall return the favour." Joan smiles with pride and attempts a curtsey to her Queen.

"Townsfolk are gonna be here in a bit," Hugo says in a gruff voice, somewhat disapprovingly. "I'm gonna get everything sorted for tonight." He walks into the kitchen.

"I'll help him out," Christian grins and follows his brother-in-law.

"I'll show you to your rooms," Joan says, speaking directly to Queen Silvia. We follow her as she leads us up the stairs. The four rooms are positioned next to each other, identical in size and furniture. "You're going to have to pair up," Joan explains, she never lifts her eye contact of Silvia, "Maria and Isaac will be in this room, next are Shakra and Silvia... I mean Your Grace, and then next will be Laveona and Christian and the last one is for you two," She says pointing at Yasmin and me, "Come back down in a couple of minutes before the customers arrive." Joan walks down the stairs.

Yasmin and I walk to the end of the corridor and enter our room. The room is pretty much just a double bed but compared to the Great Woods it seems like a palace. My eyelids go heavy just looking at the soft feather bed. Yasmin drops her scimitar and shield at the side of the room. She throws off her wet cloak and turns to face me, "We better go down." Yasmin mutters as she adjusts her turquoise earrings in the small, bronze mirror.

I nod in agreement, with the thoughts of homecooked food dancing in my head. Carefully I place Nemesis and my two quivers of arrows to one side. I take off my cloak which is full of water and toss it to the side.

"Leave the knife as well," Yasmin says bluntly.

I glare at her, "No chance," I push past her and head downstairs. She groans and follows, chuntering to herself.

Our companions are already downstairs sitting in pairs in different corners of the room. Joan tells Yasmin and me to sit down at a table in the corner next to the stairs. She then produces one of the most wonderful things I've seen since home; a bowl of goat stew with a large portion of bread to go with it. I look down at the bowl, chunks of meat, potato, carrot, turnip, and onion floating in rich gravy. Heaven.

Just as I start to tuck in the first customers arrive. Men and women pour in, quickly grab a tankard of ale then make their way to Christian and Laveona's table. I try to ignore the noise from the other side of the inn. This food is too good to be distracted from.

Yasmin looks at me in disgust as I shove down the stew, ripping chunks of bread, and soaking up the rich gravy. I ignore her looks and intentionally leave the gravy that has spilt on my chin. Yasmin sits stoically, pushing a potato around the bowl with her fork.

"You going to eat that?" I ask. Yasmin shoves her bowl to me aggressively. Grinning, I grab her stew and tuck into it without a moment of hesitation. I slurp up the meal, acting more like an animal than human. When I finish Yasmin's bowl, I am very full, dry, and warm. I can't help but smile, it almost feels like home. I grab my tankard that is filled with mead and takes a deep drink. The sweet drink warms me up inside. I lean back into my chair and get comfortable. I can barely stay awake. Yasmin still looks disgusted with me. I'm going to have to talk to her. I sigh, "What's wrong?"

Yasmin looks up at me, "Why are you still here?"

I take another sip of mead and look around the cosy tavern, "Warm food, feather bed and a roof over our heads. Why would I ever want to leave?"

"That's not what I meant," Yasmin huffs, "Why are you still here?" Yasmin repeats, spitting out every word.

I shrug my shoulders confused, "Same reason you are. The whole world wants me dead. Nowhere else to go. Fleeing for my life."

Yasmin interrupts me, "No, why you still here with us?" Yasmin hisses, "I struggle sleeping with my leg. I hear you every night, begging Maria to run off and leave us. All this time everyone has looked up to you, followed your leadership and sacrificed themselves and it just turns out you're a bloody coward."

My hand instinctively goes straight to the hilt of my knife. I pause and calm myself down then whisper, "Valouria's two most powerful nations are out for our blood. We are surrounded by people who would most likely turn us in for the cash reward. Our sanctuary is at another side of a desert. I'm scared, and I'll admit it. And you'd be a fool not to be afraid." I lock eyes with Yasmin, unwilling to back down.

"Oh," Yasmin sits back. She shrivels up with shock. After a few deep breaths Yasmin says, "I understand you're scared but we're safer as a group, we can watch each other's back."

"As safe as we were with Kelley?" I hiss.

Yasmin shoots me another look of disgust, "We seem safe enough now, and when in Arabia we will be perfectly safe. Why are you always acting so negative?"

I sigh, "Sorry, I'm just tired." Yasmin softens and looks a bit more sympathetic. I continue, "One of the major things I'm scared about is the Elves. I barely know a thing about them, yet we fought them and witnessed them cut through Klad."

"Really?" Yasmin exclaims inquisitively, "I thought all true Kladoenians knew the story of the Elves and the Wars of Old."

I shrug my shoulders. "Not Maria and I, our father would never tell us the story," I admit.

"What about your scholars?"

"I didn't grow up in a castle," I tell her bluntly.

"Oh," Yasmin pauses, she forces out a smile, "I only learnt it when I came to Klad. Would you like to hear it?"

Looking around at the wonderful drunken mess of the crowded tavern. People are clambering over each other to talk to Christian and Laveona. Songs echo from their corner and drown the rest of the bar. Ale and mead slops onto the floor as the locals dance and drink. I sigh, a story will at least pass the time before I can jump into the feather bed. "Yes, please tell."

Yasmin smiles gently, then she closes her eyes and begins speaking a deep melodic tone, "Over a thousand years ago, men arrived in Valouria from over the mountains. At the time the Great Woods covered the whole of Valouria except the desert. The men split into four colonies. The majority stayed in the North-West in what is now Vlaydom. The hunters travelled South to what is now Chevon. The traders travelled East to Arabia and finally, the soldiers travelled South-East to Klad..."

"What about Yasu?" I interrupt.

"Seriously Jacob... Yasu is a new kingdom, it wasn't around then." Yasmin explains with an air of exasperation. She sighs and continues, "The kingdoms began to take shape. They cut back the forest, claiming new lands, building castles and strongholds. This carried on for years until one day a Chevonic boy stumbled across an unfamiliar face in the Great Woods. The face he was looking at belonged to an Elven hunter. Within a fortnight there was a peace treaty formed in Arabia between the Elves and Humans to prevent war. Open trade began between the nations; it was a time of prosperity for Valouria.

But within a century that all changed at the coronation of Vlaydom's new King, King Julius II. The Prince of an Elven clan was caught making love to Vlaydom's new King's wife. In a rage, Julius cut off the Elf's head in single combat. When the Elven Clan found out they declared war on Vlaydom. The Elves viciously attacked Vlaydom in the night without warning, riding Gryphons and Pegasi, with arrows raining upon all. It was a massacre. Vlaydom claimed it was an attacked against all mankind and called on all to fight with them. Arabia and Chevon joined Vlaydom, Klad did not.

After ten years of bloody conflict, the war was stuck in a deadlock. It became a merciless battle of attrition between the three realms of Humans and the three Elven clans. Until one day the Elves foolishly killed a Kladoenian merchant in cold blood. Outraged the royal blue army of Klad marched north into the Great Woods led by the greatest ever warrior in all of Valouria's history, Elijah. Elijah claimed he was half Arabian and half Mountain Elf, making him the first *Immortal*, the most powerful beings ever to exist. Under Elijah's guidance, the Kladoenians slaughtered the three Elven Clans and the Elves disappeared from existence as did Elijah."

I sit back. Surely the all-powerful immortal Elijah can't be the same Elijah from the dream with Kyra. "What do the stories say about Elijah?"

Yasmin looks confused, "He was a great warrior and as he proclaimed, people thought he was an Immortal, that he could never age just like the Elves. He claimed he was the first of the Five Immortals and each one would be more powerful than the last. He wielded some sort of spear with five points, think they called it a quindent, plus he used a net as well. Scholars also say that he had some mystical ability that had something to do with entering people's dreams and talking inside their heads. But what is definitely true is that Elijah was the hero from the Wars of Old. He single-handedly won the war."

236

I feel sick. The Elijah that Yasmin had just described seems uncannily like the Elijah I had met in previous visions. Maybe he was truly immortal, "Were there any others, any other Immortals?" I ask, trying to mask my fear.

Yasmin pauses to think, "Yeah, there was another claim of an Immortal. A couple of hundred years ago, a girl named Enyo was born. Her mother was a Chevonic priestess who claimed that Enyo's father was an Elf. No one believed the priestess and locked her away in the church on account of her madness. A young Enyo was sold to a master who discovered she had a talent in the fighting pits. She became an undefeated heroine. When she made enough money, she bought back her freedom then paid for her mother to be released from the church's asylum. When she was reunited with her mother, she saw how badly her mother had been mistreated. Enyo magically healed all her mother's wounds right there in the street. She then entered the church again, furious with her mother's mistreatment and slaughtered everyone inside. Upon leaving the asylum she saw what the naïve and scared world thought of her. Her freshly healed mother was hanging dead from a tree with the word 'Witch' written on her chest. There was a second noose waiting for Enyo. Enyo went wild and killed all in her path. The mob didn't stand a chance. Enyo cut her mother down but couldn't heal her from death. In her rage, she killed the entire village. Men, women, and children. Scholars claim she killed just under two hundred and fifty people that night. Then she disappeared from Valouria."

"She could heal others?" I ask.

"I believe so," Yasmin says.

"Handy talent," I mutter. Yasmin doesn't hear, obviously not interested in telling me more stories about the Immortals, something else had taken her attention. Silvia has slid around her booth to sit next to Shakra. He doesn't seem too pleased about this and is sat right at the edge of the booth, trying to get away, shooting me and Yasmin a pained look. I smirk under my breath. Yasmin gives me an angry glare, then turns her back on me.

Looking around I notice the bar is finally starting to quiet down. More and more people are finishing their last drinks, shaking Christian's hand, giving Laveona a peck on the cheek, then turning around to leave the tavern and face the storm. On the nearest table, Maria and Isaac are sitting opposite each other in fits of laughter. I sigh. So much for laying low. At least they are having a good time. Poor Isaac has been dragged through hell and back. I finish my mead in silence, watching the last few patrons head out into the storm.

Yasmin continues to ignore me until Joan appears holding a ceramic jug which has the design of the map of Valouria decorating it, "Fresh milk before bed?" She offers.

Yasmin smiles, "Thank you, Joan, that will be great." Joan produces two cups and pours. I drink all the milk from the cup in one gulp. It is lovely and warm.

Joan quickly looks around, "You two better go and wash up and get some sleep, I'll bring up a hot bowl of water." Yasmin and I thank Joan once more and leave our table. Without a word to each other, we head up to our room.

I sit on the bed watching the storm through the window. Yasmin stands at the far side of the room, leaning against the wall. There is a knock on the door. Yasmin opens the door and gracefully accepts the basin of hot water from Joan and carries it over to the small bronze mirror. I let Yasmin wash up first. She quickly washes her face and neck then undresses to her undergarments and clambers under the quilt into bed.

Reluctantly, I stumble over to the bowl and catch a glimpse of myself in the mirror. I look a shade of my former self. My eyes are wild and hungry; I look like I've lost a couple of pounds that I couldn't afford to lose; I am covered in scars, scratches and bruises and my skin seems to be stretched tightly over my bones. These days of running and fighting don't seem to agree with me. I wash my face quickly. Even though I had washed with soap earlier today, the water ends up brown and full of grit.

I stretch and feel my joints crack. I take off my shirt and walk to bed. Yasmin sits up, "Er... Jacob, I don't think it is proper for us to share a bed."

I roll my eyes. "You're joking. After all, we've been through, you're scared to share a bed. I don't mean to offend but nothing is going to happen." I say in jest.

Yasmin tries to act firm, "No Jacob. I am a lady. I am betrothed."

I smile at her discomfort, "Who you betrothed to?"

Yasmin frowns, "Well I was betrothed. The war between Klad and that horrid alliance between Vlaydom, Chevon and the Elves has put a stop to that."

"I'm sorry for your loss," I say taken aback slightly. Who was she betrothed to? Must have been some poor Kladoenian lad.

Yasmin softens. "It's ok Jacob." She sighs, "You're right. Get into bed."

I smile and get under the covers. Yasmin rolls away and faces the opposite direction. The bed feels fantastic even if I have to share it will Yasmin. I have a full belly, I am nice and warm, and I am unbelievably comfortable. I could be lying in my old bed in Rochton after a perfect evening spent by the fire with my Dad and Maria. I close my eyes and listen to the rain pound against the roof and the window. It doesn't take long for me to drift off. Unfortunately, I don't get much sleep...

We are going to have to fight throughout the night.

Chapter 16

Rosalyn's sweet voice is there to greet me in my dream, "Come on Jacob. It's getting away." She leads me through the forest holding my hand. I look ahead, pass her cinnamon hair to see a beautiful dove made purely out of radiant white light. We chase the dove, running and jumping through the thick forest at full speed.

Then; darkness.

We have fallen into the hole in the ground. Rosalyn smirks as she brushes the dirt off her front. "We need to get out or we'll lose it." I look to the top of the hole. The Shadow Warriors are out there waiting. I can't give Rosalyn a foot up into peril.

It doesn't matter. I have spent too long thinking to myself. Rosalyn is already halfway out. I try to follow her quickly but stumble. As I get up, I see her just climb out. I hear swords clash. I try to scramble out of the hole, but I seem to be moving in slow motion.

I then hear the sickening thud. Rosalyn can barely whisper, "H-h-h-h-help-p-p-p." I manage to escape the damn hole. Rosalyn is lying in a heap on the floor with a nasty wound on her head.

This time I don't call out. Instead, I nock an arrow, gripping the bow so tight my knuckles turn white. The warrior of pure shadow steps out from the bushes. He doesn't even have time to raise his bossed shield. My arrow lodges deep into his left shoulder. He roars with agony and drops his shield. He expects the second arrow and swipes it out of the air easily with the shaft of his trident. In one quick movement, he pulls the first arrow out of his arm.

I charge and swing for his neck. He manages to drop to the deck at the last moment. I stab down but he manages to roll out of the way at the last second. He tries to swipe my legs with his trident. I catch the trident in the hooks of Nemesis. With one swift twist, I send his weapon flying out of his hands. The Shadow Warrior quickly gets to his feet. He draws his sword and lunges for my chest. I parry and kick him in the stomach. He buckles and drops one knee to the floor, gasping for air. I swing a kick to his wounded arm. He roars once again in agonising pain.

"Jacob!" Rosalyn screams. The second Shadow Warrior throws his trident at me. I take one step to the side and watch it sail past me. I charge at the oncoming enemy. He raises his shield. I jump and kick the shield with all my might. The force of the dropkick knocks the Shadow Warrior flying. The first Shadow Warrior runs towards me, sword in hand. I parry his stab with ease. I feint a strike to his head then stab down on his foot. The first Shadow Warrior tries to swing his sword, but I am too close. I barge my shoulder into him and take my blade out of his foot. He stumbles backwards and drops his sword.

I turn to the second Shadow Warrior. He is cowering behind his shield again. I go for the kick a second time. This time he is expecting it and stabs with his sword. He catches the side of my chest. It is only a graze, but I can feel the warm sensation of blood soaking my shirt. I take a step back in shock. The second Shadow Warrior senses a victory. I position myself between him and Rosalyn. The first Shadow Warrior is struggling to find his feet. I draw an arrow and fire it at Shadow Warrior one but the second Shadow Warrior dives across and blocks it with his shield. I reach for another arrow, but both are hidden behind the shield.

I curse. Everything hurts. The cut is deeper than I thought. Blood is continuing to seep out of the wound. I can't help but smile despite myself. This is the furthest I have ever gotten. I get ready to finish the fight. The Shadow Warriors are poised to strike.

I am about to attack when there is a roar from behind me. I turn. A third Shadow Warrior is standing regally behind me. This one is different. It is female even though she must've been around seven feet tall. She is wearing rusty bronze armour and a bronze tiara. Instead of wielding the usual weapons of trident and shield, she carries two *sai,* dagger-like weapons almost like mini tridents. She walks gracefully like a dancer. I am frozen in fear. Without hesitation, she stabs Rosalyn in the back. I watch the life slip out of her eyes. The She-Warrior walks round elegantly until she is standing between me and the other warriors. The other Shadow Warriors look in awe. She speaks with a deep, raspy voice, as if there are thirty people, all speaking at once in a harsh whisper, "He's mine."

Rage builds up inside me. I swing my blade down towards the She-Warrior's face. She is too fast though and easily sidesteps. I spin and wildly swipe at her midriff with all my might. The She-Warrior seems to smirk as she catches Nemesis between the blades one of her sai. I push against Nemesis hoping to overpower her. The She-Warrior bares her fangs as all my strength cannot push her one blade back.

In one swift movement the She-Warrior flicks her sai, throwing Nemesis out of my hands and into the bushes. Before I can do anything, the She-Warrior has pirouetted around me, stabbing me in the back twenty times with her sai. I drop to my knees. Pain surges through my body. The She-warrior kicks me in my face. I collapse to the side, dead.

*****

SMACK!

I curse quietly. Whilst rolling over Yasmin has managed to hit me square in the face. A metallic taste covers my tongue. I click my jaw and spit the blood out of my mouth. My lip is bust. I sigh as I roll out of bed.

Shivering, I tiptoe over to the mirror, every single floorboard seems to creak. I pull down my lip to get a better look; thankfully, it is only a small cut. I yawn, I must have only been asleep a couple of hours. I quickly wash my face in the now freezing water. I shiver some more and wipe off the cold water, spitting out more blood into the small basin.

The storm is still raging outside the window. The rain seems to be giving the inn a beating. I can barely hear myself think over the noise. An arc of lightning illuminates the village of Stonemarsh. The thunder rumbles almost immediately afterwards, shaking the Humble Hearth. I watch a silhouette run across the street in the rain, trying to shelter from the storm.

I am about to head back to bed when I hear a knock next door. I raise my eyebrows; I grab my knife and slowly open our door. The hall is empty. The rain continues to beat the window at the end of the hall.

I must have been imagining things. Turning back around, I shut the door and walk towards my side of the bed. I lift the covers and climb under. Just as my eyes close there is a second knock on the wall between our room and Christian and Laveona's room. Then another knock. Then another.

I nudge Yasmin. She wakes confuses. I put my finger to my bloody lip to tell her to stay silent. She looks confused but thankfully trusts me enough to stay quiet. We climb out of bed and grab our weapons. There is another knock. We sneak over to the door and open it slowly. I nock an arrow. Another knock. The corridor is dark and empty. We silently creep round to Christian and Laveona's room. I draw back the arrow and aim it at the door. Yasmin grasps the handle of the door and looks at me to check if I am ready. I take a deep breath then nod. Yasmin flings open the door.

What we see shocks me. Laveona is on the floor next to her bed with a big red welt on her forehead, proudly pulsating through her red hair. Her right pupil is twice the size of her left. Her mouth is gagged, and her hands are tied. Christian is nowhere in sight. Yasmin runs over and takes off her gag. I stay by the door cautiously, bow still drawn.

Laveona is in shock and has a concussion, "Christian... Christian... Christian..."

Yasmin stays calm, trying to comfort the distressed Laveona. "Did Christian do this to you?" Laveona's eyes full of fear, she nods. I curse, I never should've let him come with us. "Where is he now?"

"I don't know. He accidentally woke me up when he got out of bed. When I tried to stop him, he attacked me." Laveona is struggling to hold back the tears.

I turn to Yasmin, "We need to get out of here fast," Yasmin nods solemnly as she cuts the ropes that bind Laveona, "I'll wake the others." I tell her. I run down the hall and start thumping on the doors, "Wake up!" I yell.

I can hear the others fumbling around in their rooms. Panic engulfs the tavern. I hear my companions jump out of bed and scramble to grab their weapons. Maria and Isaac stumble out of their room.

"What's wrong?" Maria asks.

"Christian..." I spit out as Shakra and Silvia manage to climb out of their room, "He's betrayed us."

Isaac swears loudly. Maria manages to stay calm, "Grab your stuff, we're leaving now."

A gruff voice pipes up from the stairwell, "We can't let you go." I turn with my bow drawn. My arrow is facing the unarmed Joan and Hugo. Both are terrified, you can see it in their eyes, but Hugo somehow musters a strong voice, "Christian said he would kill us if you all got away,"

I look at my arrow, "If you try and stop us, we will kill you." I say sympathetically.

"Come with us," Maria pleads. "If we go now, we can disappear."

Joan shakes her head, tears roll down her cheeks, "Christian always brags that he is one of the best trackers in the world, and from the looks at all the gold he has, it seems he's right. There is no running away. He's going to kill us." She sobs as her hand rubs her pregnant belly.

A wave of fear hit me. Joan is right. I look around the room. Laveona is unconscious, not sure if it's the shock or the nasty knock on her forehead. Silvia looks like she is about to throw up. Shakra's hand was gripped to his sword handle. Shakra seems to be nervously eyeing up Hugo, ready to strike him down if necessary. I desperately look to Maria for guidance, but she looks as lost as I feel. Christian could lead an army right to us. Even if we somehow escape Stonemarsh, Vlaydom's Outpost is not far away and may catch us. And should we pull off another miracle, there is still the Arabian Desert blocking our path.

Isaac doesn't seem phased. He strides forward with confidence and power, "We can outrun them. We only have to make it to the Arabian Desert." Everyone turns and looks at him. "I have an idea."

Silvia trembles, "Isaac the Arabian Desert is suicide. In the Wars of Old, a Vlaydom army was lost forever, buried in the sand. It is as treacherous as the Great Woods. Plus, we'll never make it to the Arabian Desert as we'll never outrun them."

Isaac remains stoic and self-assured, "Not all of us will be running. Trust me, my plan will work." He almost seems excited, "Yes... it'll work. Joan and Hugo, we can keep you safe. We can protect you. You have to trust us; Christian will not follow us."

"Whatever your idea is lad, make it quick," Hugo says, snapping Isaac out of his roll. Hugo points to the window; outside through the storm, there is the faint glow of orange light coming from the other side of Stonemarsh. Christian must have recruited some troops to follow him. He has mustered enough men to easily outnumber us.

Isaac is unfazed, "Grab the essentials and take them to the cart. Shakra, leave two horses, preferably Lena as one of them. Take Joan and Hugo and head north to Arabia. Do not wait for us. Maria and Jacob, you're staying here with me." We stand, shocked. Isaac shouts, "Come on, get going."

Our companions rush to their rooms, grab their gear and rush down the stairs to the stables. Hugo picks up Joan with ease and carries her down the stairs. I turn to Isaac, "Why are we the ones staying?"

Maria shoots me an angry look, but Isaac turns and says softly, "You two are who Christian wants. That'll keep his attention here rather than going after the others. We need to make sure we kill Christian; Joan wasn't wrong about his tracking skills. He kept on bragging about them to me as we hunted. We need him to be dead. After we kill him, we have to get away fast."

Unfortunately, Isaac is right. We don't need to fight all of Christian's troops, just him. I quickly run to my room passing Yasmin who bolts downstairs towards the stables. I throw on some clothes on and sling a quiver of arrows over my shoulder. I curse, there is no time to put on what little armour I have. Isaac and Maria run downstairs. I go to the big window at the end of the upstairs hallway, facing the street. I kick it open. The rain is still lashing down but at least the thunder and lightning has stopped.

The orange torchlight glow of Christian's troops creeps closer to the tavern. He must have planned this out from the start, his bounty hunter friends would cut into his share of the gold, but the men here are Vlaydom soldiers who wouldn't take any of his rewards. I hear the cart filled with my friends frantically rattle into the darkness behind us. I am feeling sick; will I ever see them again?

I start to make out the group of Vlaydom soldiers marching towards the Humble Hearth. I count the number of silhouettes. There are twenty-seven in total, leading the mob is the tall skinny figure of Christian. Even though he is so far away in the dark, I am sure I can see the cruel smile carved into his face. He is expecting us to be asleep, ready to take us by surprise.

Slowly, I reach back to my quiver and pull out an arrow. The soldiers must be about two hundred metres away. I nock the arrow and draw the string back. I let them march closer and closer. I hold and wait and wait and wait. The rain is starting to flood in through the open window. I follow Christian with my aim. I am waiting until I am right on top of him to ensure it will be the killing shot. There is no way we will survive this without a miracle. I just want to make sure Christian wouldn't be able to chase the others. Christian must die.

Christian's mob is about fifty metres away. I slow my breaths. The point of my arrow is aiming straight for

Christian's eye. I am just about to release when Christian freezes.

"Take cover!" he screams.

He must have caught a glimpse of either Isaac or Maria. I fire my arrow. Christian dives out of the way at the last second. My arrow sinks into the stomach of the soldier standing behind him. He falls to the ground mortally wounded.

The enemy soldiers panic and run in every direction. I rain arrows upon them. I manage to kill three other soldiers and wounded another. Unfortunately, the initial fear and surprise cease very quickly. The soldiers are dispersed, hiding from my arrows. Invisible to me. The rain continues to flood Stonemarsh.

I stop firing. The street is empty. All the soldiers are hidden away. I can hear the troops barking orders to each other, but I can't make out what they're saying. The storm is too loud. A soldier tries to run to a building on the other side of the street. I take my aim and put my arrow through his neck.

Silence.

Where are they?

I stick my head out of the window to check that they aren't trying to flank and get behind us. I can't see anything. The soldier who tried to run across the road lies still, blood soaking the ground. They aren't anywhere in sight. I stand up and squint. There is a faint whistling, cutting through the storm. Instinctively I drop to the ground. A javelin flew over my head and impaled into the ceiling above me.

I still can't see anyone. I hear Christian yelling, "Don't kill the Da Nesta's. I need them alive." This is my advantage; I can kill them, but they can't kill me: for now, at least. I stand up with confidence and move right to the window ledge. I nock an arrow and wait for another target to emerge. One unfortunate soldier pops his head out from behind a wall. My arrow enters through his eye.

The rain keeps falling. The street is starting to soak red due to the six men lying in the street, two of whom are bleeding out. I look out for any movement. I have a vague idea where the soldiers are hiding because of the faint orange light coming from their torches. No one dares ventures out. I count my blessing that not one of them has a shield. If they did, they would've easily been able to walk safely down the road. I continue to patrol the street with my arrows, waiting for the next soldier to foolishly appear.

To my surprise, Christian steps out, spear in one hand, torch in the other. I fire an arrow towards his heart. He swipes it out of the air with his spear. He then runs forward a few metres and grunts, throwing his torch. I sidestep as it sails through my window into the corridor. The other soldiers follow suit and come out of hiding, throwing their torches at the Humble Hearth. A wave of orange crashes into the inn. Most of the torches smash through the ground floor windows.

I can hear the panic of Maria and Isaac downstairs. I choose to ignore the flames and retaliate by firing my arrows mercilessly, killing three as they retreat. They quiver and hide as they watch the building burn. Regrouping and waiting. Smoke begins rising and circles around my corridor. I move closer to the window, forcing myself not to lose focus. They will attack soon. Christian is trying to force us out into the street. We must hold firm.

Christian gives the order to charge, not allowing Maria and Isaac time to deal with the fire. The soldiers race towards the inn. I see Isaac's javelin soar through the air and find its target in a soldier's chest, knocking the enemy off his feet. I bring down as many as I can. Four soldiers jump through the downstairs window. One immediately is thrown out with a red slash across his chest. I look down to see a soldier trying to scale the wall and grab me. My arrow lodges into his shoulder causing him to fall.

The flames are growing inside and fast. I am drenched in sweat. Smoke is starting to sting my lungs and eyes. I can't make a shot, I'm too busy trying to stamp out flames around my feet. I rub my eyes. A group of the soldiers stand back, taunting us, leering us, trying to make us act rash and foolish. I can still hear fighting downstairs. The heat is becoming intense. Orange dances across the wall. The dry wood inside the inn is combusting too easily. Christian is just waiting in the rain. He knows we must leave the safety of the inn soon. Outside we are vulnerable. Their numbers will surround us with ease.

I try to think. There must be a way we can keep the enemy in front of us. We have to leave this building but where can we go. Most importantly we need to find a way to kill Christian. Our companions have no chance if he is left alive.

Before I can come up with any sort of plan, Isaac does the unthinkable. He charges straight at Christian. Christian

cracks a wry smile and gets ready to fight. Maria follows
Isaac out of the inn, but she is too far behind. The soldiers
move around Isaac towards Maria.

I try to ready an arrow and offer some support, but the
Humble Hearth is starting to groan. I turn to run down the
hallway to the stairs, but a wall of fire blocks my path. I
hear the clash of steel as Maria and Isaac fight against
insurmountable odds. In desperation, I run and leap out of
the window and land heavily on the ground.

Christian and Isaac are battling ferociously about thirty
metres away. Two soldiers stand cautiously near them
waiting for an opportunity to strike. Between them and me,
Maria stands with both swords at arm's length, warding off
the six soldiers that surround her. Four soldiers march
over to me. It is hopeless. There is only one thing keeping
me going: I must stop Christian. He has to die so the others
can escape. I stand up proudly, ready for the fight.

I bolt towards the four men approaching, slashing wildly
at the first soldier. He manages to block but the swing is
filled with so much rage that it knocks him to his knees. A
well-placed knee to the head knocks the soldier out cold.
The second tries to sweep my legs with his spear. I jump
over it and stab the man in the thigh. The other two
soldiers hesitate for a split-second. I use this opportunity
to push past them to try and help Maria.

Maria has currently disposed of two soldiers but is down
to one sword. The other is stuck in the chest of a fallen foe.
She is desperately trying to reach Isaac who is losing his
fight. But the enemy soldiers know this and block her path
at every turn.

I look ahead at Isaac. He is bleeding quite heavily from his right arm. He can barely raise his sword. Christian is toying with him, savouring the kill. He keeps slamming his spear down upon Isaac's shield. It's hopeless, I can't get to either of them in time. We're too far apart. The enemy are too many. I try to ready an arrow, but another soldier engages me, swinging his sword towards my face. I duck and stumble backwards onto my arse.

I watch helplessly as Christian finally manages to knock away Isaac's shield. The storm beats down as Isaac drops to his knees, defeated, and silently begs for mercy. Christian raises his spear for the killing strike.

I am paralysed. Time seems to slow. Maria drops her sword and dives between Isaac and Christian. Christian is in mid-strike. Maria grabs her knife and covers Isaac's eyes with her spare hand. Maria thrusts her knife into the air, towards Christian's spear. Her knife starts to glow brighter and brighter. A ball of white light starts to form around the blade. The ball grows and grows at a rapid speed until the brilliant light illuminates the night, engulfing all of Stonemarsh.

The light appears to pass around me as if there is some invisible barrier. For a moment, I can't see anything except white. I grip Nemesis a little tighter. My eyes burn from the light. The other soldiers seem to have disappeared, as has the storm, only a wall of white light exists.

The light slowly begins to fade. My eyes adjust as the stormy streets of Stonemarsh reappear. I make out a few silhouettes of the soldier's ahead of me. They are screaming maniacally. One is frantically waving his hand in front of his face. All of the enemies have dropped their weapons and are acting panicked. The light continues to fade until it disappears completely.

I take a closer look at the Vlaydom soldiers. Their eyes have clouded over. They are blind. The intense light has blinded them. I turn to see Maria lying collapsed in the mud next to Isaac. Christian stands away from them yelling with fear and anger. He swipes his spear wildly, fighting a foe that is not there. Christian has been blinded along with his men. Isaac grabs his sword and struggles to his feet. Christian swings at Isaac's direction. Isaac catches the weapon in his empty hand, with one quick movement he slices the spear in two. Christian screams until Isaac silences him forever.

I rush over to Maria. I put my hand near her mouth, thankfully she is still breathing. The blind Vlaydom soldiers stumble around helplessly trying to get away. Isaac runs over. He has a dark tan from Maria's light but has a white hand-shaped print from where Maria had covered his eyes. The blind soldiers have the same burns and tans, covering their skin. I look at my hands, as pale as ever.

Isaac stands up, bewildered; cursing loudly before asking "What happened?"

"Maria has a secret," I say, not able to meet his eyes. I can't stop myself from telling the truth, "Using her blade she can manipulate and create light. She created a light so bright that it blinded our enemies."

Isaac takes a step back, afraid that Maria is some sort of monster. He crouches and picks up Maria's knife which is lying in the waterlogged street. He yelps and immediately drops the knife, "It's red hot!"

I ignore him, "We need to get moving."

Isaac is still in shock, "How long have you known about the light?" I don't answer. He continues, "How does she do it? Can you do the same? How come you weren't blinded?"

The last question takes me off guard. How come I wasn't blinded?

"I shut my eyes." I lie. Isaac knows it is a lie, it is painfully obvious by the lack of tan and burns from the light exposure. Thankfully, he lets it pass. He turns his focus to Maria, obviously his fear of Maria has quickly dissipated.

Maria groans. I cradle her head. She can barely open her eyes. "Isaac..." She moans.

Isaac crouches down next to her and takes her hand, "I'm here,"

Maria reaches up and put her hands on his shoulders. She pulls him close and plants a kiss on his lips. I sit awkwardly. Maria's knife and swords start to glow again. After what seems forever, they finally stop kissing. "Don't ever scare me like that again.," Maria tells Isaac firmly. Isaac sits up with a silly grin. He is tongue-tied.

I look at the blinded soldiers. The clouding in their eyes is slowly starting to fade. "It's time to go," I tell the others.

Once again, I rip off my sleeve and tie it around Isaac's wounded arm as a bandage. He manages to scoop up Maria with ease even with a wounded arm. Maria's light or maybe her kiss has given him a new lease of energy. Maria has slipped out of consciousness. I grab Maria's knife and swords. We run pass the burning remnants of the Humble Hearth to the stables where the poor horses are still tied up, petrified of the flames. Shakra has left us two horses; Lena and the second strongest. I am surprised that he has so much faith in us, leaving Lena. Isaac lifts Maria onto Lena's back, then climbs on himself. I mount the other horse.

The rain is slowly ceasing as we set off north at full speed. The night is starting to end, and the first signs of the morning are beginning to appear. The tracks from the caravan are easy to find as the wheels had cut into the saturated earth. We follow the tracks at a frantic pace. As we ride, I can't help but think it; he knows too much...

I must kill Isaac.

Chapter 17

A bloody red dawn is slowly starting to climb over the horizon. The rain has stopped. The oranges, reds and purples of today's sunrise paint the sky. Maria is still out cold, lying across Isaac's lap. I follow Isaac, Maria, and Lena in a solemn silence. I look back to the direction of Stonemarsh. I can still see the smoke billowing in the sky from the Humble Hearth. I have no idea if we are being followed.

I should be enjoying the sight of a new day. We've once again cheated death, but my hands are trembling. I must do something heinous and terrible. How am I going to kill Isaac? He has always been the kindest out of the group and he never has done me or Maria any wrong. But he knows Maria's secret. He would tell the others. People are scared of what they don't understand. Not even Maria and I can work out Maria's powers. I have to kill him. The best way to keep a secret is to not let anyone know.

Maria will hate me for it but one day she will thank me. I am doing this for her. I take an arrow out of my quiver and nock it. I draw back the bowstring slowly. It is difficult to aim while riding on horseback. I'm sleep deprived and aching. What if I missed? I could hit Maria. I sigh and put the arrow back into the quiver and sling Nemesis over my shoulder. I will have to wait for the right opportunity.

About twenty-five minutes of riding later an opportunity presents itself. Isaac pulls on Lena's reins until she halts to a stop. I move alongside him and halt. Isaac turns to me,

"I need a break." I agree, we have been riding for over four hours straight. Isaac climbs off Lena's back, then he turns and picks up Maria. He gently places her down, using the remnants of his tattered shield as a makeshift pillow. He walks thirty yards and stops to take a leak. This is my chance to silence Isaac forever. I jump down from my steed silently. There is a slight scrape as I pull the arrow from my quiver. I step over Maria and get in position to fire. This has to be done.

I steady my breathing. Thank goodness Isaac has taken his shield off his back. He is a clear target. I pull back my bowstring. A bead of sweat trickled down my brow. This needs to happen. He must die. This is the only way. "I'm sorry Isaac," I whisper.

I try to let go of the string. I can't. I am frozen. I can't kill Isaac. He's a friend. Maria trusts him. He has to die but I can't do it. Too many times Isaac has helped save our lives. He is a good loyal man. I put the arrow back in my quiver and sling Nemesis over my shoulder again, ashamed of myself. Not sure what I'm more ashamed of: not having the guts to kill Isaac or the fact I've even contemplated his death. How did I allow an outsider to get so close with me?

Isaac finishes his leak and turns to face me. His ever-present smile disappears when he sees me standing, pale and guilt-ridden, "You ok Jacob? You look sick."

"I'm fine," I lie. I feel sick. I am so ashamed of myself. I am dirt.

"You sure?" He asks.

259

I lock eyes with him. My voice is full of desperate sincerity, "Promise me that you won't tell a soul about Maria's ability."

Before Isaac can answer, Maria's pipes up, "He doesn't have to promise anything. I'm telling them." Maria sits up. She looks a little tired but ok.

I can't control my shock when I retort, "You can't tell them, what if they..."

"What if they what?" Maria interrupts, her green eyes full of determination, "Jacob I trust these people with my life, they deserve to know the truth. There's no other way to explain Isaac's tan" She points at Isaac's face. He is still very bronze apart from the white handprint that covers his eyes. Maria continues, her temper rising, "They are our friends. Jacob, you should trust them. Not everyone is like Gwen."

My vision goes red, "What do you mean?"

"You know exactly what I mean." Maria screams angrily, "Since she broke your heart you've never been the same. You need to grow up, it was over a year ago."

Before I can throw an insult back at her, Isaac jumps between us. "Whoa, whoa. Maria, there's no need for that."

Maria wipes away a tear, "You're taking his side!"

Isaac stays calm, "I'm not taking either side. We need to stick together." I go to open my mouth, but Isaac shushes me, "You two are brother and sister, start acting like it. I don't care who this Gwen is. I don't care what she's done. Right now, there are more important things, such as finding the others."

Maria shoots me a hateful look, "Fine, let's go." She pushes herself to her feet, she is still a little shaky from using her knife's power last night. She turns her back to me and storms over to the horses. Isaac gives me a look; I can't tell if it is sympathy or anger. He follows Maria wordlessly.

I stay silent. Sweat is trickling down my brow. Somehow my right hand has made its way around my back and is tightly gripping the hilt of my knife. I let go, even more disgusted with myself. Why did I grab my knife?

I take a second to calm down. Maybe Maria is right. Since Gwen left, I haven't been the same. I miss her so much. It actually hurts just thinking about her. No one else has ever made me feel like this. I'll never get to see her again, she lives in Vlaydom. I can't just show up there. I wouldn't make it five metres until someone spotted me, and I would be arrested or killed. I sigh and head to my horse. Right now, it seems worth the risk. I would rather face all of Vlaydom than speak to Maria.

I climb into the saddle of my horse. Maria sits behind Isaac on Lena's back, arms around his waist. She still has a tear glistening on her cheek. Neither Maria nor Isaac looks at me, they just set off. I follow them but keep my distance.

We canter for about an hour before we stumble across fresh tracks made by the cart that contains our allies. The wheels of the cart have continued to cut straight through the soft, wet earth. It takes us a further thirty minutes to spot our friends. At this point, my stomach is growling. I am starting to get very drowsy; everything aches. Our friends have set up a makeshift camp for a quick break.

Shakra runs over ecstatic when he sees us, "You all made it!" He pauses when he sees our scowls. Then he spots the white handprint on Isaac's face, "What happened to Isaac?"

Isaac grunts. He and Maria both dismount Lena. Shakra embraces the pair of them with a hug. He looks quite ridiculous. He can barely wrap his little arms around one of them let alone both. Shakra grabs Lena's reins and leads Maria and Isaac over to the camp.

Silvia and Yasmin are sat next to a small fire. Opposite them sits Joan and Hugo. Joan is half-heartedly stoking the fire. Laveona is sitting away from the others. She is slumped up against the front left wheel of the cart, sitting in the shade. The lump on her forehead that Christian had given her, has gone from red and angry to an awful shade of purple. She locks eyes with me. She can immediately tell that something is wrong and pats the ground next to her, inviting me to sit.

I dismount and put my horse with the others. I walk around the makeshift camp as Isaac starts to tell the story of our fight against Christian and the Vlaydom soldiers. Maria stays silent. She sits next to Isaac, leaning against his shoulder. She pays no attention to the story. Instead, she just holds her knife in her hand, analysing it. I sit down next to Laveona and watch the others.

Isaac has gotten to the point in his tale where he is duelling Christian, admitting he was beaten. Our allies are enthralled in his tale, hanging on every word. I brace myself for the shock and disgust from the others. Isaac pauses and looks at Maria. She sighs and nods. Isaac takes a deep breath, "Maria used her knife's power to blind the Vlaydom soldiers."

A collective gasp echoes around the camp. My hand finds the hilt of my knife immediately. The camp falls silent as a few allies exchange awkward looks. Maria leans further into Isaac's chest. He puts his arm around her. The silence continues longer and longer.

Eventually, Silvia speaks, "What power? How did you blind those soldiers?"

Maria's hands are shaking, "I'm not sure." She admits, "It's something to do with creating and manipulating light." To prove her point, she flicks her knife. A small orb of radiant white light floats and hits the fire. For a second the flames rise and brighten. Warmth spreads through me as if everything bad that has happened has been washed away. The rest of our comrades are obviously experiencing the same warmth. Hugo and Joan smile at each other, Hugo's hand on Joan's baby bump. Silvia sits with a silly grin. Isaac pulls Maria closer for a hug.

I am taken away from the camp and gifted a vision. Gwen and I are sitting facing Rochton. It is the night she will leave. The King of Kings' chariot is rolling towards my village. I feel the tears on my cheek. Gwen curls up a bit more and snuggles into my chest.

"We should do it," Gwen says, "Just run away and live our lives together. We'd go anywhere we like, free from responsibility. We could live on a small patch of land or be lord and lady in some kingdom. I don't care where, but we have to leave now."

The memory strays from the truth. I finally get to give her the answer I have always wanted to give. "Yes, let's do it. Let's run away."

Gwen turns to face me. She wears a huge grin, her eyes water up some more. She wraps both arms around my neck and plants a kiss on my lips. My insides seem to melt with joy. She pulls me in tight for an embrace. Her long, brown hair brushes against my cheek. She whispers into my ear the words I have always wanted to hear, *"I love you."* She stands up, holding my hand. We run downhill at full speed towards the forest, laughing as we run away from responsibilities.

The vision starts to become fuzzy. One second, I am being led by Gwen to a lifetime of happiness, the next second, I am sitting in a miserable field waiting for the next passer-by to try and kill me. The flames start to die down. Chills race down my spine. The happiness is gone from the camp. The silly smiles leave the faces of my friends.

Once again Silvia speaks first, "That was incredible Maria." There are nods around the camp. I wonder what everyone else saw.

"What else can you do?" Shakra asks feverishly.

Maria is taken back by that question, "I'm not sure. I've never really pushed it. All I know is that it increases and makes light, and somehow it can lift people's spirits. It's not especially useful."

"It was useful against Christian and his men," Isaac points out, "You saved my life."

Maria turns red with embarrassment, "I guess..."

264

Shakra wheels round to face me, "Can you do the same, Jacob?" The eyes of our camp all turn onto me.

I draw my knife and show the others. "Sorry to disappoint but my blade doesn't create light or feelings of joy."

Yasmin chips in, "Maybe it doesn't do the exact same thing. I mean, your knives are pretty different."

Everyone stares at me intently, expecting me to miraculously perform some magic. Even Maria looks curious. I don't know what to do or say. Thankfully Laveona comes to my aid, "We can discuss this later. Right now, kids, we need to put some more distance between us and Stonemarsh."

There is a half-hearted mumble of agreement. Our companions stand up and get ready to move out. Isaac still has his arm around Maria. Shakra and Silvia go to collect Lena and my steed. Yasmin turns to Maria and Isaac, "You two get some sleep in the caravan." She pauses, "You too Jacob."

I want to argue but sleep sound fantastic. Every muscle in my body aches. My eyelids are starting to get heavy and are barely open. "Wake me if there's any trouble," I say. Yasmin nods. I follow Isaac and Maria into the back of the caravan. It is a bit of a squeeze for the three of us to lie down in, but we manage.

Lying in the caravan with the bedding of Razak's *'finest silks'*, back-to-back with Maria, is incredibly comfortable. We have just set off when I start to fall asleep.

*****

Luckily, this sleep isn't plagued with the nightmares of the Shadow Warriors. Instead, I am sitting crossed-legged in a small clearing in the Great Woods. I curse, I am dressed in the same attire as when I had met my mother and Kyra; the floaty, silvery shirt and trousers. Barefoot again. I look right. To my surprise, I see that Maria has joined me this time. She is wearing the same clothing. We are both unarmed and sat waiting.

I am about to say something to Maria when a soldier appears in front of us. The bronze armour, bronze and amber quindent, bronze and amber net, dark skin, and slightly greying dreadlocks immediately tells me who it is.

The Immortal, Elijah.

Elijah approaches silently, then sits down just in front of us. He speaks with a rich, deep voice, "Maria, Jacob, it's so good to speak to the two of you at the same time."

Maria asks confused, "Wait, I've seen you before. Who are you? How are we here? Why are we here?"

Elijah simply smiles, "Well my dear, my name is Elijah. You are here because I brought you here," From behind his back he draws a knife. Maria gasps. It is identical in shape and size as the knives Maria and I own. The only difference is that his blade is made from the same, bronze-steel as Elijah's armour and quindent, and instead of a ruby or sapphire in the hilt, his knife has an amber stone. His knife has a slight glow of orange. I know immediately that he is using his knife to bring us here, in the same way, that Maria's knife can create and control light. Elijah can see the shock on our faces but continues, "Why you are here is simple, it is so I can finally have a chat with you."

Maria looks confused, "Your knife, it is the same ours."

Elijah smiles, "You have a keen eye, Maria. Our knives are similar. But is this what you really want to chat about?"

I open my mouth to ask more about our similarities, but Maria manages to get her question out first, "What is our mother like?" I can't help but sigh and roll my eyes. Maria shoots me an angry look to shut up.

Elijah doesn't spot Maria's disgusted look at me and answers, "Your mother... I never quite saw eye to eye with her. She obviously is under pressure, but she could try and relax a little. But Kyra, your aunt, she is the opposite, so laidback and that rebellious streak of hers does make me smile. I'm going to miss them both."

Maria raises an eyebrow, "Miss them? Why are you going to miss them?"

Elijah simply shrugs his shoulders, "I had been there for a while, it is time to move on." Elijah has a guilty look on his face, but continues, "You'll be glad to know that I have managed to spot the young princesses Elizabeth and Mary. They're doing well. They were handed over to the Vlaydom army, they were given their own carriage and are currently on their way to Vlaydom." Elijah notices that this news has lifts Maria's spirits, "Maria, I vow to look after the girls to the best of my abilities. I will follow them from afar and make sure they come to no harm."

I can't help but smile. Somehow, I know that we can trust Elijah. When he speaks about protecting Elizabeth and Mary, I know he is telling the truth, that he really means it.

Maria is beaming with awe, "Thank you."

Elijah's smile slowly disappears, "I'm afraid I do have some bad news as well."

I sit forward, "What is it?"

Elijah sighs, "I've been informed that soldiers from Vlaydom's Outpost have been camped out on the Arabian Pass. This prevented the Kladoenian messengers from reaching Arabia to call for aid. Arabia has been informed by Vlaydom about the Kladoenian massacre and they have been encouraged to hand over yourselves to the Vlaydom forces. Luckily for you, Arabia will do no such thing and King Joseph of Vlaydom knows this. He cannot declare war on Arabia as he did on Klad, he relies on Arabia's trade too heavily. But he knows that you have nowhere to go except Arabia. Yasu won't take you and it is quite amazing you survived your journey through the Great Woods. Therefore, he ordered the men from the Outpost to march up the Arabian Pass to prevent anyone from entering Arabia. They have been searching every traveller and trader to enter or leave Arabia along the Arabian Pass. This leaves you with no choice but to cross the Arabian Desert." He pauses, "I fear that some of your company is not fit to make this journey."

Maria curses, "Joan, she's pregnant"

Elijah nods gravely.

Maria pauses, "Wait, how can you possibly know all this?"

Elijah shrugs again, "Is it important my dear?"

Before Maria could politely respond I butt in, "Yes. How can you do all this?"

Elijah smiles a wry smile, "I have a gift. It lets me bring you here when you sleep. It lets me carry out conversations when you are miles away."

Maria raises an eyebrow, "You can read people's minds?"

Elijah chuckles, "Not quite. I can talk to someone and if they reply I can gather information. If they refuse to answer, I gain nothing."

I shake my head in confusion, "Then how are we here? I didn't agree to be here."

"When you're asleep your mind is more vulnerable," Elijah explains, "This allows me to drag you here or it allows me to enter your dreams." Elijah grins, "You two have such vivid dreams."

Maria goes bright red, "How dare you? What gives you the right to look inside our heads?"

Elijah remains calm, "I wanted to get to know you before I spoke to you. I know how you feel lost Maria, how you long to find your mother and reunite as a family. How you're sick of trying to keep everyone's spirits up when you're terrified yourself. How you need someone to rely on. How you feel like you're losing Jacob."

I spin and look at Maria. She avoids eye contact with me. Maria looks on the verge of tears. "Stay out of my head." She spits. Her hand is firmly behind her back, trying to grab the knife that isn't there. "Wake us up now." She demands.

Elijah drops his head, looking guilty that he struck a nerve, "I am sorry my dear, I'll send you back,"

I look at Maria, she starts to glow orange. The orange glow forms a bubble around Maria. The orange glow becomes stronger and stronger until I can no longer make out Maria. Suddenly the orange bubble dissipates, along with Maria.

I look down at myself. No orange glow. I look up at Elijah. I want to be furious at him for upsetting Maria, but I am too curious, "Why am I still here?"

Elijah smiles, "I have a gift for you."

"A gift?" I ask, "What is it?"

Elijah doesn't say anything. He just closes his eyes and starts to meditate. Nothing happens. I just sit there waiting in the clearing. I am about to make some smart comment when a small orange orb appears just behind Elijah's right shoulder. The orb grows slowly. The shape begins to change. A figure of a girl starts to appear. When the orange disappears, I gasp.

It is Gwen!

She is even more beautiful than I remember. Her soft, long, brown hair is flowing effortlessly in the gentle breeze. She is wearing a silver gown that hugs her slim figure. Her ice-blue eyes light up when she sees me. A huge smile appears on her face, making my heart do a backflip.

She runs over at full speed. I just manage to stand before she clatters into me and knocks us both over with an embrace. Gwen smothers me with kisses. Tears appear in the corners of her eyes, "Jacob, you have no idea how much I've missed you," Even her voice is perfect, it is like a gentle stream that makes me feel all warm inside.

I wrap my arms around her and hold her close. Tears start to trickle down my cheeks. I plant a kiss on her forehead, "I've missed you so much too."

Gwen sits up and put her hands on either side of my face. Her fingers are ice cold. Her gorgeous eyes are bloodshot from the tears. I lie stunned by her beauty. She runs her fingers through my hair. She speaks, almost a whisper, "When I heard about the attack on Klad I was so scared that I had lost you." Gwen tries to stem the river of tears, "I prayed and prayed to every god and goddess known." She turns and looks at Elijah who is sat frozen in deep meditation, "I couldn't believe it when the Immortal Elijah answered them. He showed me visions of your camp whilst I slept. And now he has brought you here." Her red lips form a wonderful smile, showing off her radiant white teeth.

I sit up so we are face to face. I am awestruck. I can't speak. My heart pounds my chest. My cheeks ache, I'm grinning so much. I reach out and hold her hand. Even though I know I'm in a dream controlled by Elijah, I know she is real. After all this time Gwen is with me.

Taking a deep breath, I manage to pull myself together, "You were right. We should've run away together. That night watching the sunset, we should have just left everything behind and escaped together."

Gwen's eyes shine with happiness. "We really should have."

Elijah grunts. I turn and look at him. He is starting to grimace and sweat. Bringing us here is exhausting him.

Gwen's smile disappears, "We don't have long," She says hurrying, "Come and find me. Come to Vlaydom. No harm will come to you. I am the one who put the bounty on you and Maria to be taken alive." She begins to glow orange. She holds my hands tightly, "I wanted to make sure that if you were alive no harm would come to you or your sister. Hand yourself over and we can be together."

I can't help but notice that the straining Elijah seems a little shocked about Gwen's last comment. He just told us how to avoid the Vlaydom guards. I don't care though; I'm too happy.

The orange orb is once again growing around her. I look down at myself and see that the same is happening to me. This gift is ending. I am being dragged back to reality. "I will come," I promise. Gwen begins to fade. The image of the forest is starting to melt away. "I love you," I call desperately.

I sit up, awake and alone in the back of the caravan; drenched in sweat. The sun is beginning to set. A huge smile is etched into my face. Just before Elijah's vision ended, Gwen said three words. Three little words that have made my life infinitely better...

"Love you too."

Chapter 18

I climb out of the back of the caravan. The evening is warm with a gentle, cooling breeze keeping the air fresh. Vibrant oranges and gentle purples paint the night sky as the sun sets. I look off into the distance, south towards Stonemarsh. There is not a soul following us. This evening is peaceful. Smiling at the tranquillity of it all, I turn around to face our makeshift camp. My friends are sitting around in a huddle.

Looking past them, I am greeted by a stunning view that takes my breath away. The Arabian Desert. Miles of rolling hills crafted out of golden sand stand between us and Arabia. There is no way we can make it through there. I watch as the Arabian Desert changes in front of my eyes, the slight breeze moves the hills of fine sand with effortless ease. The Arabian Desert is so dangerous as no two days are ever the same.

I try not to think about the Desert and look back to my companions. There is no fire in our camp, there isn't a tree in sight to cut down. A quiet mumble floats amongst the group. Maria's eyes are bloodshot as she leans into Isaac who has his arm firmly wrapped around her. Shakra sits with Yasmin and Silvia either side of him. Joan and Hugo are already curled up asleep with plenty of layers of Razak's finest silks covering them. Laveona sits alone, away from the camp. She seems anxious, slowing rubbing her thumb along the edge of her axe blade. The purple lump on her forehead now has hints of blue and yellow.

I head towards the group, still walking on air. My throat is parched, and my stomach is growling, but nothing can upset me. Gwen awaits me. She loves me. No one in my cohort notices me until I am only a few steps away.

"Evening Jacob," Shakra mocks, "Good of you to join us."

I force myself to grin, conscious of everyone's eyes fixated upon me. Well, everyone's eyes apart from Maria's. She has a scowl etched onto her face. I try to ignore her and sit down next to Laveona, away from the group. "Got any food?" I ask.

Shakra is his usual upbeat self, he laughs as he says, "You're in for a treat, daisy leaves and dandelions,"

Yasmin passes me a handful of greens. I am too hungry to complain. Quickly, I shove the leaves down and swallow a gulp of water. Thankfully, the greens stay down. I am still ravenous though. Everyone is still watching me intently. Silence fills our makeshift camp.

After an age, I decide to break the deafening silence, "What's the plan for tomorrow?"

There is an exchange of nervous looks before Silvia speaks up, doing her queen impression, "Maria reckons that the army from Vlaydom's Outpost will be positioned between us and the Arabian Pass." I glance at Maria. She knows that Vlaydom soldiers are blocking the pass. She obviously hasn't told them about our meeting with Elijah. Silvia carries on somewhat nervously, "Which gives us no choice but to travel through the Arabian Desert."

Silvia pauses. She is petrified just at the thought of the Arabian Desert. Why shouldn't she be? The ever-changing hills of sand are a maze, impossible to navigate. Arabia itself is only a dot in the vastness of the desert. No one knows how far the Desert goes past Arabia, many claim it is endless. If we miss Arabia, we would never be able to find it. Luckily, Maria and I have a way out thanks to Gwen.

Silvia continues, "The journey through the desert will be dangerous. Since they are not wanted by the Vlaydom soldiers: Laveona, Joan and Hugo will take the horses and the caravan and follow the edge of the desert east to the Arabian Pass. The Vlaydom soldiers will assume they are traders and allow them to continue to Arabia. This will be a longer route but much, much safer."

I nod in agreement. It must be why Laveona looks so anxious. It is a good plan; therefore, definitely not Silvia's. Going around the desert is easily the better option for Laveona, Joan, and Hugo. Maria has heeded Elijah's words.

"How long will the trek through the desert take?" Isaac asks apprehensively. "We've got no food and only one small waterskin each."

There is a murmur around the camp before Yasmin pipes up, "I can't be sure, but I reckon it'll take a day and a half."

Silvia turns to her handmaiden, "Are you sure you know the way?"

"Yes." Yasmin mumbles, "We'll head north for half a day, then after that east. With some luck, we'll spot the Arabian Pass in the distance and use that as a guide to lead us to

Arabia." Yasmin doesn't sound confident. She seems quite down about the prospect of returning to her homeland.

Shakra sits up and grins, attempting to keep everyone's spirits up, "See, it'll be nice and easy. A few days from now we will be able to relax in the safety of Arabia. Comfortable beds, fine food and the best wines are all waiting for us."

Few smiles bounce around the camp. It did sound fantastic not to be running tomorrow. I am almost tempted to go with them. But Arabia is missing one thing, Gwen. I can find her in Vlaydom and be happy for the rest of my life. Just the thought of her is making me giddy. I can't help but smile at the idea of being with her.

I take a deep breath and calm down. The sun has set now, and darkness is slowly starting to creep in. A few of our companions curl up for a night's sleep. Laveona leans against me and with moments is snoring gently. Maria locks eyes with me from across the camp. She gestures to her right. I sigh and excuse myself from the group. I walk past Maria and carry on until I'm out of sight from the camp. I quickly take a leak, then wait.

A few moments later I see Maria storm down the hill. Even at dusk, I can see one thing clearly, Maria is furious. "What did you and your buddy Elijah chat about after I left?" Maria spits, "I left the dream and woke up. You stayed and schemed with your new *friend*. What did that invasive parasite say?"

Instinctively my right-hand goes behind me back and loosely grips to the hilt of my knife. I take a step back. How could she be this angry at Elijah? "Calm down Maria."

Maria's face is bright red. Her shoulders are tense. I notice her hands are fists. I try and stay relaxed, "I was given some good news."

Maria takes another step forward, snarling, "What? What could that cockroach have told you that could even be considered as good news?"

My anger starts to build, "How can you call Elijah a cockroach? He's been nothing but helpful. He told us about the Vlaydom soldiers guarding the Pass. You obviously thought that information was useful, you told the camp about that." I try and laugh it off, through my rage. I tense up as I continue, "Elijah wasn't the bearer of the good news, someone else was there." The darkness of the night sharply surrounds us. The air turns bitterly cold.

Maria scowls, her breath fogging in front of her face, "Who told you this *good* news?"

Fear takes over my anger. The cold and the dark haunt me. Chills raced down my spine. I brace myself, "Gwen."

Before I can react, Maria's right-hand swings round at full speed and slaps my left cheek. She hits me hard. I stumble onto one knee. The metallic taste of blood floods my mouth, my cheek is already swelling. I spit out blood, "What was that for? Gwen is going to save us."

Maria interrupts me, shaking with rage, "I don't want to hear it, Jacob. Gwen and Elijah are just manipulating you. You'll do anything Gwen says. She could make up anything and you would just follow blindly."

I stand up fully and spit out some more blood. My vision turns red with rage, "Why do you think we're wanted alive? Gwen has been protecting us."

"Do you even hear yourself, Jacob? Don't you remember that she left you, forget about her." Maria retorts.

Maria turns her back on me and starts to walk back to camp. My anger is uncontrollable. Fear fills my lungs. Although terrified, I have never felt so powerful. I feel out of my own body. My hate and anger are fuelling me. "Maria!" I shout.

Maria jumps; petrified. She is as white as a sheet. Her eyes are wide and hollow. Her short, sharp, shallow breaths cloud in front of her. "J-Ja-Jacob... Your kn-knife!" She stammers.

I look down in shock. I have drawn my knife and am gripping is so tightly that my knuckles have turned white. All the light and happiness in the world seems to be sucked into a void of darkness. The jet-black blade has somehow become a shade darker.

Maria drops to the ground and starts writhing and screaming. "No!" She screeches. Her eyes are pure black. She starts foaming at the mouth. Maria continues to yell wildly, "How could you do this to me?" Maria thrashes about desperately. She throws desperate punches and kicks at an imaginary target. She suddenly recoils as if she has been hit in the gut.

I am frozen with fear. I just watch Maria struggle on the floor. A cold chill creeps up my spine whispering, *'it's your fault...'*

Black tears stream down Maria's cheeks. Maria's voice is filled with hopeless desperation, "Dad... Jacob... Isaac..." She curls up into a ball, "Don't leave me. Please don't leave me." She looks so helpless and weak. I watch her fight with this unknown entity. I am helpless. This horror just continues to devour her soul.

'it's your fault...'

She continues to fight what seems a losing battle. Blood trickles out of her nose after she recoiled from an imaginary enemy. She screams with fear. Her mouth continues to foam as she chokes on her own words. But the most horrifying image are her eyes. Maria's eyes are black voids, pouring black tears down her face.

'it's your fault...'

Finally, I come to my senses. I drop my knife and run over to help. Maria stops still. I cradle her head in my lap. "Please be ok. Please be ok..." I pray. Her body is ice cold and limp. I curse. Have I killed her? I feel sick. Tears pour down my face.

Maria stays still and frozen. She isn't breathing. Her pulse has stopped. "Wake up," I plead. "Please wake up." She doesn't hear me. I hold her limp body. Her black eyes stare ominously at the night sky. Her freezing cold skin is still pale.

I retch. I've killed my sister. I don't know how but this was my doing. I made her cry the black tears. This was my fault. I hang my head with sorrow and fear. First, I lost Dad and now I've caused Maria's demise.

Suddenly the green returns to Maria's eyes. Colour returns to her cheeks. She coughs and splutters. Maria sits up, shakily and looks me in the eyes, "What the hell happened?"

I breathe a sigh of relief. "No idea," I admit. "Thank goodness you're alive." I smile uncontrollably, thanking my luck. Maria chuckles weakly.

Maria is still pale and drenched with sweat. She wipes away the black tears and nosebleed with her sleeve. I wrap my arms around her, she is still frozen. We sit there in silence for a few minutes, trying to comprehend what had happened. I have no idea what has happened to Maria or what she is thinking but I know now isn't the time to ask. I just stay still and watch her, silently praying to Gods I will never believe in.

Maria finally stops shivering then speaks, "Jacob?"

"Yes Maria," I respond.

"Firstly, sorry for hitting you."

I rub my swollen cheek and smirk. In the grand scheme of things, it is nothing. "It's fine. You didn't hit me that hard."

"Still... I'm sorry. I don't know what came over me." Maria admits. There is another pause of silence until Maria takes a deep breath, "Promise you won't leave." I go to reply but Maria gets in first, "I know you want to find Gwen and someday when we're safe we will journey out and find her. But right now, Silvia, Isaac, Shakra and Yasmin need us. We are their strength. I can't do this on my own, I need you."

I sigh. Maria is right. I have been selfish. My heart aches for Gwen and missing an opportunity to see her is unbearable. But Maria is my sister and best friend. With Dad working all the time, Maria has practically raised me and has always been there for me. I soften and say, "Maria, I promise to stay with you."

Maria manages a weak smile. Colour pours back into her cheeks. Her knife slowly starts to glow from behind her back. Warmth spreads through my body, lifting my spirits. Maria draws the blade from its scabbard. She closes her eyes and focuses. Slowly her blade glows brighter and brighter. Within moments the whole clearing lights up. Maria flicks her wrist and a perfect sphere of radiant white light drifts forward; it easily is a metre in diameter.

Maria leans forward and places her palms on either side of the radiant orb. Her eyes tell me to copy her. Tentatively I reach out and position my hands just above Maria's. As soon as I touch the orb, my aches and pains melt away as I am transported to a new vision.

I awake in the last place that I ever expected to see again. Home. Our old home in Rochton. I am sitting on the bench in the living room. The hazy sunlight pours in through the window. I look around the room. All the furniture is exactly how I remember it; worn down and cosy. The fireplace has the logs and kindling set up but there is no need, it is a beautiful summer's evening. The smell of warm beef stew fills the air.

This isn't a memory; this is a dream. Maria is curled up in Dad's chair with Isaac. He is sitting reading to her and methodically stroking her hair. Maria is nestled into his chest and is looking up at Isaac with big eyes, filled with adoration. The pair of them have smiles etched into their faces.

In the kitchen, I hear a familiar deep laugh. My Dad is joking around, making a mess. He is not alone. Also, in the kitchen stands a tall, elegant, blonde lady. The lady is dressed in humble clothes and has no jewellery, but she oozes beauty and class; even the flour on her face and apron can't dampen that. It is our mother. She is in fits of giggles, messing around with Dad. Dad wraps his arms around her. I have no idea what has just happened but the pair of them can't stop laughing.

I sit back. This is what Maria longs for. She just wants a safe and happy home. It hits me that I have been so focused on seeing Gwen that I have pushed my sister aside. A feeling of guilt rush down into the pit of my stomach. Fortunately, the orb immediately replaces the guilt with overwhelming happiness. I sit back and enjoy the family home.

"Kids; dinner," Dad calls.

Maria and Isaac grin at each other and walk hand in hand to the dinner table. I follow at a distance into the next room. Maria and Isaac sit next to each other, whilst our mother sits at the head of the table.

I stop. The table is set out for six. Six knives, six forks, six mugs of mead.

"Watch out son," Dad says. I step to the side as he places the pot of stew and dumplings in the middle of the table. He starts to ladle out six portions of the greatest smelling meal imaginable. I take my seat opposite Maria and next to our mother. I keep looking at the empty seat next to me as my father hands me a bowl of stew.

Who was the extra seat for? I am in Maria's dream. Surely it can't be Gwen. It mustn't be Gwen. Maria has never liked Gwen. Footsteps echo down the stairs. I wait to see the sixth person in Maria's dream. I find myself making a silent prayer. I am so desperate for it to be Gwen.

The footsteps finally reach the bottom of the stairs. My heart sinks. Kyra, my aunt, walks around the corner. My heart sinks.

"This all smells great Tatiana," Kyra exclaims. My mother smiles. Kyra sits down next to me and nudges me playfully. "Why are you looking so glum Jacob?"

Everyone's attention turns to me. I shrug my shoulders. "I'm not glum."

Dad starts to chuckle. "He's just lovesick Kyra. He's not seeing Gwen until next week."

My heart skips a beat. In Maria's ideal world I am with Gwen. Despite her disapproval of Gwen, Maria wants me to be happy, even after all the pain I have caused her. I smile uncontrollably.

I grab my spoon and prepare to tuck into dinner with my family when the image becomes faint. I start to panic. I don't want this memory to end. I spot Maria opposite me becoming a little agitated. Maria starts to mutter to herself, "No, no, no, no..." She is frantically trying to hold onto the dream.

Within seconds Maria and I are sitting in the dark field on the edge of the Arabian Desert. I sigh. The use of Maria's knife is always bittersweet, a fleeting moment of happiness followed by the disappointment of reality. It just seems to highlight what's missing from our lives.

"Thank you," I say. "That was really personal what you shared."

"You know Jacob, you're not the only who's lost with their feelings." Maria smiles through her tears, "You can always share anything with me."

I grin. Maria is right. Maria has always been there for me and always has my back. I wrap an arm around her shoulder and give her a light squeeze. "Let's get back to the others."

I stand up laboriously. Everything aches. This whole ordeal since the destruction of Rochton seems to hit me all at once. The memory of home and what it could have been has hit me hard. I want to live in that dream. I take a deep breath and try not to cry. I will trade anything to make Maria's dream a reality for myself. But even more so I'm desperate for Maria to be that happy. She deserves a break like that. I am going to get her to Arabia where she will be safe to have a normal life. Who knows, maybe our mum will be there. I shudder, that is a scary thought.

I pull Maria to her feet. When she's up I take a few tired strides, bend down, and pick up my knife. It is freezing cold. The grass around it has frosted ever so slightly. Hastily, I sheath the blade and brush away the ice before Maria could catch a glimpse.

Maria and I trudge back to the camp. Joan and Hugo are still sound asleep. Laveona is slumped up against a pack, asleep and drooling. The purple lump on her forehead that Christian gave her seems to be pulsating. Silvia, Shakra, Isaac and Yasmin are sat in a small circle, talking in hushed voices. Shakra is fiddling with his beads in the back of his hair. He does that when he is nervous. It is obvious why; Queen Silvia is attempting to cuddle up to him and put her head on his chest. It is so painful to watch. Shakra clearly isn't enamoured by his betrothed.

Isaac spots us first, his eyes light up when he sees Maria. A relieved Shakra pipes up first, "Hey, what took you guys so long?"

Maria perches herself down next to Isaac and Shakra. "Sorry, we were just having a chat."

I sit myself down next to Yasmin and Silvia. Shakra analyses me for a second, looking at the swollen cheek which Maria had slapped. "Was it a good chat?" Shakra asks inquisitively, probing to find out the truth. He doesn't like it on the rare occasions when he isn't in the know.

Maria locks eyes with me and answers, "Jacob and I just made sure we were on the same page."

Isaac smiles and speaks before Shakra has a chance to quiz us some more, "Glad everything is straightened out." There is a murmur around camp in agreement. "But there is one thing concerning me," Isaac continues. I sit forward. If Isaac, the one with the most positive outlook on life, is concerned, it must be serious. "What is the actual plan for when we get to Arabia?"

"What do you mean?" Yasmin says quite defensively.

"Well, we aren't exactly a welcome sight." Isaac points out, "If Arabia takes us in, they will be defying Vlaydom, putting the whole nation in danger." Isaac is attempting to be diplomatic, ensuring he doesn't offend Yasmin. "It would be much easier for the Arabian King Tufail to just hand us over to Vlaydom. It certainly would be much safer." Silvia sits up. Maria starts shuffling uneasily. Isaac is making a good point. He continues preaching what we are all thinking, "Even if we are accepted by Arabia what happens then. Do we live out our days in hiding or do we try and get revenge for those we have lost?"

Yasmin's face has a blank expression, but her eyes scream anger and frustration. She manages to stay calm, "Arabia *will* help."

Maria interjects and speaks softly, "Isaac is right. Our whole plan rests on the Arabians sheltering us. If they refuse us, it's over."

Yasmin growls. She goes to speak but Shakra gets in first, "Arabia is fiercely loyal to Klad. They will protect us. As for the after that who knows; that problem can wait."

Silvia tries to resume leadership, "Well that is good enough for me. I trust Yasmin, she has been extremely loyal to me since the day we met. If she believes Arabia will protect us, then so do I."

Tears glisten in Yasmin's eyes. Small grins bounce around camp, it looks clear that Silvia has cheered Yasmin up. Everyone smiles except me; Yasmin's tears seem filled with guilt. There is something she hasn't told us, and I know that Shakra knows what it is. Whenever it seems that she is about to finally tell me, something has interrupted us. I want to believe it is nothing serious, but these last few days have made it even harder not to suspect betrayal.

Yasmin leans over and hugs Silvia. A sense of joy spreads around the camp. I decide to bury my suspicion for now. We are only a day and a half away from safety. Soon we won't be running. Featherbeds and hot baths are waiting for us. I couldn't help but feel positive despite myself.

Isaac whispers something into Maria's ear and she starts to howl with laughter. Her knife and swords are glowing so brightly from the top of their scabbards. It is clear Maria is happy, the nightmare of before with Maria and I, seems like a distant memory.

Shakra announces he would take the first watch. There are a few half-hearted complaints but Shakra shrugs them off. He stands up, obviously keen to get some distance between himself and Silvia, and walks over to Lena, making sure she is fed and watered.

We all curl up for the night, smiles upon our faces. I lie back, head in hands and look up at the bright full moon and stars. I don't need Gwen, I tell myself. One day I'll find her but right now the important thing is getting everyone to safety. I need to focus on family first. Maria has always been there for me. I sigh and close my eyes. I need to rest; we have a long day ahead of us. A trek through the desert is the last obstacle before Arabia and safety.

A twang of anxiety appears in my stomach. I can't help but take notice. The buried suspicion of Yasmin comes to the forefront of my thoughts. Isaac may have had a point; how can we trust Arabia?

I am too tired of this stress. I roll over and get some sleep. After all, I need to be fully fit for tomorrow, because tomorrow...

We face the Arabian Desert.

Chapter 19

It's freezing. No matter how much I toss and turn, sleep continues to evade me. I sit up. Maria and Isaac are curled up together using each other for warmth. I curse them. I have no idea how long it will be until dawn. The full moon shines brightly, directly overhead.

"Would it be rude to wake Maria?" I mutter to myself. With one flick of her knife, she could form a ball of light. The warmth and happy memories it can create surely would help me sleep. Would that be too selfish? She looks very content and peaceful. A faint smile is stuck on her face, her fingers are interlaced with Isaac's. I curse for a second time, after the stress Maria has been put through today, I couldn't wake her now.

I shudder. That same cold chill from earlier races up my spine, *It's your fault... you cannot save her'*

I jump up to my feet knife drawn. What is that voice? Who does it belong to? Frantically I search the surroundings. I grip my knife tighter. "Calm down Jacob," I whisper to myself, "It's all inside your head."

"Hey," A voice behind me makes me jump. I turn to find the tip of my blade pointing at Shakra's chest. "Whoa, calm mate," He says in a mixture of panic and a smirk. "What's got you on edge?" The small Chevonic Prince asks.

I force myself to take slow breaths and eventually relax. "Nothing," I lie as I sheath my knife. It is an obvious lie.

Shakra isn't fooled. He quickly checks that everyone is sound asleep and whispers, "Has it got something to do with your swollen cheek?"

I touch my cheek tentatively. It is red hot with inflammation and incredibly sore. "No." Another obvious lie.

Shakra takes a few steps away from the group and sits down. He pats the spot just to his right, inviting me to sit with him. Reluctantly, I trudge over and sit next to him.

Shakra breaks the brief silence, "Jacob, I can't pretend there's nothing odd about Maria and yourself." He speaks softly, treading carefully, "You two obviously aren't just some regular Kladoenians, there's something different. What Maria can do with her knife," He pauses. "It's like nothing I've ever seen before."

I nod in silent agreement. He's right. Maria's power is unnatural. "Maybe it's just her blade?" I suggest.

"Maybe," Shakra ponders, "I guess no one else has tried but it's still not normal." I nod again. He was half right. I have tried before and failed, but Shakra doesn't need to know that. Shakra gestures with his head towards my knife, "What about your blade? Can it do the same as Maria's?"

Tentatively, I unsheathe my knife again. After what happened to Maria earlier, the worn leather of my blade doesn't feel as comforting as usual. I close my eyes and attempt to meditate, willing my knife to glow bright and warm. I strain my arm. Beads of sweat run down from my forehead and neck. I open one eye and take a glimpse.

The blade is as jet black as ever. No majestic white glow radiates from it. No warmth reaches out and comforts me. No happy memories sought me out and fill me up with happiness. The knife is just my knife. Cold and black.

I sigh and re-sheath the blade. I look at Shakra, who's eyes are full of disappointment. "I'm sorry," I mumble.

Shakra cracks his same old cocky smile, "Don't worry about it. At least we know not to put you on campfire duties." I can't help but laugh. After all the crazy stuff we've been through, Shakra still manages to make a joke. We chuckle for a little while and look out to the night sky over Stonemarsh.

Shakra slaps his lap, breaking the silence once more, "Well if you're not going to sleep, I will." He rises to his feet and lies down next to Yasmin. Not Silvia, Yasmin.

I don't know if that made me smirk or annoys me. There is definitely a history between Shakra and Yasmin. They must have met before King Edward announced Shakra's engagement to Silvia. It is the main thing that has prevented me from ever fully trusting Shakra. It feels like I am treading on thin ice around them. Yasmin has come close to telling me a few times, but we've always been interrupted.

I sigh. The truth always seems to unfold itself at one point. I sit back and look at the night sky, trying to make shapes out of the stars.

"Do you think everyone's asleep?"

The voice makes me jump; again. I curse, "People need to stop doing that,"

Maria sits down next to me, amused with herself that she had given me a little scare. "After all we been through, you're terrified of a little voice in the dark." She mocks.

I smile, "Probably because of what we've been through that makes me a little on edge." Maria grins and nods in agreement. I look at her, "Why you awake?"

"I've got too much on my mind,"

"Like what?" I enquire.

Maria takes a deep breath, "Well firstly the silver arrows,"

"What silver arrows?"

"Remember when we thwarted the bandits' ambush..."

I interrupt, "Where Flint died?"

Sadness fills Maria's voice, "Yes, where Flint died. When the rest of us were praying you and Shakra scavenged for weapons and found Laveona."

The memory of those damned silver arrows floods back, "Yeah, what about them?"

Maria locks eyes with me, "Are you not curious about who fired them?"

I shrug my shoulders, "With all the crazy stuff that's happened, I haven't really," I admit.

Maria sits up, "Well I think I've worked it out."

"Who was it then?" I ask, my voice filled with trepidation.

Maria took a deep breath, "Our people."

"Our people?" I am taken aback, "Our people are dead, Maria. Klad is dead. The few people here are the last of our people."

"But our mother's people are not dead," Maria says, frankly. She sees my dazed look. "Hear me out, Jacob. Each time we have been gifted a vision by *your friend* Elijah, the setting has always been the woodland. Therefore, when we were fleeing the Chevon riders, we must have past whatever haven they live at. Plus, *your friend* Elijah once gifted me a vision where our aunt Kyra wore a quiver which bore arrows with the same flight as the silver arrows you scavenged. They've watched over us without directly intervening."

I am a bit annoyed about how she calls Elijah my friend in such a condescending way. I ignore the dig and entertain the possibility. We have certainly faced many dangers in the Great Woods but not half as many as we should have. Everyone knows trying to cross the Great Woods was near suicidal. Throughout the journey, only Flint and Joshua had died, and Joshua's death isn't due to any woodland creature or bandits. It does seem we had some luck on our side.

"Who are our people then?" I say.

Maria looks me in the eye and calmly says, "Elves."

294

I curse loudly. Maria frantically tries to get me to be silent, trying to make sure I don't wake anyone. She looks around the camp who lie, blissfully unaware.

"Elves!" I exclaim, "Do you not remember who slaughtered our real people? The damned Elves are the ones who got us into this mess."

Maria somehow manages to stay calm, "Jacob, please listen." She grasps my wrist tightly. I take a few controlled and deep breaths. Maria continues, "When we were having the meal at the Humble Hearth, Isaac told me stories about the Wars of Old. He told me there were three Elven kingdoms. First were the Mountain Elves who lived high up in the North-West mountains; clad in golden armour and rode gryphons. They are the ones who slaughtered Klad. Second were an Elvish race called the Fiends. Apparently, they lived purely out of hate, and lust for war. They rivalled Klad for the military power of Valouria, luckily for Humans, their numbers were too few. And finally, there were the Woodland Elves who live in the Great Woods. They wore silver and rode Pegasi, winged horses, famed for their skill with a bow."

I brush Maria's grip off my wrist and sit back to collect my thoughts. "What are you suggesting? That our mother is a Woodland Elf."

Maria nods slowly, "I believe so. It would explain why we've always been different."

For the first time in years, Maria pulls back her hair revealing something both Maria and I have tried to hide all our lives. Her ear has a slight point, nothing compared to the Elves, but her ears are still pointed. Instinctively, I put my hair behind my ear to reveal the same.

I curse. Maria must be right. Our mother must be a Woodland Elf. That's why we never saw her. That's why our father would never talk about her, he was trying to protect us. If anyone in Rochton had found out we would have been run out of town, or worse.

Suddenly a wave of nausea hits me. What had Yasmin said about Elijah and Enyo? They were half Elven and half Human. "Immortals," I whisper.

"What?" Maria turns and looks me in the eye.

"Immortals. If we are half Elven that means we are part of the Immortals." I mutter, somewhat frightened of what I was saying.

Maria scratches her chin. "I think Isaac mentioned something about them. He said that there was a golden giant who is an Immortal."

"He must be the third Immortal," I explain. Maria looks confused. I continue, "Yasmin told me how Elijah was the first Immortal and was the main reason that Humans defeated the Elves in the Wars of Old. Elijah claimed he was the first of the Five Immortals. Then some girl named Enyo managed to slaughter over two hundred people in one night and they claimed she was the second Immortal. This golden giant must be the third. Making you and I the fourth and fifth Immortals."

Maria sits thinking. After an age, she finally spoke, "You think we're immortal as in we can't die?"

"I have no idea," I admit, "I think that is just the name given to them."

"But the Wars of Old happened hundreds of years ago. If the Elijah that has been giving us visions is the same Elijah; he must be ancient, he should be dead."

"I guess." I mutter, "But who knows, maybe it means we don't age like the Elves. Honestly, I'm not sure whether we even are part of the Immortals. For now, let's avoid being killed under the assumption that we are mortal like everyone else."

Maria smirks, "After cheating death for the last few days I'm not desperate to try it."

I smile. She is right, we have cheated death a few times. I look over towards the Arabian Desert. If we survive that we may be safe. I'm filled with a warmth like that of Maria's knife's magic. Maria lays back and stares at the stars. For a rare moment, I am genuinely happy. I think of our father, of Rochton, and despite myself, I couldn't help but think of our mother. If she is truly Elven, could this mean I am one of the Immortals?

My hand instinctively finds the handle of my knife. Do I have powers like Maria or would mine be different? Maria seems to be able to control light, happiness, and warmth. Elijah somehow can speak in our heads and enter our dreams. And from what Yasmin had told me it sounded like Enyo has some sort of healing power.

"The Behemoth!" Maria exclaims, interrupting the tranquillity of my own thoughts.

I shush her this time. Hopefully, we haven't woken anyone. "The Behemoth?" I whisper.

"The golden giant. Gwen's bodyguard. The Behemoth." She says anxiously.

"What are you going on about?"

Maria takes a deep breath and calms. "I've figured out who the third immortal is. It's the Behemoth, Gwen's bodyguard."

I feel an empty pit in my stomach. He is huge; a towering giant, seven-foot-tall at least. He wears some golden-steel armour. His ear that hadn't been severed is pointed like mine and Maria's. "I think you're right."

"Elijah, Enyo and The Behemoth." Maria mumbles, "Don't you find it weird that Gwen has connections to at least two of them."

I start fiddling with blades of grass, avoiding eye contact, "What do you mean?"

"If we truly are part of the Immortals, Gwen has had contact with four of five that we know of. I mean she has the Behemoth as her bodyguard. Elijah brought you a vision of her. She then has stayed in our home. Plus, she has you under her heel." I fill with rage, but I don't bite. I decide to stay quiet. Maria continues, "It seems that she is connected to the Immortals. Either that or she's gone out of her way to find them."

I remain quiet. I don't want to cause another argument with Maria, especially after what happened last time. The image of her writhing with fear, crying black tears is a haunting image I'll never be able to un-see.

Maria is about to carry on slating Gwen, but she is thankfully interrupted by Silvia yawning and sitting up. I thank my luck. Tension leaves my shoulders as our Queen shuffles over to sit with us.

"You two get some sleep." Silvia chuckles as she rubs the sleep from her eyes, "That's a command from your Queen."

I grin to myself; Silvia looks extremely regal with her brown hair sticking out in every direction.

Maria smiles, "Yes your majesty." Maria gives Silvia a hug and goes to lie next to Isaac.

Silvia locks eyes with me, "You get some sleep too Jacob, we need you well rested for tomorrow, we have a long day ahead."

I nod and lie down. Sleep finds me within seconds, and I drift off into a dreamless slumber.

*****

I awake to find Laveona prodding me with the butt of her axe. "Wake up hun."

I moan with disapproval; the sun hasn't made an appearance yet. I twist, cracking my back. I yawn as I stand up. My companions are up and about, filling waterskins and packing the essentials for our trek into the desert.

Yasmin smiles at me, "We need to get a good head start into the desert before the sun is overhead." I nod in agreement. I gulp down my warm water and refill my skin with cool water from the stream.

There is an air of trepidation around the group. No one speaks. Everyone just stays silent. Shakra is standing away from camp attaching the horses to the cart. Laveona leads Joan and Hugo to Razak's caravan. I watch from the distance as they climb onto the cart.

Shakra resentfully hands over the reins to Laveona. I saw him mouth '*If you hurt Lena, I will come for you*'. Poor Laveona gulps down her nerves. Silvia, Isaac, and Maria head over and say their farewells, wishing them the best of luck. I walk over next to Yasmin in silence as I watch Laveona give a quick flick of the reins. The cart gently pulls off East, towards the Arabian Pass, into the sunrise.

Yasmin gives a small sigh. She turns North and begins to trudge towards the desert. Shakra jogs over to walk with her. Maria and Isaac follow them. Silvia appears by my side. She is wide-eyed with fear at the prospect of the task that lies ahead. I ignore her and take my first step into the sand. My feet sink and the coarse sand fills my boot. This is going to be a nightmare.

It takes precisely five minutes for me to feel lost. The slightest breeze causes the sand dunes to completely change. Fine sand attacks my eyes. I stumble around blind. The swirling sand burns my skin. Any exposed body part is brutally sought out by the flying sand.

My feet continue to sink in the soft sand. It feels like I'm sinking into soft mud. My calves burn as I drag my feet out of the sand to make my next step. It takes all my will not to give in. We move far too slowly in this sand.

To climb up the steep dunes I'm forced to go on all fours. I can't get any grip on the loose sand. My hands burn in the sand. As I climb Isaac falls over in front of me. When I finally reach the top of a dune. I look around. The sea of sand is endless. The route behind me has already changed. There is no trace of where we've been or where we are going.

I look up to the sky, desperate to try and get some bearings, but the sweltering sun is just directly overhead. If it weren't for Yasmin, our group would be well and truly doomed. She manages to power ahead, even with an injured leg. She seems to float on the top of the stand. An internal compass guides Yasmin through the endless ever-changing maze of sand. Systematically, Yasmin doubles back to help us, making sure we knew which routes to take through the hills, pulling us up the scorching dunes.

Silvia sticks closely by my side through the mountains of sand. She keeps on going to say something then backing off. Then, she would try again but seems somewhat scared. Trudging around in the unbearable heat is making me frustrated and Silvia tentatively looking for a conversation was only flaring my temper. After an hour or so, I begrudgingly start a conversation, "What are the Arabian Royals like?"

Silvia looks at me and smiles, "Well King Tufail loves three things: his family, Arabia, and good business. He would rarely visit Klad and leave his family unless it was needed. King Tufail and father never got on well, but they had a lot of respect for each other. Father would always speak highly of him. And then King Tufail's wife is Queen Amira, she would always travel with Tufail to Klad. And I think they have five children, but honestly must be six or seven years since I last visited there. Think the oldest one is Prince Naseem, who must be in his late twenties by now. Then it's the Princesses: Aisha, Jamila, and Nadia. I remember Nadia, she is about my age, we use to play together when we were little, but she was terribly ill, and bedridden for years. I didn't get to see her very often. Then finally he has a young son, Tufail junior."

I smile, masking my mild frustration in the heat, "Well hopefully tomorrow you'll get to see Nadia."

Silvia grins, "Yeah, I hope so. I must be over ten years since I last saw her." She chuckles to herself, "We had so much fun as children. Hope she is well enough to meet us."

After all the trauma of the last few days, to see Silvia smile at the premise of seeing an old friend brings a calmness to me. The world does carry on after the destruction of Klad and there was some joy to be found. I just hope Yasmin can deliver on her promise of getting us through this desert and guarantee our safety in Arabia.

The sand continues to swirl around us. The sun continues beats down upon us. It seems to stay directly overhead all day. I have no clue which way is north. We carry on trudging through the sand. Poor Isaac is really struggling. He is twice the size of everyone else. Each step causes him to sink into the fine sand which he has to claw himself out of. Maria and Shakra keep on having to pull him up the dunes. He chunters to himself, cursing the sand. He kicks sand into my face as I give him one final push over the brow of the hill.

As we struggle on through the sand, I start to notice how the Desert is sapping my strength. Sweat pours down the back of my neck. Precious water is leaving my body fast. My head is thumping. My throat is parched and feels like it is cracking. I am dehydrated. I take one tiny sip from my waterskin. I am desperate to drink it all.

Next to me, Silvia has wrapped any spare item of clothing around her head. She had left on a small slit to see through. I look ahead an see why. A wall of sand is approaching fast. Yasmin wets a rag and then covers her mouth and nose with it. She gestures for us to do the same and then ploughs on ahead, straight into the storm. I quickly use my knife to remove my only sleeve, the other is still tied around Isaac's arm, and pour some of my water onto it. I quickly manage to tie it around my face just as the sandstorm hits.

I can't open my eyes. I blindly walk in the storm. Any exposed skin is taking a beating from the sand. It feels like the skin is being ripped off my body. I feel Silvia grab my hand as I lead her further into the tempest. The storm continues to blast us with sand. I can't see any of the others. My eyes are raw, each grain of sand seems to dig deep into them. This is hopeless, I think as I drag Silvia aimlessly.

But thankfully some good luck finally appears, as the storm vanishes as soon as it had arrived. The unbearable sun reappears.

I look around. Where the hell is everyone? Silvia grips my hand tighter as we look around, seeing nothing but the vastness of the Arabian Desert. I curse.

I drag Silva up the nearest dune, desperate for a vantage point. We scour the horizon, trying to find a sign of our allies when Silvia exclaims, "Over there." She points at Yasmin and Shakra in the distance. She gives the pair a friendly wave. I ignore them and keep looking. "Maria!" I shout. Where is she?

Shakra waves at me, "She's over here. Behind the dunes."

I run over, pulling Silvia down with me. We tumble down our dune but are alright. When we manage to get around to Maria and Isaac the cohort's spirits lift. Maria and Isaac are unharmed, just have taken a beating from the sandstorm like the rest of us. I notice that I still have my fingers interlaced with Silvia's. I hastily let go. Isaac had spotted it though and he has a smug smile plastered on his face.

I go to sit down to take a five-minute break, but Yasmin speaks up, "No rest till sundown. We keep moving." She turns on her heels as if nothing had happened and carries on. I curse silently and follow. We keep on walking.

Eventually, the sun begins to set. At first, it is a blessing. The low sun allows some of the dunes to provide shade, a temporary respite from the heat. But when the sun disappears it is hell. We stop and make camp. With no wood for a fire, it is pitch black and incredibly cold. The six of us nearly freeze to death in our barebones camp. We all cuddle together to try and share some warmth but fail miserably. Maria tries to use her knife, but she was far too preoccupied with the cold and couldn't even manage a shimmer from her blade.

No songs are sung. No conversation is had. We can almost taste safety, but the Arabian Desert has sucked all the hope and joy from us all. I try to sleep on the sand but it's just too cold. Everything aches. My calves are cramped up. My quadriceps spasm with fatigue. Sand has found its way into all my clothing. Blisters paint my feet.

When a dreamless sleep eventually finds me, it isn't restful at all. And before I know it, the sun is up again. I get up, brushing off the layers of sand that have buried me. I am shattered. I feel less rested than when I had laid down last night. My back is in agony. I take a swig of water whilst Yasmin maps out how we are heading east to hopefully find Arabia.

We set off on our second day of trekking through this hellhole. I am too hot, too tired, too hungry, and especially too thirsty. Shakra is burnt red raw from the day before but carries on without a word of complaint. Everyone is too fed up with their own situation to care about someone else's moans.

Yasmin leads the way again, determined to make it to Arabia before the heat of the day. We walk in single file over the mountains of sand. I bring up the rear. The Arabian Desert continues to echo eerily with silence. I like quiet, but this lifeless wasteland is unbearable. "Just keep going Jacob," I mutter to myself.

I few metres ahead of me Isaac is really struggling again. He can't find any footing when climbing the dunes. The fine sand just isn't enough to support him. I take over from an exhausted Maria and pull him up the next few dunes.

It was easy to imagine an army becoming stuck and buried here. If any one of us was wearing full armour, there is no way we would be able to climb up the dunes. The sheer weight of the metal would drag you down into the sand. I sympathise with the Vlaydom soldiers who had lost their lives here, hundreds of years ago in the Wars of Old. I stop allowing my mind to wander as Isaac stumbles again. I curse as I heave with all my might, pulling him over the brow of another mountain of sand.

By what I assume is around midday we find our salvation. At first, I thought it was a mirage, but my eyes don't deceive me, Arabia stands proud on the horizon. Smooth white stone has been used to form beautiful towers and temples, which over the years the locals had painted. Even from this distance, I could see the vibrant purples, reds, and blues of the painted town. It is beautiful.

The spirits of myself, Maria, Shakra, Silvia and Isaac immediately lift. We have almost made it. We keep on hiking through the sand, almost breaking into a run. Yasmin follows at some distance looking tense and nervous. Within an hour, we reach the glorious front gates of the busy market kingdom. I take a deep breath. Surely after all the trauma and hell the group has been through, there would be no more surprises awaiting us...

Once again, I am wrong.

Chapter 20

As we join onto the last few hundred metres of the Arabian Pass, the road that leads directly to Arabia's main gate, I have to stop and admire the breath-taking kingdom. Arabia is easily the most beautiful place I've ever seen. The gate is over three times the height of any man and could comfortably allow twenty people through at once. Made from a rich, dark wood the gate was gilded with gold designs of animals, landscapes, and heroes. The walls tower over us. Guards patrol the walls, longbows in hand and scimitars on their belts. Huge catapults sit atop the highest towers. I can't help but compare it to Klad which had paled in comparison. This place could never be sacked. A sanctuary amongst the sea of sand. The wealth of Arabia has provided them with the best of everything and the Arabians were not ashamed to flaunt it.

The gates are wide open. Trading carts pour in and out of Arabia. Each cart is instantly searched by a team of Arabian guards. A small cohort of guards approaches as we wander to the gates. I can't help but realise that Yasmin has slunk to the back of our group, head hanging low. Why is she trying to hide?

Before I have time to think the guards have reached us. Each guard is dressed in light armour, with a lilac purple headscarf, many with their faces hidden behind bushy beards. Every single guard has a hand resting gently on the hilt of their scimitar, which is hanging low on their belt. They aren't taking any chances; twenty guards greet us.

The soldier leading the cohort of guards is dressed differently from the other men. He wears a red headscarf, and the hilt of his scimitar is golden rather than the wooden handles. The lead Arabian soldier is tall and lean. Rather than sporting a bushier, untamed beard like the rest of his allies, the lean guard is very well-groomed, sporting a well-sheared goatee. He greets us with a warm smile. He bows, then speaks with a rich accent, "I am Zahir, Captain of the guards. I have sent a messenger to inform King Tufail of your arrival."

Silvia stands up a little straighter, "Thank you, Captain Zahir," I smirk quietly to myself. Silvia loves her phoney royalty act. She acts as if she has everything under control. She continues as regally as possible, "My people have trekked far and been through many hardships. With your permission, I would ask if they can eat, drink, and freshen up before meeting the great King Tufail if that is not too much trouble."

Zahir seems a little shocked that it is Silvia that spoke, but he simply smiles, "Of course Your Highness, it will be an honour." I am impressed that Captain Zahir manages to recognise Silvia just by sight. Zahir clicks his fingers and his men approach, each giving us waterskins. I gulp down as much water I as physically could. We thank the soldiers.

"Captain Zahir, I am lost to find the words to thank you enough. On behalf of the kingdom of Klad, we are eternally grateful." Our Queen is in full swing. I roll my eyes.

Zahir bows his head. He seems to quickly glance over at Yasmin. My eyes may have deceived me, but I'm sure that

Yasmin ever so slightly shakes her head as if they are having a silent conversation. I am about to brush off what I had seen but the look I receive from Maria tells me that my paranoid fears are right. Maria looks scared. Zahir definitely looked towards Yasmin and Yasmin definitely responded. What are Zahir and Yasmin gesturing about?

Zahir straightens his armour, "Me and my men will escort you to the palace. It is a couple of miles walk. I expect there to be crowds, once word spreads of your arrival. Don't stop, just keep your head down and keep walking." Zahir gives a short sharp whistle and his men rush to form a circle around us. Although it is for our protection, it doesn't make me feel any safer at all. Zahir turns and proceeds to walk into Arabia with us following obediently.

Nothing could have prepared me for the wonderful diversity and beauty of Arabia. The city is alive with colour and fragrance. The main road leads straight to the palace, a spot in the distance. Small market stalls fill the entire road. People haggle tirelessly with the business owners, kids play in the street, performers breathe fire and swallow swords, music fills my ears and incredible food smells fill my lungs.

Zahir is right though. Someone manages to spot our group after only a minute. He yells something that I couldn't make out. Whatever he shouted has gotten the people excited. Crowds come running over, leavings their stalls and homes. They swamp us, clambering over each other just to get a look. The crowd is cheering, people throw flowers, give us fresh baked good. I am in heaven when someone manages to pass me bread and honeycomb. The bread is delicious, but the honeycomb is unbelievable. So sweet and wonderful. I scoff it all in a heartbeat.

Zahir keeps us moving forward pushing his way through the crowd. Silvia stands directly behind him, waving at the crowd, soaking up all the cheers and applause. She is acting as if she is a triumphant, all-conquering hero. But Silvia isn't who the masses are cheering. The crowd seems to be cheering either Shakra or Yasmin. I can't figure out why the Arabian public would be particularly overjoyed to see either. Is the Chevonic Prince really that popular here? Who is Yasmin and why is she being celebrated? Do Arabians just love their own?

I can't help but feel anxious. My right hand keeps reaching for the handle of my knife. I struggle to make a conscious effort not to grab the hilt. Even if did grab my knife, what could I do? I am surrounded by armed guards. They seem to be guarding the common folk from us rather than the other way around. It doesn't make me feel very safe. I feel claustrophobic, even amongst these happy people in this beautiful kingdom.

We keep on pushing forward, forcing our way through the masses. The palace is getting closer and closer, growing bigger on the horizon. All the surrounding Arabia pales in comparison to the palace. A huge white temple, with huge white pillars, stands proudly, looking down over the busy market street. Everything inch of the glorious palace is gilded with purple and gold designs, the colours of Arabia. A giant ivory statue of a simple trading cart is positioned outside the front of the palace, honouring the kingdom's humble beginnings.

Behind the gates is an even greater statue situated halfway up the palace steps. Crafted out of bronze, an immense figure of a warrior stands heroically. In his left hand, an intricate bronze net is held, and in his right hand, his bronze quindent is poised to strike. The statue's bronze dreadlocks are decorated with amber. His face I know too well. Elijah stands protecting the palace from anyone who dares to approach. I spot Maria shudder and pull a face when she sees his likeness.

As we pass the statue of Elijah, the crowd stops. They stand in front of the statue, watching us take each step up to the palace. Our armed escorts are still in a tight circle around us.

When we reach the top step, Silvia turns to face the crowd and gives one last wave, which is received with a roar of applause. Her smile is ear to ear as we walk through the vast palace entrance. The marble palace entrance is very spacious and eerily empty. Unlike the main gates, no one is here to greet us. Our footsteps echo on the marble floor. The sounds of the crowd seem to dissipate as soon as we pass the pillars into the palace.

We finally reach the far side of the empty, open marble room. A small wooden door stands there. Nothing fancy, just a small wooden door. Two heavily armoured guards proudly stand either side. A further three guards wait nearby to the right of the door, stood behind a small table.

As we approach the five guards, Zahir calls us to a halt and says firmly, "Before we enter, I will ask you all hand over whatever weapons you have in your possession. I can assure you they will be taken care of and returned to you as soon as you leave the throne room."

There are a few uneasy looks amongst our group. These weapons have too often been the difference between life and death for us. Yasmin and Shakra hand over their blades almost immediately. I can't help but distrust them. What are they hiding? I reluctantly take Nemesis off my shoulder, then my quiver of arrows. I hand them to the nearest guard. I pull the back of my shirt down, ensuring it hides my knife.

Unfortunately, Shakra spots me, "Jacob relax, you can trust them." Zahir and the other guards all lock their eyes on me. I curse Shakra silently. I slowly unsheathe my blade, then throw it into the table with the other weapons, making my feelings known. I feel so naked and vulnerable without it.

"You too Maria," Yasmin pipes up. I catch my breath. Maria is thinking the same as me. She scowls and places her knife next to mine.

I have an urge to bolt out of the palace grounds. I also have a desperate urge to hit Yasmin and Shakra square in the jaw. I have the time to do neither. I curse a thousand times under my breath. Zahir opens the small wooden door and walks through. Yasmin and Shakra follow without hesitation. Silvia takes a deep breath and steps forward. Isaac takes Maria's hand, "Well, what's the worst that could happen?" He chuckles.

"Death," Maria mutters as Isaac whisks her through the door.

I sigh. The next few moments are going to determine whether the entire escape of Klad and our desperate fight for freedom was just in vain or if we had a real opportunity of salvation. If I were King Tufail I would execute us all on the spot and send our heads to Vlaydom, keeping his country safe. I make a silent prayer that King Tufail isn't that smart, and I walk through the doorway.

Luckily, our judgment isn't imminent. The small door leads to a washroom, not the throne room. A small bronze brazier stands in the middle of the of eight large baths built into the ground. Six have been filled with water, flower petals and fragrant oils. Zahir walks to the brazier and turns to face us, "You must be weary from your ordeal. Please relax and I'll come to fetch you when you are ready." And with that, he walks to the far side of the room and out through another small door.

We look at each other nervously. Shakra shrugs his shoulders, "I don't know about you guys, but a bath sounds amazing." He walks over to the far-left bath. Strips off all his clothes and cannonballs into the water.

We stand in stunned silence. I'm not sure whether it is because of how calm Shakra is or the mental scarring of seeing him nude without warning. His head appears out of the bath, overconfident smile on his face, "Come on, get into one, it's lovely,"

Isaac sighs, "He's right, we may as well have a bath, we're filthy." He follows suit and steps into the bath next to Shakra, leaving his clothes in a heap by his bath. Before Silvia can react, Yasmin runs to the bath at the far-right, opposite Shakra, and has slipped into the water.

I look at the bath next to Isaac on my left. I shrug my shoulders, after all we've been through, who cares about them seeing me naked. I take off my clothes and dive into the water. All the aches and pains instantly dissipate. The warm, fragrant water is heavenly. My muscles relax. I push my feet on the floor of the pool and stand up. I flick the wet hair from my eyes. I can't stop the huge grin. If we were going to die, they wouldn't bother washing us. I relax and sink underwater. This is what safety feels like. No more surprises, no more terror, no more death.

I stand up and look around at the others. Maria and Silvia have jumped into their own pools. All I can see is the head and neck of each of them. Smiles adorn my companions. Laughter fills the bathhouse. Uncontrollable laughter. Shakra starts and one by one we all join in, unable to prevent ourselves from showing our joy. Pure unbridled joy. We have done it; we have made it to Arabia. We have survived against all the odds. We didn't need Maria to use her powers to create an artificial happiness.

For once I am genuinely happy. No dream, no vision, no Gwen. Just me; happy.

But then the realisation kicks in. All those we have lost. Dad, Flint, Joshua, the entirety of Klad. So much death and carnage. Plus, the poor twin princesses, Elizabeth, and Mary, are hostages of Vlaydom and Chevon. I sink my head under the water to block out all the noise of laughter and conversation. I take a moment to get out a tear or two. I compose myself and resurface.

I have a shock waiting for me. Two Arabian maids are stood by my bath. The first is a short lady with greying hair who holds a folded towel. The second is much younger, maybe in her early twenties. She holds freshly laundered clothes. I look around at my friends. Each has two maids standing over their bath. Plus, another two maids are taking away our dirty clothes and for some reason our shoes.

I give myself a quick scrub then climb out of the bath. "Thank you," I say as I grab the towel off the first maid. I dry myself then wrap the towel around my waist, conscious how exposed I am. The second maid passes me a pair of fresh, white linen trousers; then a fresh, white linen shirt, and finally a pair of leather sandals. I put them on and feel comfortable. The clothes are simple and light. Everyone is dressed in similar attire of white linens.

A maid knocks on the door at the far side of the room. Zahir appears again. "Ahh," He exclaims, "Good to see you all cleaned and freshened up. Time to go and see the King." He leads us out the door we came in. The blinding light of the sun bounces on the marble floor.

We walk across the vast marbled floor until we came to a corridor on our left. Zahir turns and heads down the corridor. As I turn to follow him my breath is taken away. A huge door made of ivory and gold is at the end of the corridor. I smile, this door must lead to the throne room.

Five guards armed with pikes stands guard. The guard in the middle steps forwards and speaks, "Halt, who goes there? Who seeks an audience with King Tufail?"

I can't help but think it is painfully obvious but Zahir answers without hesitation. "It is I, Zahir, captain of guards."

The guard turns without a word and pushes open the door. The guards step aside and Zahir strides through the open door. Then Shakra and Yasmin. Isaac and Maria closely follow. Silvia grabs my hand. For once I am grateful. My stomach is doing somersaults. We walk through the entrance. The guard slams the door shut behind us. Silva squeezes my hand a little too tightly.

The throne room is stunning. A mirrored marble floor. Pillars of purple and gold. Arabian banners hung wherever possible, there is no bare wall visible. The throne room is twice the size of the great hall of Klad and is packed full of Arabian nobility dressed in all their finery. All eyes are on us as we walk behind Zahir towards the thrones. I can't pick up on what they all seem to be whispering.

The grandest throne in the middle sits a large, fat bearded man, dressed all in purple with a golden crown resting upon on his balding head. His face is littered with smile lines and he has a huge grin as he watches us approach. The large, jolly man must be King Tufail, king of Arabia. On his left sits a slender woman who is at least ten years younger than him. She too seems to be smiling. She wears a purple dress and a small tiara. She must be Queen Amira.

On the other side of Queen Amira sits her son Prince Naseem. He is a much slimmer version of his father, he sprawled across his throne bored, picking his nails with a small knife. Beside him is the young Prince Tufail junior who must only be ten, yet he sits attentively with his parents watching. His dark hair keeps falling over his eyes.

On King Tufail's right sit the Princess's Aisha and Jamila. They are almost identical to their mother apart from the fact they are dressed in turquoise not purple. Aisha is slightly shorter and plumper than her mother. Whereas Jamila seems unhealthily thin. Both Aisha and

Jamila look excited, craning their necks to get a better look at us. On Jamila's right sits an empty throne, belonging to Princess Nadia who I assume is still too ill to accompany her family.

Zahir leads us past the packed court until we reach the foot of the thrones. He drops to one knee and bows his head. The entire congregation of nobles do the same, honouring the Arabian royalty. I am pulled down to one knee by Silvia, desperate not to offend the Arabian King.

"All rise," King Tufail says in a booming baritone voice.

Zahir stands up and gestures towards us, "My King, may I present to you the survivors of Klad." An applause breaks out through the court. I look at Maria confused. Why are we being applauded? Luckily, the applause dies down quickly.

King Tufail gets up on his feet with great effort. His large belly bounces up and down. "Queen Silvia, what a pleasure it is to marvel at your beauty again."

Silvia musters her nerves and releases hold of my hand. She triumphantly steps forwards, "King Tufail, it's been too long." She responds.

"Indeed, it has." He agrees.

Silvia drops to her knees once more, "King Tufail, I beg you to let me and my companions stay in the safety of your great nation." The Queen of Klad pleas, "Also we have three allies who are travelling by cart and will arrive in a few days, I hope they can have safe passage into your kingdom."

King Tufail smiles, "It will be an honour to accommodate you all."

Silvia grins. She has done well. Tufail seems pleased with himself also. He turns to Isaac, "You must be Joshua,"

"Isaac, Your Highness," Isaac corrects him. He looks down upset, crushed by the memory of his fallen brother.

King Tufail realises his error as he spots Isaac's pained look. "I'm sorry, all of you have lost so much. I promise we will avenge them."

I stand up a little straighter. Silvia steps forward and speaks, "Your Grace, how do you mean we will avenge them?"

King Tufail stands arms raise, addressing the entire throne room, "Unfortunately, when the attack on your home occurred, we were unaware of it. We sat idly by whilst our strongest and closest ally was overwhelmed by an alliance forged from cowardly tyranny. For that, I am eternally sorry. But out of the ashes, a new opportunity has arisen. We will fight by your side in taking vengeance on the nations who broke the peace and attacked you." King Tufail roars. He is gaining momentum. He continues rousing the throne room, "Arabia will fight by Klad's side once more. We will find more allies, smith more weapons and train more soldiers. We will use Shakra's influence to turn the already discontent Chevonic people against their royals, then onto Vlaydom and victory." There is a huge cheer from the Arabian nobles and soldiers.

I can't believe it. I thought we would just hide here and grow old. Tufail proposes madness, we can't win. Against my better judgement I walk forward and speak, "King Tufail, you can't beat Vlaydom, Chevon, and the Elves. You don't have the numbers. Who are these allies?" Maria grabs my arm and tries to pull me back, but I continue. "If we try to march an army across to Vlaydom or Chevon we will be slaughtered." The throne room goes as silent as the grave.

King Tufail smiles, "You must be Jacob Da Nesta," I am taken aback. How does he know who I am? King Tufail continues, "And that must mean the beauty behind you is your sister, Maria." He directs the conversation to us personally, ignoring the rest of the room, "I know we do not have enough men. We will not fight this war stupidly in the field. You're correct, we would lose if we were to do that. But there is more than one way to win a war. Plus, you're forgetting our secret weapons; you two."

I can feel everyone's eyes glued onto myself and Maria. Maria speaks timidly, "What do you mean?"

King Tufail chuckles, "The ability of you two in combat is fabled across the entirety of Valouria. You two will be the face of the rebellion. We will attack smartly. When we are ready and prepared, we will start attacking patrols and their supplies, little and often. A war of attrition."

Queen Amira stands up and effortlessly glides over to her husband's arm, "Enough talk of war. This is a time for celebration."

The King smiles, "You're right as always my dear."

Queen Amira elegantly tiptoes towards Shakra, "It's been too long Shakra, a pleasure as always to see you,"

Shakra kisses the back of the Arabian Queen's hand and speaks coolly, "The pleasure is all mine."

The Queen smiles, "I see you brought your betrothed with you." Silvia grins and steps forward. But Queen Amira ignores Silvia and turns to Yasmin. They embrace each other with a tight hug. "You've cut your hair short," Queen Amira says as she twirled Yasmin's hair through her fingers.

I look at Yasmin, then at Queen Amira. There is something similar about them. They are a similar height. Both had the same slim builds and defined cheekbones. They both wear identical turquoise jewellery.

Isaac speaks up, voice full of confusion, "Wait a second your grace. Shakra is betrothed to Queen Silvia?"

Queen Amira turns to Isaac then looks at Shakra. Shakra speaks slowly and solemnly, "Silvia, my dear, unfortunately, I cannot marry you. I was already promised to another when I met you, a fact your late father knew well."

Silvia's eyes well up, but she manages to stay strong, "How long have you been engaged to Yasmin?"

Shakra shrugs, "Our fathers agreed to the marriage when we were very young. But I do love her, I am not doing any of this out of politics."

Yasmin steps up to Shakra's side and takes his hand, "I'm sorry we had to deceive you all. We had to keep it secret, so no one knew my true identity."

"Your true identity!" Silvia exclaims, shaking with exasperation, "You're my handmaiden. My friend. I've told you everything!" Tears start to roll down her cheeks. The nobles in the throne room shuffle awkwardly.

Yasmin tries a smile, "Yes and my friendship to you is real. But I was sent by my father to keep an eye on your father, King Edward, and offer advice to him."

"Who are you?" Silvia asks furiously.

I look up at the empty throne. It is obvious. I should have figured it out. Our friend who we used to call Yasmin sighs and says...

"My name is Nadia, Princess of Arabia."

The Jacob Da Nesta Saga will return with

Enyo

Printed in Great Britain
by Amazon